Hood Defined
Love

Hood Defined Love

Raevyn Renee

www.urbanbooks.net

Urban Books, LLC
300 Farmingdale Road, NY-Route 109
Farmingdale, NY 11735

ISBN 13: 978-1-64556-641-0

First Mass Market Printing October 2024
First Trade Paperback Printing June 2023
Printed in the United States of America

10 9 8 7 6 5 4 3 2 1

Distributed by Kensington Publishing Corp.
Submit Orders to:
Customer Service
400 Hahn Road
Westminster, MD 21157-4627
Phone: 1-800-733-3000
Fax: 1-800-659-2436

Chapter 1

Mikayla's heart pounded inside her chest as her eyes darted from left to right. She hadn't noticed how heavy her backpack was until now, as the straps dug into her shoulders. She tucked her hands under each strap, hiking it up a bit, hoping to bring herself some relief, but the wall she was pinned against and the three young men before her gave her little room to do so. With the small space she had between them, she shifted her body weight to her right, glancing up at each boy, expressionless. Her goal was to display a relaxed demeanor even though she was silently freaking out. Jason, Daniel, and Levi, three of McClane High's most popular students, had her cornered near the boys' bathroom door. And although rationality told her they wouldn't try anything crazy, she still couldn't shake the queasy feeling in her gut as the three pairs of eyes stared back at her.

"You're Mikayla, right?" Daniel, the first to speak up, looked down at her with a slight smirk. He wasn't that much taller than her, but the difference in height was enough to have her eyes upward and his head tilted down to meet them.

Though she found his question absurd, she was glad one of them finally said something to her instead of continuing to stare at her like she was a foreign object. She and Daniel had fifth period together, the class they were currently missing because he and his friends had her cornered. So she knew without a doubt that he knew exactly who she was. She'd always thought of Daniel as a good-looking guy in a "rough around the edges" sort of way. He dressed nicely and had a hard exterior, with a slice across his cheek rumored to have come from a fight in juvenile hall. Besides the scar, his chestnut complexion was smooth, and his deep-set eyes were sexy. His antics in class, though, kept him from being her type.

Deciding to humor him in hopes that her answer would prompt them to move out of her way, Mikayla nodded, confirming her identity. With her eyes still on Daniel, she slightly stretched her neck as if to say, "Now what?" His smirk switched into a full-blown smile, showing his semi-straight teeth.

Annoyed, she moved her eyes from Daniel over to Levi, then Jason, who she unintentionally allowed her eyes to linger on a bit longer, before looking at her feet. Each boy was handsome. Jason, finer than the other two, had crept into her mind a time or two due to her bulging crush on him. He reminded her of the guy who played Khalil on *Black Lightning,* just darker and maybe shorter. Still, the resemblance was enough to have her lusting for the imitation if she couldn't have the real thing. Right now, however, she couldn't see past his creepy and lustful gaze to find even a hint of joy that he was even acknowledging her. It was something he'd never done until now, and she had no idea why. Mikayla wanted to push through them and go about her business, but the wall their broad teenage shoulders built discouraged her from doing so.

"So listen, me and my boys are trying to see what's up with you. I've seen you watching me, and I'm assuming that's 'cause you like me." Jason's smooth and confident tone prompted her attention back to his face, although she purposely avoided his eyes. The way he practically told her she liked him was as if he was daring her to deny it. So she didn't. It would be a lie if she had anyway. Her admission of finding him attractive came from nodding her head, still avoiding eye contact with him and his friends.

"That's what's up. I mean, I'm trying to get to know you. Possibly like you too. I need you to do something for me first, though."

Mikayla frowned. She certainly wasn't in the mood to do any favors. Besides, she was still uncomfortable with how they had her surrounded.

"We heard what you did for that boy Greg, and ol' boy ain't even a quarter of us on our worst day. So I'm sayin' if you giving out favors like that, then you may as well do it for some real ones who can make it count for something, ya dig?"

Her eyes bulged at the mention of Greg's name. She'd heard he spread some things about her around the school, but she hadn't really taken it seriously because he didn't have anything to tell. They'd kissed behind the bleachers of the baseball field, and she vomited right after, disgusted by whatever he'd eaten that day lingering on his tongue. Either that or he naturally had some bad breath. Plus, she only kissed him because he was kind of cute, nice to her, and showed genuine interest in her. She was having one of her moments where she wanted some male attention. Those days didn't come frequently, and one day that it did, Greg was the lucky guy.

Today, however, her guard was up, and given the subtle aggressive nature of the three guys before her, it was rightfully so. She wasn't in the mood for male attention, even if one of the guys happened to be her secret crush. Mikayla opened her mouth to . . . Hell, she had no clue what she was going to say, but before any words could formulate, there was a loud squeak throughout the hallway, indicating someone was coming, which prompted the boys to shove her into the restroom.

Their lustful gazes landed on her as she backed away from them, finally having room to do so. She only wished she could back out of the bathroom door as the pungent smell of piss invaded her nostrils. Unfortunately for her, that wouldn't be happening with them blocking the way and Jason and Daniel advancing on her slowly. Her eyes shot to Levi, who began checking the stalls.

"I should be getting to class." She spoke without an ounce of confidence.

"You're already late, so you may as well kick it with us. You'll make it to next period," Daniel said as he caressed the left side of her face, causing her skin to feel as if she were getting pricked by a ton of needles.

"Ain't none of us gon' make it to our next class nor get our dicks sucked if we keep beating around the bush. I ain't miss a fuckin' quiz to miss out on my turn." Levi's words pierced her ears like nails scratching a chalkboard.

Mikayla thought her heart had been pounding before. Now it felt as if it would leap from her chest at any moment. Her mouth immediately felt dry, her cheeks heated, and she could feel sweat beads form on her forehead. Her eyes shifted toward him, widened because she couldn't believe the words from his mouth. Oddly, Levi looked the most innocent of the crew, with light brown skin, silky hair he wore in a low Afro, and one dimple near the corner of his mouth on the right side of his face. It only proved how looks could be very deceiving given the filth that had just left his mouth.

"Fuck it, let's get this over with. Mikayla, after you do this, I promise you'll be the most popular girl in the school, and you can sit at our table a couple times a week during lunch. And if you're worried about anyone finding out, don't. We won't say shit," Jason said, rushing into her. His hands immediately grasped her breasts, while another set grabbed her ass. Tears stinging her eyes caused her vision to blur while the swift movements of hands roaming her body left her unsure of which guy was touching where. It wasn't until she felt a hand between her legs that she found her voice again.

"No!" she screamed, forcing her body backward into one of them.

"Ay, what the fuck is going on in here?"

Relief washed over her as the hands that had been violating her were removed. She wasn't sure who unknowingly came to her rescue, but she was grateful.

"Mind yo' fuckin' business, dawg," Levi said, moving from behind her.

Mikayla wiped her eyes as she took two steps to her left to see who'd come into the restroom. Jeremiah, a boy from her second-period class who was known around the school as a troublemaker, had unknowingly just become one of her favorite people, especially if he could get her away from Daniel, Jason, and Levi.

"Yo, you good?" he asked, looking her over. She saw a flicker of concern in his eyes before they went dark, and he turned his attention back to the boys.

"Yeah, she good." Jason slung his arm over her shoulder, and the shiver that possessed her body couldn't be mistaken.

"Y'all some bitch-ass niggas if I've ever seen any. And we all know I'm not the nigga you want problems with." Jeremiah stepped up, his hand going toward the back of his pants as if he was reaching for something. Based on his reputation, she wouldn't put it past him if he did have a gun.

"Ay, Mikayla, we'll catch you another time." Jason removed his arm from her shoulder, and he and his crew exited the bathroom. Each mugged the hell out of Jeremiah, even going so far as to bump into him on their way out.

"You sure you good?" he asked her once they were the only two left.

"I said I was fine!" Mikayla snapped, rushing toward the door. She halted, then she went back to him as her hands flew to her face in an attempt to silence the sob escaping.

"Ay, man." Jeremiah's tone was soft and full of concern. It was also what got her feet back moving. Mikayla rushed out of the bathroom, not stopping until she reached the end of the hall. She placed her back against the lockers, shielding herself as she tried to compose herself.

"Mr. Stately, what did you do to that young lady?" The voice carried to the end of the hall where she stood frozen hoping that Jeremiah wouldn't snitch on her or Jason, Daniel, and Levi. That would open a whole other issue she wasn't interested in dealing with.

"Mr. Feng, I don't know what you saw or think you saw, but it wasn't that. Number one, I didn't do nothing to nobody, and two, I don't know who or what you're talking about," she heard Jeremiah say.

"Sure you don't. We'll finish this discussion in my office." Mr. Feng's voice boomed through the hall, and she knew he didn't buy what Jeremiah told him. In fact, she was sure he was about to dig into Jeremiah's ass, because that was the kind of stuff he lived for. Mr. Feng took his job as principal seriously, determined to instill enough fear in the students that they didn't disrupt his school. He cared about accolades and test scores and making sure to keep delinquents in check, Jeremiah being one of them.

"I'm telling you, I ain't do nothin'."

Jeremiah's protest was the last thing she heard before footsteps drew farther away from her. Mikayla knew that whatever was about to go down in the principal's office would not be good for Jeremiah. Still, she couldn't bring herself to save him the way he had her. Besides, he didn't know she was listening, and he'd already lied about knowing who she was, so there was no need to intervene.

Hoisting her backpack up onto her shoulders, she headed for the exit, not stopping until she made it behind the same bleachers where she and Greg had kissed. Mikayla sat in the dirt Indian style, not caring about the dirt stain that was sure to be left on the back of her distressed boyfriend jeans.

She couldn't believe the nerve of Jason, Levi, and Daniel. To think she would suck all or even one of them off proved that not only were they delusional but naive as well. She knew she was giving them too much credit to think that high school boys would know better than to believe a rumor. But that was what high school was pretty much about—everyone trying to prove or deny something someone else said about them. Rarely were people's high school reputations based on their own actions and not descriptions given by their peers. Still, the last thing she thought would happen was that a rumor would get her almost raped.

"Oh, my God," she cried, placing her face into her palms. The revelation of what was close to happening hit her like a ton of bricks. They were about to rape her. She said no, and no one stopped touching her. If it weren't for Jeremiah, there was no telling how far they would have gotten. She was happy she hadn't worn the corduroy skirt she originally planned to wear, as she remembered hands being forced between her legs.

Tears continued to run like a leaking faucet from Mikayla's eyes as everything played back in her head like it was stuck on repeat until the loud blaring of the school bell scared her. Pain and agony filled her so much that she'd forgotten all about the few hours left of school. Removing her phone from her back pocket, she opened the FaceTime app. Instinctively her thumb hovered over her cousin's name. She was ready to call her before she immediately decided against it. Her almond-shaped eyes were puffy, and traces of red surrounded her light brown irises. Her jet-black curly hair was all over the place, and she had no clue how her ponytail had become so loose since she couldn't remember her nor any of the guys' hands in her hair. Her disheveled look was more than enough to have her cousin ready to head to the school and take off anyone's head who even looked at her wrong.

Wiping her face with the sleeve of her Abercrombie T-shirt, she stood and dusted off as much of the dirt as possible before making her way to the bus stop. She was done with school for the day. She also knew her cousin would get messages alerting her of every class she missed, and she didn't care. Mikayla was getting as far away as possible from McClane High and its nasty-ass male students. She would deal with the repercussions of her absences later.

Chapter 2

Jeremiah held his head high as he walked through the office door Mr. Feng held open for him. He tittered slightly as he knew the gesture wasn't one of courtesy but to further establish his dominance, which didn't move Jeremiah at all. Taking a seat at Mr. Feng's desk, he sat unshaken with his legs wide as he brushed his hands down his jeans. He wasn't in the mood to be interrogated, yet he knew it was sure to come. Jeremiah was pissed that his meddling had landed him across from Mr. Feng. Since he started at McClane High, the principal seemed to have it out for him. Granted, he wasn't what one considered a model student, but he surely wasn't as bad as he was made out to be.

At least, he wasn't at first. Although he kept his grades decent enough to guarantee graduation, he'd become the school misfit they deemed him. He felt he might as well give them the kid they wanted him to be so badly, so he acted out when he felt like it. He recognized he'd get further by proving them wrong. However, he hadn't cared enough to take that route. Being rebellious was more fun anyway. He sat back, waiting for Mr. Feng to say a bunch of shit that didn't apply to him because, for once, he was in his office for being a solution and not the problem, whether Mr. Feng knew it or not.

"Mr. Stately, would you like to tell me A, who the young lady was coming out of the restroom with you, and B, what you two were doing in there?" He gave Jeremiah a stern stare, hoping it would persuade him to not only answer his question but also reveal the identity of the young woman who moved too quickly for him to catch. Given the numerous times he'd had to chastise Jeremiah, he could pick him out with his eyes closed. Besides, he was almost certain that whoever the young lady was, she had been influenced by Jeremiah. Truthfully, he wanted nothing more than to get the young woman's side of the story, but because he had no clue who she was, Jeremiah would have to do. He'd never understand why good girls seemed to be so intrigued with bad guys. He would've liked nothing more than to let whoever the girl was know that dealing with a kid like Jeremiah would do her more harm than good.

"Mr. Feng, there is honestly nothing to tell. I wasn't in the bathroom with a girl," Jeremiah said with a straight face even though he was having a fit on the inside. Subtly he shook his head as Mikayla entered his mind. The relief that washed over her face when she first locked eyes with him, then the tears that spilled from her eyes before she stormed out of the bathroom, played back as if it were happening again in real time. Still, he wouldn't admit to being in that restroom with her or any other female.

"My eyes were playing tricks on me, huh?"

Jeremiah's eyes met his as he shrugged. "I can't tell you what's going on with your eyes, sir."

Mr. Feng's face transformed to beet red, and Jeremiah did his best to keep his face even. "Why must you think everything is a game, Jeremiah?" He called him by his first name, leaving not an ounce of doubt that anger consumed him.

"Mr. Feng, I'm not. I mean, I don't. Anytime I've been in your office, it's behind something I've actually done and owned. Always. There's nothing to own up to this time, so there's no reason for me to be here. You gonna keep asking me a question I can't give you an answer to."

"Maybe if I give you a couple of days at home, it'll come to you." He slid back his chair enough to open the center drawer of his desk and removed a pink slip.

Jeremiah peered at Mr. Feng as if he'd just lost his mind. He hated the position that he was being put in, because if anyone needed any time at home, it was Jason and his bitch-ass friends.

"Last chance, Mr. Stately."

"My answer isn't going to change, Mr. Feng. The truth can't be forced into a lie no matter who don't like it." Jeremiah sat back, irritated. He refused to speak on what he walked into in that bathroom because it wasn't his business to tell. If she wanted to tell Mr. Feng what went down, then she could. She had a better chance of Mr. Feng believing her than he did anyway. He could sit there and run the entire situation down and he was sure their beloved principal would still deem him guilty until proven innocent. Not only that, but it would also be his and Mikayla's words against Jason, Levi, and Daniel, and as shady as they were, those three could flip the script on him quick. Regardless of how he thought the truth would prevail, he knew it wouldn't work in his favor.

"Three days' suspension." Mr. Feng slid the pink slip in front of Jeremiah like he was handing over a $100 bill.

"Three days? That's bullshit! I can take one, maybe two, but three days is pushing it. I have a test this week, Mr. Feng."

"You will watch your language in my office. Those three days can easily turn into five. I say three days is fairly reasonable since you broke school rules and you're failing to cooperate."

"Can I go now?" Jeremiah sat up, grabbing his backpack from the floor and slinging it onto his shoulder. He was about to leave whether Mr. Feng said it was okay or not because he was two seconds from knocking over all the shit on his desk, including the photo of Mr. Feng's funny-looking-ass family every student and even some teachers talked about. Though they weren't Jeremiah's cup of tea, nor could someone pay him to walk a day in Mr. Feng's shoes, he was one of the few people who refused to say anything negative about the man's family. But since Mr. Feng was on some bitch shit, it was fuck them kids and his wife.

"You are dismissed," Mr. Feng said to his back.

Jeremiah sucked his teeth, angrily exiting the office. The bell had already rung, indicating that he was late to class, which his teacher was going to bitch about. As he made his way down the hall, he saw a disheveled Mikayla rushing toward the main exit.

"Damn, man," he mumbled before heading to class. As much as he wanted to be pissed at her, he couldn't find it in his heart to be upset with anyone other than the dudes who had been moments away from assaulting her.

Jeremiah released an exasperated breath. If he could, he'd be exiting school early too, but he had to get his affairs in order due to the unwarranted suspension. Looking down at the pink slip in his hand that would almost serve as a valid reason for being late to class, he promised himself that if he ever caught Daniel, Levi, or Jason outside of school, he was beating their asses.

Unprepared. That was exactly what he was when he had to sit down and take the quiz for his sixth-period class early. Mrs. Josh told him he'd either take the quiz after school or miss it altogether, resulting in an F he did not want. He figured he had a better chance of getting some points rather than none. It took him almost forty-five minutes to take an eight-question multiple-choice quiz, and when he left the classroom, he wasn't sure if he felt dumb as hell or proud that he really put in some effort. A two-day suspension would have been ideal, giving him enough time to study. Three days, though, had put his back against the wall, and if he failed the quiz for lack of preparation, it would be fuck Mr. Feng for life.

"I thought you said you weren't going to skip classes anymore."

Jeremiah had barely gotten through the front door when his brother questioned him. "Damn. No 'What's up, bro? How was your day?' Just straight to the bullshit, huh?" Jeremiah flung his backpack onto the sofa before taking a seat across from his brother. He sat back using the same cool demeanor he'd possessed in Mr. Feng's office. There was no way his feathers were going to be ruffled when he wasn't in the wrong, no matter who he was sitting across from.

"Not when I'm getting an automated message from your school alerting me about some shit you said you were through with doing." Jermaine looked him square in the eyes, uninterested in whatever excuse his brother was about to hit him with. If he'd heard one of Jeremiah's bullshit reasons for cutting class, he'd heard them all.

"That's the only one you got? I'm surprised the one telling you I got suspended didn't come, too." Jeremiah shrugged, not caring about his brother's frustration.

Sometimes his brother seemed to forget he was just that—his brother, and not his father. Eight years separated them, and as much as they looked alike, they were so different. They were the spitting image of their father, although Jeremiah had their mother's caramel complexion while Jermaine shared their father's almond complexion. Their skin tones were all that really made them different, looks-wise, outside of the obvious age difference and the goatee Jermaine sported. Both men shared their father's broad nose, defined chin, and ears that were too big to be considered small but also too small to be considered big. Their hooded amber-colored eyes inherited from their mother always got them female attention.

"Suspended? What the fuck, Mouse?"

"Ay, quit calling me that shit. I told you I don't like that name no more. Damn, man, give me a little respect," Jeremiah demanded with his face scrunched in disgust. Mouse was the childhood nickname that everyone in his family called him. Unfortunately for him, some of his family couldn't move past the name. Since he and his brother lived hours away, he only had the displeasure of being called Mouse when he spoke with their mother when he took her calls, or times like now when his brother decided to be an asshole.

Jermaine dismissed Jeremiah's attitude and his foul language. Though he demanded respect as a big brother, he still tried to be his friend, although Jeremiah made that hard as hell. One thing he was certain of, though, was that if he censored Jeremiah too much or was too strict with him, his brother would only pull further away from him. His relationship with their mother was already strained, and the two of them were really all Jeremiah had. Therefore, he encouraged his brother to be himself while respecting the boundaries he set.

"This coming from the person who keeps getting in trouble at school."

"I got suspended and missed class behind some shit that didn't have anything to do with me."

"So what happened?" He elected to hear his brother out because one thing Jeremiah did was own his shit if he was in the wrong. Granted, excuses and beating around the bush were things Jeremiah did, too. However, something in his eyes told him the reason for this suspension was different.

"On the real, I was going to be late to my class regardless 'cause I got caught up talking to this girl in the hallway. I wasn't going to cut, though. Anyway, while I was heading down the hall, I noticed these three bitch-ass dudes push this girl I got another class with into the boys' bathroom. At first, I was going to mind my business 'cause there had been some shit going around the school about her, but my gut told me something wasn't right about how they shoved her in there, so I went to check it out, and I was right."

He shook his head as he felt a lump form in his throat. He still couldn't believe what had almost gone down. "I mean, even if she is a slut or whatever, being forced into the bathroom by three dudes wasn't coo'. Anyway, I get in there, and she crying and shit, and they all over her, so I called 'em out. I may have bluffed like I was holding, and they dipped. She ran off not long after, and when I came out, bitch-ass Mr. Feng caught me. I didn't tell him what he wanted to hear, so now I'm suspended."

He shrugged like it was no big deal because he didn't want Jermaine to see he was bothered by what had gone down. It had been years since he was placed in a position where he had to protect a female. Luckily for Mikayla, he was able to provide her something he couldn't provide years ago.

As he watched his brother's facial expressions reveal his feelings toward what he'd just told him, Jeremiah felt his chest tighten, and his eyes began to dry briefly before moisture replaced the dry feeling. It had been years since he'd shed a tear and even longer since he'd felt this feeling coursing through his body. If he never felt it again, he wouldn't complain. This feeling embodied fear and anger. He hated how this situation brought him back to a place he'd tucked away. But as he recalled the boys shoving Mikayla into the bathroom, he couldn't help replaying in his mind the night he saw his mother being shoved in the same manner.

"Nah, he got you fucked up. You not about to stay home for three days over some shit you didn't do, especially when you were trying to do the right thing." Jermaine stood, heated. He was angry with himself for thinking his brother was on the same ol' bullshit, and mad at the principal for not investigating harder to find that Jeremiah was actually innocent.

"He's not going to lift my suspension unless I give him names. Right now, he only wants the girl's name. If I give her name, I may as well tell on the dudes, too, and you and I both know snitching ain't my thing."

"Well, I'll tell their names. Somebody needs to dig in their ass for the bitch-ass shit they were trying to pull anyway."

"Come on, bro, that's not even you. I'm not saying shit, and neither are you. No matter whose mouth it comes out of, I'm the one who'll be stamped a snitch. Let the shit play out. At the end of the day, it's that girl's story to tell." He knew his brother meant well, but he abided by a code. He couldn't go his last year of high school being viewed as a snitch or a liar, depending on how people chose to twist the story.

"You're not about to be punished for some shit you didn't do." Jermaine was insistent. Though he was in agreement with his brother's viewpoint, it didn't feel right to accept the punishment given to his brother. At this point, it was Jeremiah or those other kids, and he'd choose his young'un first every time.

"That's done already. You asked me what happened, and I told you. I didn't ask you to bail me out of the shit. Just let it go, man." Jeremiah shook his head, feeling defeated. Usually, when Jermaine made his mind up, he knew there was little he could do to change it. It was a trait the two of them shared.

"I won't give up no names, but I'm not about to let you live with this suspension, either. I'll find a way to make something shake without having to reveal any names," he vowed.

Peering at his brother, Jeremiah shook his head before grabbing his backpack and storming off to his room. It irked him how his brother constantly seemed to forget where they came from. His brother was one of the toughest street dudes around their way back in their hometown, and since moving, he showed to be squarer than anything.

After placing his backpack into his closet, he opened his bedroom window and exited. He could have taken the front door, but it would have led to another exchange with Jermaine he wasn't in the mood to have. He wanted to go hang with his boys, people who understood him and stuck by the code of the streets.

Jeremiah grimaced as the lukewarm alcohol burned his throat. Drinking was surely something he could live without, but since his homeboys were doing it, he decided to indulge some too. He wasn't a fan of dark liquor, yet that was all the crew seemed to drink.

"What you get into today?" his homeboy KJ inquired. He was posted against the brick wall with his left foot propped against it, looking just as cool as he felt.

"Shit, went to school, then got suspended for something that ain't have anything to do with me."

"Damn, that's crazy." He pulled his body from the wall and turned to face Jeremiah. "See, that's one of the reasons I stopped going to school. Them officials don't care about us underprivileged youth like that," added a kid known as H-Town who was a part of his gang. He was from Houston, hence the name, and Jeremiah still hadn't found out what landed him in California. Not that he cared much. Still, it was odd he didn't know the story.

"Exactly. I already know your brother is pissed." KJ chuckled. "Ain't no money at school, no way. You should be out here getting this gwap with us full-time," KJ inserted, pulling a wad of money from his pocket to show what cutting school had gotten him.

"Yeah, my brother tripping, but I ain't worried about him too much. And school ain't that bad. It's easy, honestly. Plus, I go for my moms, ya know?" He half told the truth. Finishing school was more for himself and his father. He did a lot of things his parents wouldn't be happy about, but his studies weren't one of them. He meant it when he said school was easy, and for that reason, he found no reason to drop out. He also did not want to burst H-Town's bubble, because he was far from underprivileged. His brother worked hard and made sure they had all they wanted and then some. He didn't need to cut school to hustle. The truth was, KJ's knot of money did not move him because he'd seen way more than that from his brother's bank statement. The kind of money Jermaine pulled in for their household couldn't fit in any of their palms.

"What you gon' do while you free from the system for a bit?" asked a kid named Arnold.

"Not sure. My brother said he's going to have a talk with the principal because he's not feeling me getting suspended for nothing."

"Damn, your brother fight your battles?"

"Nah, it ain't like that. I told him not to say shit. Like me, he does what he wants to do, so it is what it is." He shrugged, hoping to hide how embarrassed and upset he was that his brother was hell-bent on going to his school. This was one of the reasons he hung out with a crowd he knew his brother wouldn't approve of, because they understood him. They made him look powerful, unlike a punk who needed his big brother, which was exactly the vibe his peers would get after Jermaine went to the school and overreacted.

"Hey, you ever held a gun before?"

"Yeah." His admission made him feel butterflies in the pit of his stomach. A question like that would only lead to a follow-up he wasn't sure he was ready for.

"We got something popping soon. We'll get paid for a few cars to move to a chop shop," H-Town informed him.

"Oh, okay."

"You not scared, are you?"

"No. Why'd you say something crazy like that?" His voice unintentionally rose an octave.

"You seemed nervous, that's all. It's time for you to earn a few more stripes, though."

"Y'all got me. I got y'all." He slapped hands with KJ and braced himself to ride with his boys when they were ready.

Chapter 3

With her knees pulled to her chest and her head resting there, Mikayla tried controlling the flow of her tears, to no avail. Her heart was slowly shattering inside her chest, and she swore she felt every piece crack and fall off, and it was the worst feeling in the world. She wanted nothing more than to forget what had happened at school, but she knew it wouldn't be easy. Too many things could keep today alive, and there was enough ammunition from the guys that could drag her name through the mud. A loud sob escaped her lips as she thought about another rumor being aimed her way at school. What would Jason, Levi, and Daniel say about her? Would they tell people she was going to service them until Jeremiah came along and hated? And Jeremiah, what if he told Mr. Feng what transpired and gave all their names? There were so many things going through her head as she continued to cry loudly. In the comfort of her bedroom, alone in the home she shared with her cousin, she could cry without restriction or judgment.

"Mikayla." Riley's voice was three octaves higher than normal as she burst into Mikayla's bedroom.

Riley's unexpected bursting into her room startled Mikayla to the other side of her bed, and she hit the floor headfirst. "Ouch," she groaned, placing her right hand on her forehead.

"Mikayla, what's wrong with you?" It had taken Riley two steps to get to her cousin. She knelt, taking Mikayla by the elbows, assisting her up. Before she could look at her baby cousin's face, Mikayla's arms were wrapped around her waist tightly as she wept into her chest.

Riley could feel Mikayla's agony through her sobs, and it hurt. She wondered what had her cousin so distraught, and as badly as she needed Mikayla to reveal what was wrong, she knew Mikayla needed even more to finish crying. Vulnerability like this was not a quality of either of theirs. So for a moment like this, she knew something major had happened. Riley hugged her back tightly, doing her best to comfort Mikayla and reassure her that, no matter the situation, she had her back, good, bad, right, or wrong. As tears welled in her eyes, Mikayla shook as she sobbed, wetting Riley's shirt and evoking a million worst-case scenarios in Riley's mind. In fact, they seemed to get worse with each thought. Hesitantly, Riley pulled back from Mikayla, taking her hands to unlatch her cousin's from around her.

"Baby girl, please tell me why you're crying like this. And the truth, Mikayla. There's nothing you can tell me right now that will make me want to do anything other than protect you, as always." Riley placed her forehead on Mikayla's and waited as she took multiple deep breaths in an attempt to calm herself down. With her eyes closed, she prayed for her cousin.

"At school today . . . these boys . . . I think they were going to try to . . ." She couldn't finish the sentence. Saying the word "rape" out loud was torturing, so she didn't. Instead, her cries replaced the word, and Riley felt sick. She felt her stomach twist and the day's lunch rushing to her throat, and it took a ton of willpower to swallow it back down.

"Mikayla, do you know the kids? Do they go to your school?"

"Yeah, I know them." Mikayla wiped her tears before looking at the ground.

Riley looked at her and recognized shame and defeat in her cousin. She hated that, for a split second, she wondered what Mikayla may have said or done to the boys to even try her. Mikayla's past was supposed to be just that, and Riley hated that she even considered it. She stepped back from Mikayla, heading straight for her desk drawer, removing a notepad and pen before she sat down.

Frowning, Mikayla looked at her cousin, confused. "Riley, what are you doing?"

"About to send a kite to our dads. Those boys need to disappear," she said seriously.

Although this wasn't a smiling matter, Mikayla couldn't help the one that spread across her lips. Her cousin was a true rider, and she loved her for it. But even through her grief, she knew she couldn't allow Riley to send a letter to the prison asking them to put a hit out on some teenage boys. Then she too would be taken from her, and she knew she couldn't handle that.

"Riley, don't. You'll get in trouble and them. I don't think they'll mess with me anymore. Some kid from my class came and stopped them before they could really hurt me," she told her, walking up to her and taking the notebook from her hand. She looked at the chicken scratches and shook her head. Riley had immaculate handwriting, so she knew her cousin was upset. The words on the paper were barely legible.

"That's nice and all, but I need pain inflicted on them. You know where any of them stay?" Riley stood from the desk and began pacing the room.

Mikayla knew she was ready to take off the heads of everyone who violated her. "No. Riley, I just want to forget this happened."

"I can't do that. This cannot go unpunished, and as much as I wish you could forget it happened, you won't. Not something like this." She spoke as gently as she could. There was no way she wouldn't see to it that whoever had tried her cousin in such a horrific way would pay.

"But I want to. They'll make the rest of my days in high school hell if this gets out. I don't want you to do anything. Please let it go."

"I'm not. And what I got for them, trust me, they won't even look your way after."

"Riley," she whined.

"I'm calling our cousins from the Bay. You're going to give me names and faces, and they are getting their asses whipped. I won't handle it through the school, but we are for damn sure taking it to the streets. Now tell me as much as you feel comfortable with, including about the boy who came through and helped you."

The air in Mr. Feng's office seemed stale as Mikayla sat across from him, her throat feeling like a million ants were running rapidly over her esophagus. She had never felt so thirsty in her life, yet the courage to ask for water, which he kept available to any of his office visitors, was nonexistent. Not only that, but Mikayla wasn't sure her voice worked. Her heart was racing, and her hands felt clammy as she silently encouraged herself to calm down. Her eyes purposely avoided his as he continued to stare a hole into her. This was the first time she had been in his office afraid. She and

Mr. Feng had a decent relationship. She was one of the top students in the school, so whenever he saw her, it was always for good reason. Today, she was sure that would change. The past twenty-four hours showed her anything was possible.

"I did some investigating and come to find out the young lady coming out of the bathroom was you, Ms. Triumph."

Mikayla's eyes shot toward Jeremiah, who sat cool as a cucumber, a demeanor she couldn't understand since he had snitched on her. She couldn't give a damn that Mr. Feng said he'd done his research. She knew he was only trying to cover for Jeremiah's snitching ass. She never pegged Mr. Feng as the type to try to protect a student's street cred, but maybe that was the deal he made with Jeremiah to get information.

"Okay, you found the person you were looking for. I'm already suspended, so what am I here for?" Jeremiah asked, slumped in his chair, a horrible posture he was sure irked Mr. Feng. He might have shown a little more respect if he hadn't already been suspended. He wasn't due back to school until Friday, and since he'd already taken the quiz he thought he was going to miss, he was tempted not to return until Monday. He had gotten suspended yesterday, and before the bell was due to ring this morning, Mr. Feng was calling Jermaine.

"And with no cooperation from you, Mr. Stately. Your three days of suspension may have been shorter had you cooperated. This moves me to the reason I reached out to your guardians." Mr. Feng's eyes shifted to the other two adults in the room and immediately back to his desk as he swallowed the lump in his throat. He hadn't expected the frowns on their faces and quickly wondered what he'd said to warrant such looks. In his mind, the other adults in the room should have been displaying their disappointment toward the teenagers who were up to no good, not him. Granted, Mr. Feng had never had two guardians young enough to be his children in a principal-parent meeting. This was new to him, and as far as Jeremiah was concerned, he was sure his rude behavior came from not having a solid father figure. Being raised by his brother did not seem like the best route for a teenage boy. As he sat trying to figure out the best way to approach his students' guardians, he could only hope their age did not determine their level of maturity.

Jermaine was the first to speak. "You called, but I was coming up here anyway. You suspended my brother for nothing, and I would think that, as the head of this school, you'd be more interested in getting to the bottom of a problem rather than throwing around punishments because you feel like it." He sat back in the chair, composed like his brother, yet his eyes told a different story. He was ready to go to war behind his brother.

The uncanny resemblance irritated Mr. Feng because he wasn't confident he would get the results he was seeking from Jeremiah's brother. As of right now, it was looking like the apple hadn't fallen too far from the tree.

"I can assure you, Mr. Stately, I had probable cause to suspend Jeremiah. And I tried to get to the bottom of the issue. However, Jeremiah refused to tell me what happened. Students should not mix genders in the restrooms, which he and Ms. Triumph had done, although he refuses to admit it. Therefore, I had no alternative other than suspension."

"There's always a choice. Y'all do have a study hall and detention area here, am I right? You chose to suspend my brother rather than take his word. Hell, you didn't have to take his word. The least you could have done was wait until you had all the information before suspending him. You investigated after suspending him, which feels like targeting."

"I, uh, no, that's not the case." Mr. Feng's face turned red as he pulled his lips together. There were valid points made, and if Jeremiah had been any other student, that might have been the route to take. Since he wasn't, a suspension was suitable, he thought.

"This was the males' restroom, right?"

"It was."

"And my brother is a male, correct? So of the two, he was the only one who belonged in there."

"Yes, but—"

"There are no buts to be added. He wasn't the one in the wrong."

"Hold the hell up." Riley sat up in her seat, turning to face Jermaine. She couldn't believe what he was implying. Then the nerve of him to do so while she and Mikayla were right there, as if they didn't matter. She understood him taking up for his brother. She was there to do the same for Mikayla. She didn't have to throw anyone under the bus to do so. She knew they could both defend their kids without putting another down. Riley eventually wanted to thank Jeremiah because Mikayla let her know how he came to her aid, but his brother's attitude was about to get that gratitude voided.

Mikayla sank in her seat, knowing her cousin was about to let the men in the room have it. They may have been outnumbered in testosterone, and that meant nothing to Riley. It was a trait Mikayla truly admired and a quality that, if she had, might have allowed her to come out of yesterday's situation much better.

"I'm sorry, Ms. Belter, you have something to say?" Mr. Feng spoke up.

Riley rolled her eyes at Jermaine, then nodded at Mr. Feng before taking a deep breath. She had a lot to say, and they were going to hear it. "Yes. Number one, I don't know what the hell you're trying to imply about my cousin, but you need to rephrase that shit right now." She rolled her neck and pointed at Jermaine. Riley had never considered herself ghetto fabulous, though right now one would have assumed that was precisely who she was: a ghetto-fabulous cousin ready to go off about her baby cousin. "And you!" She turned toward the principal. "You claim to have done some investigating, yet you still don't know what the hell happened in that bathroom. If this so-called meeting is going to continue, I need facts to be straightened out ASAP." She sat back in her seat, folding her arms across her chest because she knew without a doubt that she had just gathered every dick in the room.

Jeremiah chuckled, causing both Jermaine and Mr. Feng to cut their eyes at him.

"I assure you that's why we're here, Ms. Belter. To find out exactly what happened. I never thought that Mikayla was in the wrong. She's a good kid. Her grades are great, and she has never given me nor her teachers any problems—"

"This what the fuck you not about to do," Jermaine once again interrupted. He could see the principal's mind was already made up about

Jeremiah, and it pissed him off. He wouldn't say Jeremiah was a great student and did not act out in school. Even still, the principal was not supposed to be showing favoritism. "You not about to make her seem so innocent and my brother the bad guy. If it weren't for him, the three niggas she was in the bathroom with probably would've had their way with her. Since she still hasn't spoken up to talk about that, one can only wonder if her ass—"

"Ay, bro, the fuck?" Jeremiah sat up, looking at Jermaine like he'd lost his mind. He understood his brother was taking up for him. He was taking it too far, though.

"Excuse me? Three? Is this true, Ms. Triumph?" The color seemed to drain from Mr. Feng's face.

"Why the hell did you call us here with these two? Clearly somebody's home training was done under a fucking rock. I'm trying not to lose my cool, but homeboy got one more time." Riley lifted her right index finger to emphasize Jermaine's last chance. If he came for Mikayla again, she couldn't promise that the police wouldn't have to come and peel her from on top of Jermaine. She'd say Mr. Feng, however, looked as if she could flick him and he'd fold.

"Please, let's all calm down. Mikayla, so we can get to the bottom of this and end all the speculation, please tell me what happened." Looking at Mikayla, he believed she was the only one in the room with some sense. Nothing he said about her characteristics as a student was a lie, and he could only hope it showed through honestly about what went down yesterday.

Mikayla could hear her heart beating through her ears, sounding like a symphony of drums. Her eyes traveled up Mr. Feng's black dress shoes, blue slacks, and gray button-up. They landed on his face. His French vanilla skin tone and intense black and Asian features made him resemble an older and lighter version of Tiger Woods. His eyes bore back into hers with pure sympathy, which she found odd because he had no idea about what had happened to her or about the rumors being spread about her around the school, which were sure to get worse if she told the whole truth, including names.

"Um, first I want to say that Jeremiah did nothing wrong. He shouldn't be suspended. He told some fellow students to leave me alone, and they did."

Clearing Jeremiah's name meant more to her than ratting out Daniel, Levi, and Jason. Besides, she had already begged Riley not to give their names because she didn't want the rest of her high school days to become so tortuous she'd need to transfer. Though she wasn't too happy with the decision, Riley had given her word that she wouldn't say anything as long as she could call their cousins from Richmond to come down and beat the boys' asses.

"Who were the boys, Ms. Triumph?"

"Mr. Feng, I'd rather not say. They're not going to bother me anymore, and I wasn't hurt. I honestly want to put this all behind me. I can't do that knowing Jeremiah got in trouble for helping me."

"That's not why he's suspended. His suspension comes from not complying. He could have told me the same thing you did, yesterday."

"Look, man, I know you the principal and all, but I'm really starting to feel like you have it out for my brother. If that's the case, I'm ready to change the tune of this entire meeting. At this point, if you're not talking about lifting his suspension, then you need to be suspending her too." Jermaine was fed up. Mikayla had cleared his brother's name, damn near announced him as the good guy, and the principal was still trying to justify a suspension he didn't deserve. And if Mr. Feng still felt the suspension was warranted after Mikayla's confession, then she needed to be held accountable too.

"Excuse me. And why would my cousin need to be suspended?" Riley was back, leaning forward in her seat, body turned toward him with a mug on her face he would have found extremely sexy under different circumstances.

"Shit, for the same reasons my brother got suspended, apparently. Not complying, mixing genders in the bathroom and shit."

"You know what?" Those were the last three words Mikayla made out clearly before Riley, Jermaine, and even Mr. Feng began talking over each other. Well, arguing. She couldn't stand arguments, especially those that involved men and women. Mikayla tried tuning them out by covering her ears, which no one seemed to notice her do but Jeremiah. It was also he who noticed her get up and leave the office.

"Hold up." He stopped her right outside the office's main door. "You okay?" he asked her.

"Yeah. Funny how we never said two words to each other all school year, and the first two from you happen to be you making sure I'm okay. Twice." She chuckled at the peculiarity while also trying to lighten the mood.

"It's cool. Unless you're going to lie like you did yesterday."

"Today, I am okay. I just don't like arguing and yelling."

"Really? The way your cousin in there is going in on my brother, one would think she argued for sport and you were used to it."

"She only gets like that when people come for me. She's really a chill person."

"If you say so. Anyway, thanks for trying to get me out of trouble. Mr. Feng will probably keep me on suspension even though his bitch ass knows the truth now."

"I hope not. I'll write a letter to the school board for you if he does."

Chuckling, Jeremiah shook his head. "Nah, I'm good. My brother will handle it. If not, I'm good with that too."

"Thank you for, um, what you did yesterday. I'm sure anyone else would have decided to mind their business." Mikayla avoided his eyes as she placed her hands in the pockets of her jeans and slightly hiked up her shoulders. Jeremiah couldn't tell if her posture came from being embarrassed or shy, or maybe it was both.

"And they would have been bigger bitches than Dan . . . than them dudes." He caught himself from saying their names, not knowing who was listening.

"Yeah. Still, thank you."

"It's good. You know they not gon' bother you again, right?"

"Yeah. And just in case, my people coming from out of town to make sure of it. Riley wouldn't have it any other way."

"Your cousin is a real gangsta." He laughed.

"No, really, she isn't. She only gets like this behind me and family."

"As she should. Um, you catch the bus home?"

"I do."

"Well, I'm going to wait at the exit for you and walk you to the bus stop as an added piece of protection, if that's cool."

Mikayla smiled. She didn't want to, but her lips betrayed her, stretching from ear to ear. Jeremiah was handsome. There was no denying that. Still, she shouldn't have been entertaining him further than giving the apology. However, something told her he wasn't out to get her, so she agreed.

"You don't have to, but okay. I need to get to class. I thought Riley would have come out here by now, but they are obviously still going at it."

"I'll let her know you went to class. Since technically I'm still suspended, I'll be right here 'til my brother comes out."

"Thanks. I'm going to text her as well."

"All right. Well, I'll see you after school."

"Okay." Mikayla provided him one last smile before removing her phone to text Riley while walking toward her second-period class. She hoped like hell that when fifth period arrived, Daniel wouldn't be there. If he was, she would ignore him like Riley told her to do, because soon he and his crew weren't going to even feel comfortable walking the hall at the same time she did.

"Where'd my cousin go?" Riley asked as she stepped into the hall where Jeremiah was posted against the wall. His back rested against it, arms folded and right leg propped up.

"She went to class. Said she would text you."

Standing in front of him, Riley extended her hand. "Thank you for what you did for my cousin."

Jeremiah removed his body from the wall, accepting Riley's hand. "No problem. Real ones do real thangs. Plus, my mama would have a fit if I didn't intervene in something like that."

"You and your brother have the same mama?" Riley asked seriously, causing Jeremiah to double over in laughter.

"Yeah. I grew up in the same house as my brother, but I must've missed that rock he was under."

"Be thankful you did. Well, thanks again."

The door exiting the office and leading to the hall opened, revealing Jermaine. Riley immediately rolled her eyes, and though Jermaine saw her, he chose to act as if he didn't.

"You can go to class. The suspension is lifted."

"Nah. I don't have none of my materials."

"That shit is in the trunk of my car. Let's grab it. Then you go to class. Had me in here getting out of character and shit. You going to class today. All of 'em."

"Hey, thanks again, Jeremiah. And stay away from rocks." Riley winked, walking off. She could hear one or both of them whisper, "Damn," under their breath, but she continued as if she hadn't. Removing her phone, she read Mikayla's message and replied, letting her know she was proud of her and to go straight home after school and to not hesitate to reach out if she needed something.

As she made her way to her car, she was grateful things hadn't escalated yesterday and wondered if Mikayla had said or done something to make the boys think it was okay to even approach her in such a manner. As quickly as the thought entered her mind, guilt wiped it away. Mikayla had been through some things growing up. Being touched inappropriately by an 18-year-old boy when she was only 13 was one. That changed her, making her have this thing where she either wanted male attention or didn't. At the time, Mikayla knew right from wrong, but it wasn't until the boy was arrested that Mikayla fully understood what had happened to her. For a while, she felt like the cool girl who had older boys lusting after her. Then everyone around her kept expressing how wrong the boy was, and that changed things for Mikayla.

The need to start over and be away from the judgment of others—her mother, mainly—was how Mikayla came to live with Riley. After speaking with her uncle, Mikayla's father, who at the time was in prison with her own father, she knew it was best that Mikayla come to stay with her. That was four years ago, and as rocky as things had been, she wouldn't have changed her decision.

Chapter 4

"You said you would walk me to the bus, not ride the bus with me all the way to my stop."

"Yeah, and then I figured a walk to the bus wouldn't ensure your safety. The only way to do that is to see you get to your stop. So that's what I'm doing." He shrugged as if going out of his way was no big deal.

"I would've been fine."

"Maybe, but we don't know that for sure." He winked at her, causing her heart to flutter.

She was trying not to become attracted to him. But his caring spirit, and the sly yet sexy looks he was giving her, was not making it an easy task. For the rest of the bus ride, they sat in silence. Mikayla wondered why Jeremiah was being so nice and why he was grateful to have a reason not to go straight home from school, even though that was what Jermaine wanted him to do.

"This is my stop," Mikayla announced, interrupting the silence between the two of them as she pulled down on the lever, alerting the bus driver she wanted to get off at the upcoming stop. She stood, hiking her bag over her left shoulder. When she noticed Jeremiah do the same, she unintentionally frowned.

"You're getting off too?" Mikayla's question came out with every bit of nervousness that she felt.

"Yeah, if that's cool with you. Only to walk you to the door. After that, I'll dip."

"You already came all this way, so I guess it's okay." She shrugged, then looked around the bus nervously. Silently, she hoped none of the other riders were paying them any attention. She already had one rumor that she knew of floating around the school about her. She didn't need any more.

Jeremiah noticed Mikayla's shift and immediately knew she was in her head. He had no ill intentions when it came to her and only wanted her to know she was safe with him. Gently, he took her hand and led her off the bus. A part of him knew he should have just stayed on the bus. He wasn't sure how far she lived from the bus stop, but he was certain she could have and would have made it home safely.

On the other hand, there was also a part of him too selfish to change his course because she was feeling indifferent. While he intended to make sure she got home safe, he also needed this detour to stall him from going home.

"All right, which way?" he asked once the bus pulled off from in front of them.

Mikayla looked down, noticing their hands were still intertwined, and gently pulled hers away before she began walking in the direction of her home. All kinds of thoughts raced through her mind as she walked ahead of Jeremiah.

"Ay, Mikayla, did you hear me?" Jeremiah's voice finally penetrated through her sea of thoughts.

"Uh, no. What'd you say?"

"I said that I'm happy your cousin tore into my brother. That shit was funny. She's a real G."

"Oh, yeah. Well, she's not at the house," she blurted, and the unprovoked information left Jeremiah slightly confused. He wasn't sure why she volunteered the information, because he didn't care either way. Riley was cool in his book until she showed otherwise. She'd probably like him more, seeing how he cared enough to make sure Mikayla made it home safely.

Instead of commenting, he began rapping low, Big Sean's "Sunday Morning Jetpack," to be exact. It was one of his favorite songs from the Detroit artist. The lyrics always resonated with him, inspiring and helping him keep focus when needed. He had made it to the end of the second verse when Mikayla stopped walking.

"We're here," she announced.

Jeremiah looked at the tan and black two-story duplex with minimal adoration. It wasn't because the place wasn't nice. It was because he expected them to live like this. The lawn was perfectly manicured. There wasn't any brown in the grass, unlike the grass in front of his and Jermaine's home. There was also an array of flowers lined against the home directly underneath the windows—an assortment of colors perfectly blended. Jeremiah made a mental note of all the things that stood out about the home so that he'd have no problem finding it next time.

"All right, well, I'll see you at school tomorrow," he told her as he removed his phone. He wasn't about to get back on the bus. He planned to sit in front of her home and wait for an Uber.

"Um, you want to come inside? Get something to drink or something?" Since he had come all this way, Mikayla decided the least she could do was make the offer.

"Shit, why not?" He shrugged. "I can do that while I wait for my Uber." Jeremiah followed a few steps behind Mikayla, pausing while she opened the front door.

Once again, his expectations were met, as the home was nicely decorated—soft gray walls, with photos of people he assumed to be family and some African art pieces, all strategically placed. There was a silver oval-shaped coffee table in front of the smoke gray sofa set, and the home smelled like strawberries.

"Juice, soda, or water?" Mikayla asked as she watched him look around her home. His hands were clasped behind his back, and his lips pursed together as he nodded in approval. She turned her head from him, not wanting to be caught smirking at his mannerisms. He'd be pissed if he knew she could see a resemblance to Mr. Feng with his posture and facial expression. Of course, they did not look alike, but Jeremiah was giving principal approval as he looked around her home. She wondered if he was aware of his body language or was so comfortable that he hadn't thought twice about his stance. Even she, on many occasions, looked around this same room in awe, even though she lived there, because there was no denying that Riley had decorated the hell out of their living room.

"I'll have a soda with a bottle of water."

"Oh, wow, you do that too?" she chuckled, finding humor in the odd similarity. At least, it was odd to her because she didn't know many people who did that.

"Wait, do what?" Jeremiah's brows pinched together as he looked at her, trying to figure out what she was talking about.

"Have a soda and then a water not long after."

"Oh, yeah. I've been doing it since I was a little kid 'cause my mom always said soda was bad for me. So I made a deal that for every soda, I'd have two glasses of water. A way to balance the bad stuff with the good." He shrugged.

"That's kind of the same reason I do it. My cousin laughs because she says there's no way one water will wash out all the sugar in the soda, so I upped it to two glasses of water." She laughed. "Plus, I know soda isn't the best for you, but it's so good. A guilty pleasure I do not feel guilty about."

"It's dope I'm not the only one on that hype. Well, my brother be on it a little bit, but I think it's more of a way to have something to bond with me about rather than him actually believing in it."

"My cousin does stuff like that," she admitted before walking off in the direction of what Jeremiah assumed was the kitchen.

"Can I have a seat in here?" he yelled out to her as he stretched his neck in an attempt to see the back area she'd ventured to.

"Yeah," she replied, and immediately he allowed himself to get comfortable on the sofa.

Mikayla walked back into the living room holding a can of Sprite and a bottled water, locking eyes with him. Mikayla's eyes bore into him, making him feel a strange tingling in the pit of his stomach, and he quickly pulled his eyes away from her. Then, like magnets, they found themselves right back on her. Oddly, it was the first time Jeremiah really got a good look at her. There was no doubt that she was a pretty girl. He could tell that in passing. However, as he looked at her now, really getting a good look at her, he realized that subjecting her to a title as simple as "pretty" was a disservice to the beauty she actually possessed. If he had to call it, Mikayla was the prettiest girl in their school and the baddest chick he'd hung out with. And he kicked it with some fine-ass young women.

"Why are you looking at me like that?" she asked nervously, interrupting his thoughts and stepping out of his direct view. Before sitting next to him, she placed the drinks on coasters on the coffee table.

"Looking at you like what? I was just looking. Wasn't nothing behind it," he lied.

Mikayla wanted to protest and tell him there was something behind the look in his eyes because she'd seen it before. It was less lustful than she had often encountered. Still, it was familiar. Her too-old ex looked at her similarly, and her mother's "friend's" son did too. Both had had their way with her.

The silence made the space they were sharing uncomfortable for Jeremiah, making him assume that his reply made her uncomfortable, something he didn't want.

"What do you like to do? What's your favorite subject in school?" he asked, interrupting the silence. He hoped the generic questions would ease the tension in the room.

"I mainly chill here around the house. I'm a homebody more than anything. I think, well, my favorite subject is science. Not that I want to be a scientist or anything. I just like how it works. Everything deals with science in one way or another."

"I like math. Numbers is my thing, but science is cool, too." He smirked as he sat back. He noticed how her body relaxed, and he felt comfortable enough to do so too. Her arms had been tight at her side like she was purposely keeping them still. Her shoulders had been closer to her ears as well. His question changed her posture. Her arms swayed slightly, and her shoulders were no longer near her ears. He wondered if she noticed how her body reacted to her getting tense like he did.

Mikayla smiled, glad he liked something else that she did. No, it wasn't his favorite, like hers, but it was on her radar, which she could appreciate.

"Thank you again for taking up for me in the bathroom, running after me when I stormed out of Mr. Feng's office, and making sure I got home safe. Wow." She chuckled.

"What's so wow about it?"

"It's just that you've done a lot for me in such a short time." Mikayla scooted closer to him, closing the small gap that separated them and placing her hand on his thigh.

"Wh . . . who's your favorite rapper?" The simple gesture of putting her hand on his thigh had him very close to getting aroused. He honestly hadn't come to her home to get anything from her, and he certainly wasn't trying to leave with blue balls.

"I like Wale, Kendrick Lamar, J. Cole, Rick Ross, and Lil Wayne. Oh, and of course, Lil' Kim."

"I like all of them too." He was already trying to calm his nerves, so when she squeezed his thigh, it only made the fight harder.

"You like Lil' Kim too?" She giggled, not expecting him to be a fan of the female rapper.

"I mean, her Bad Boy and Junior M.A.F.I.A. days were solid. Ay, look, Mikayla—"

The protest he was about to voice instantly halted as Mikayla straddled him in what seemed like one swift motion. Her lips met his, forcing her tongue into his mouth, breaking through his resistance. Jeremiah's hands moved to her hips with the intent of removing her, yet her kiss was like a forceful magnet, keeping him drawn in.

"Mikayla," he whispered through her lips slightly, distorting her name.

"It's okay. I want to do this." She could feel the tension in his body, how he stiffened up when she kissed him, let her know he was unsure of her motives. The only thing she needed him to know was that she wanted to give her body to him. Not only as a way to thank him, but also because she thought he genuinely liked her.

"I know, but—"

"What in the entire hell?"

Jeremiah's second protest was interrupted by Riley. Neither heard her enter the home, and that was because she came in through the garage. Had Mikayla not been straddling him, he would have seen her walk toward them. The entrance into the home from the garage was in clear view. It was off to the left, down the hallway right before the floor changed to the marbled square tile, dividing the front of the house from the kitchen. This door was the way Riley entered their home most of the time, something Mikayla should have been on top of, given her persistence for Jeremiah to have her.

Riley's angered tone had been exactly what he needed to find the strength to remove Mikayla from on top of him.

"I know y'all not attempting to do what I think you were about to do—in my house on my damn couch." Riley paced, staring at the two of them as if she'd walked in on them and they were already ass naked. It was apparent she'd been caught off guard and was pissed, as her words, as unconventional as they were, made sense to the three of them.

"What is wrong with you?" The question was aimed at Mikayla, but her eyes bounced between them. Riley's heart felt like it was on the verge of cracking into a million pieces. It hadn't been long since she'd come from McClane High defending Mikayla, and now she was in a compromising position with another boy. Things like this were why she wanted Mikayla to get outside help, which she constantly refused.

"We were only kissing. You can relax, Riley."

"Don't tell me to relax when the two of you shouldn't even be doing that. Jeremiah, it's time for you to leave." Although her voice presented full-on anger, it hadn't resonated in her facial expression. At least, not yet. Had her tone not been so stern, he wouldn't have been able to tell what she was feeling. She looked defeated more than anything, and Jeremiah felt terrible.

Nodding, Jeremiah stood, embarrassment written all over his face. He turned to look at Mikayla and was surprised by her attitude. Her arms were folded across her chest as she mugged the hell out of Riley. He wasn't sure if the mood was to save face because they had gotten caught, or if she was agitated that Riley interrupted what she was trying to do.

"I'll see you at school tomorrow," he told her before turning his attention to Riley. "I know we just met and all, but I want you to know that I'm not trying to take it there with your cousin. Real talk, I have a lot of respect for you, so nothing was going to happen."

He didn't need a reply, so he departed quickly, relieved when his phone alerted him that his Uber was less than a minute away. He hadn't even realized he'd requested it so long ago. So much had transpired in such a short amount of time that he almost forgot he ordered the ride. He was shocked Mikayla had come at him in a sexual manner, especially after what she'd been through. It made him wonder if Daniel, Levi, and Jason had the right idea about her. She was scared, he thought, recalling the look on her face and the tears flowing from her eyes. There was no way she was a willing participant. "Then why come at me like that?" he mumbled as he entered the car. He allowed his head to rest against the car's headrest. Jeremiah saw something in Mikayla that made him want to keep her around as a friend. So he hoped eventually they could clear things up.

Jeremiah's exit pulled Mikayla's and Riley's attention back to one another. For a moment they just stared, eyes locked, as they attempted to gather their thoughts. Riley wanted to go easy on her, but she felt that the easy route had landed them in this moment.

Knowing she was wrong, Mikayla was the first to break eye contact as she rolled her eyes and stood.

"You may as well sit back down because we're about to talk about this."

Blowing out an irritated breath, Mikayla plopped back down on the sofa, folded her arms across her chest, and glared at Riley.

"You know you're not supposed to have guys over here, especially when I'm not here or haven't okayed it. Then for me to walk in on you straddling his lap and you have no regard for me is fucked up."

"You're acting like you walked in on us having sex. There's no reason for you to be upset, because you heard him. He's not feeling me like that."

Riley was taken aback by the sadness in her tone. She hated this for her cousin, hated that Mikayla was still unaware that a male's attention or affection didn't validate her.

"I highly doubt he dislikes you. It's possible he only likes you as a friend, and nothing is wrong with that."

"Boys and girls can't be just 'friends.'" She made air quotes with her hands while rolling her eyes.

"That's not true. Look, Jeremiah seems like a cool kid. He's easy on the eyes as well." Riley smiled as she took a seat next to Mikayla. "Him saying what he said was in no way to hurt or insult you. He was only clearing the air so that no lines were crossed in the future. I'm sure he kissed you back, because who wouldn't? You're gorgeous, Maki. A boy only wanting friendship doesn't mean anything is wrong with you. It means everything is right. The best relationships start from friendships." Though Riley initially wanted to tear into Mikayla's ass, this approach was better. She didn't want Jeremiah's words to affect Mikayla's confidence, nor did she want Mikayla to think she was defined by what a guy accepted from her. She hoped Jeremiah was sincere and hadn't only spoken those words because he didn't want her pissed.

"Maybe. But it doesn't matter. Jeremiah doesn't like me like that, nor as a friend, I'm sure. You don't have to worry about catching him here again. I have homework." Mikayla stood, picking her backpack up off the floor before heading up the stairs to her bedroom.

Riley's heart broke for her cousin and herself as she hoped Mikayla would see her worth at some point. She would continue to love and guide her as best as possible until then.

Chapter 5

"You're adding a stop?" the driver asked Jeremiah as their eyes met through the rearview mirror.

"Yeah, it's cool, right?"

"Yes, there's no problem. Am I waiting for you or is this a drop-off?"

"A drop-off."

The driver nodded, and Jeremiah turned to look out the window. He watched as they passed the street they would have taken if he were going home. He knew Jermaine was going to be pissed at him, but he had already disobeyed him when he rode the bus home with Mikayla, so one more stop wouldn't make much of a difference. His orders were to go straight home after school, but he hadn't done that, so he decided to enjoy whatever freedom he had left before his brother banned him from everything.

Jeremiah wasn't shocked to see his boys occupying the corner when the Uber driver pulled onto the block. He hung on with his boys. It was after

4:00 p.m. on a Thursday and, according to KJ, the best time to make money.

"Thanks again, man. I left you a nice tip," Jeremiah said as he exited the vehicle.

"I see. I appreciate it, man. You be safe out here." The driver looked out the window, and Jeremiah noticed a glimpse of disdain cross the man's face. His driver was a Middle Eastern man who looked to be in his forties. He hadn't spoken much during the ride, but his change in mood was apparent. Sadly, Jeremiah wasn't surprised, not because he thought the man was being racist or anything, but because right now his boys looked every bit the stereotype placed on them, and once he walked over there, he would too.

"I will, thanks, man." He shut the door and waited until the man drove off before making his way to KJ and the rest of their crew.

"What's up, young'un?" KJ greeted Jeremiah with his hand extended for a shake, which Jeremiah took.

"You're not that much older than me. But everything is good."

"Until you've lived in the fast lane, the numbers they identify our ages with mean nothing. I'm an OG compared to you. Don't trip, though. After tonight, you'll earn a couple stripes that'll put at least a year on your age. And a little hair on your chest." He chuckled before raising his fist for Jeremiah to pound.

Hesitantly, Jeremiah met his fist with his own as he felt his stomach turn.

"What's happening tonight?" He tried to ask the question with confidence, not wanting to give away how nervous he was feeling. KJ hadn't revealed what they would be doing, but his tone let him know that it wasn't something he was ready for. However, he'd signed up to be a gang member and knew that everything wouldn't be peaches and cream to be part of the crew. He even knew he'd wind up doing some things he wouldn't be proud of, but if there was one thing he was big on, it was standing by his choices, so that was what he was going to do. He just planned to be smart about how he moved.

Jeremiah looked around as H-Town pulled into the parking lot of a shopping center on the other side of town. It was an area that his boys considered to be the rich side of town. Jeremiah frequented some of the stores with Jermaine. He'd never noticed a difference in prices between those stores and those closer to the hood where he and his homeboys hung. What was different was the types of people who shopped in the area. The cars were nicer, the streets were not flooded with trash, and everyone seemed to mind their business.

"What we doing over here?" he asked, knowing they looked out of place in the raggedy Honda they rolled up in.

"About to get some money. Come on." KJ exited the car with his hand in his pocket and began walking toward a black BMW X4. "Keep your eyes open. If you see anyone coming, tap my shoulder. Don't yell or no shit like that, making it obvious, all right?"

"Uh, okay." Jeremiah's heart raced as his eyes darted around the parking lot. He was scared shitless and couldn't believe how bold KJ was to be doing this in such a public place.

"Fuck," KJ yelled, having difficulty getting into the vehicle and setting off the car's alarm.

"What's wrong?" Jeremiah panicked as he turned his attention back to KJ. Unfortunately for both of them, that second cost them a lot.

"Hey, get the hell away from my car." An older white man charged toward them.

"I got it," KJ said as he opened the car door. He tried getting in but was stopped by the man pulling his arm.

"Fuck off me," he said before turning and punching the man in the face.

Horrified, Jeremiah watched, unsure of what to do as blood splattered from the man's nose and he fell to the ground.

"Get the fuck in the car," KJ told him, pulling him from his frozen stance.

Jeremiah hadn't felt his feet move, nor did he know how he'd gotten inside the vehicle KJ seemed to be doing 100 miles per hour in.

"We about to get paid for this mothafucka," KJ boasted, hitting the steering wheel.

"You know that whole place has cameras?" Jeremiah said, shaken. He could feel in his gut that this would not end well.

"Hold on, this H-town," KJ said, silencing Jeremiah before he could whine some more. "Yo," he answered the phone, putting it on speaker so he could focus on driving.

"Police behind me, and this piece of shit car not moving fast enough. If I'm not at the spot, you know they got me."

"Fuck," KJ yelled, and Jeremiah's heart dropped. There was no way they would be getting away with this, and he knew it.

Mikayla sat at her desk with her head on a swivel. She couldn't concentrate on a word the teacher was saying because she was waiting for the classroom door to open. Class had already been in session for fifteen minutes, and Ms. Remi had a tardiness policy that really left no one room to be late. Being late to her class was the equivalent of an absence, so missing the course was more appealing. Still, she held out hope because *he* had told her he would see her today.

She had barely gotten any sleep, wondering what she would say to him once she saw him. She'd rehearsed an apology, an attitude, and a million excuses she could present him with before she called it a night. Although she and Riley had talked things out, she was still upset with her because her intrusion left her and Jeremiah in a gray area. Well, her at least. He'd made his intentions clear before he left her house. So why was she having a hard time believing he only wanted to be her friend? Sadly, she contemplated the idea that he didn't want anything to do with her at all. Calling her a friend was more than likely a cop-out, a way to nicely say that he'd never date her in a million years. Mikayla wasn't sure if it was her ego taking the hit or her past coming back to haunt her. She hadn't met a guy who didn't want to take advantage of her, so it was hard to see Jeremiah any other way.

The sounds of squeaking coming from the hall grabbed Mikayla's attention. Just like everyone else in the room, she knew the sound could only come from someone's sneakers on the linoleum. Her heart stopped as her eyes moved to the knob, silently willing it to turn. However, whoever walked the hall continued until she could no longer hear the sound. Disappointed was an understatement.

Still, she held out hope because he told her he would see her today. Like a dummy, she hadn't gotten his phone number. With him revealing his lack of interest in her on a romantic level, she wasn't even sure if exchanging numbers was an option. After he embarrassed her, she was unsure why she even cared to see him.

"Mikayla."

She jumped, unintentionally sliding the chair across the floor. She was frightened. Fear flooded through her as if she'd just gotten caught stealing. Ms. Remi had caught her slipping.

"Yes?" Mikayla pulled herself together, sitting up in her seat and giving the teacher her undivided attention while trying to calm her rapidly beating heart.

"Did you have your definition? It's your turn to tell the class what circumvention means." The assignment was to take a word with a definition different from what one would assume. Her word instantly would make one think of a circumcision. At least, she did when she first heard it. How wrong she was.

"Um, yes, I do." She gathered her notebook, flipping to the page where her sentence and definition were written down. She completed the assignment last night, although she'd had it for a few days. She was glad she had waited until the last minute because it gave her a chance to stop thinking about Jeremiah and how she made a fool of herself momentarily.

"Circumvention has many definitions, but the two I chose were 'avoiding something' and 'deceives.'"

"Good job," Ms. Remi said before turning to address the whole class. She went on with a lecture Mikayla barely paid attention to because she kept looking toward the door. It wasn't until the bell rang, dismissing the class, that she accepted she wouldn't see Jeremiah in class.

Maybe he's sick or his suspension isn't lifted like we thought, Mikayla thought as she gathered her belongings.

She exited the classroom and headed to her locker, walking past Jason. This was the first time she'd seen him since the incident, and though she knew he wouldn't try anything again, he still sent chills down her spine from just a look. The quick glance he gave—well, the one she could see before averting her eyes—wasn't a menacing one. It looked almost like remorse. Or maybe it was pity. She couldn't be sure and had no plans of trying to find out. Her mind was occupied with other things.

"Mikayla, how are you?" The unexpected hand on her shoulder startled her, and her body tensed. Although the familiar voice hadn't frightened her, the unexpected touch had.

"I'm fine, Mr. Feng," she said as she relaxed.

"Okay. You know there is never a time limit on when you can come to me to report those young men."

"I know." Her eyes roamed the halls, and she felt like everyone was watching her interaction with the principal. However, that was far from the truth. The students were doing what they always had done during a period change.

"All right, young lady, have a great day." Mr. Feng produced a thin-lipped smile before walking away.

Mikayla, feeling exposed, hurriedly opened her locker and replaced the book she had with the one she needed. As she slammed her locker door shut, she could still feel eyes on her. She looked up and down the hall, and when her eyes landed on him, her heart skipped a beat.

"Jeremiah," she mouthed, taking off in his direction. He wasn't too far from her, but his failure to stay put was disheartening. Now she could surely say he was avoiding her. He watched as she was approaching and took off in the other direction as she got closer. She wanted to run after him, but the bell ringing stopped her. Besides, what was the point if he was going to run off? Mikayla went to her next class with a heavy heart.

"If he's not out here, then I give up."

It was now lunchtime. She had spent the entire class period wondering what was happening with Jeremiah. She refused to let him disown her. Even if he didn't want to take it there romantically, she wanted him as a friend. She needed him as one because he made her feel safe.

"Jeremiah." She called his name softly but loud enough for him to hear her.

His head shot up as he was obviously surprised to see her. He also looked as if he wanted to take off, but the warning look she gave kept him in place.

"I feel like you're avoiding me," she said, sitting next to him on the bench. Though she never had lunch outside, in passing she'd usually see Jeremiah in this exact spot, sometimes alone, sometimes with a few of his boys. Luckily for her, today it was only him.

"I got a lot going on." He shrugged.

Mikayla fought the urge to roll her eyes. She doubted he'd inherited a ton of shit on his plate in twenty-four hours, but she decided to humor him. "I'm a good listener."

"Fuck, man!" Jeremiah's bellow of frustration caused her to jump and back away from him. Although he wasn't directing his frustration at her, his tone unnerved her.

"My bad. I forgot you have a thing about yelling." He remembered she'd told him that the day she rushed out of the office.

"It's . . . I'm okay. What's going on?"

"I gotta lie low for a little bit. I'm not gon' be around for a while. I'm not avoiding you. I figured it would be better if I helped you get used to me not being around."

Mikayla frowned, unsure of what he was trying to say because he was speaking in circles. "Why do you have to go? Suspended again? I don't understand."

"Nah, I got into some shit with my potnas, and it could land me in jail if we get caught, so I need to lie low until the heat dies down." When the words left his mouth, he realized he shouldn't have even brought his ass to school. He only came because he didn't want to hear Jermaine's mouth. But given that he had already cut one class, the school would let his brother know. He was going to hear Jermaine complain either way.

"Where will you go?" Mikayla asked, and her question reminded him that he had nowhere to go. Most of his boys were hanging out in trap houses and with random chicks. He could've done the same, but if he did that, he might as well turn himself in.

"I'm still working that out," he said smoothly, although internally he was panicking.

"You can come stay with me," she blurted out so easily.

"Your cousin is not having that," he chuckled.

"She doesn't have to know. Plus, there are two places in the house she rarely goes: the basement and my room."

"I don't know, man. I'm not trying to get you caught up in my shit."

"We'd be even if you do." She smiled.

"Ay, about yesterday . . ."

"It's okay. I know you don't like me like that."

Jeremiah could hear in her tone how the rejection hurt her. "Nah, it's not okay. Mikayla, you're a beautiful girl. 'Bout one of the finest I done seen. It's just that I got a lot of shit going on right now. I'm not even ready for relationship shit, but I can be the bestest friend you'll ever have." He smiled at her before winking.

Chuckling, Mikayla quickly thought about his offer. "Best friends it is then." Mikayla extended her hand, waiting only a moment for him to reciprocate so they could seal the deal.

"Cool." Jeremiah was relieved she made things easy. He felt terrible about how he left things yesterday, and had he more time, he would've explained to her that she didn't owe him her body because he came to her aid. Had he not gone with his friends to indulge in some shit that would land him in jail, he probably would have obsessed more with Mikayla and her actions. His gut told him there was more to her and more to why she reacted to him the way she had. Truthfully, he would have taken analyzing her over his current situation. Both were things he was too young to be dealing with, but the outcome of one was far better than the other.

"Okay, well, since we're best friends now, you have to let me help you." Mikayla smiled before nudging him with her shoulder, hoping to lighten the mood. She could see the anxiety on his face, and although he hadn't disclosed the details to her, she could see it. Whatever he'd done was weighing on him.

"I already told you."

"I heard what you said, and still, I'm not taking no for an answer. You can either come with me to my house after school, or you can head there now. Either way, you're hiding out there. I refuse to let you go from place to place or, even worse, sleep on the streets." Her heart broke at the thought of him not having anyplace secure to go. He was a safety net for her when she needed it, and there was no way she wouldn't be the same for him if she could.

Jeremiah's shoulders relaxed as he blew out his breath in frustration. As much as he hated to accept her offer, he had to because he had nowhere else to go.

"All right. We'll meet at your place after school. I'm not sure who may be watching, so I'll meet you there. I promise."

"Okay." She easily believed him. There was something about Jeremiah she didn't doubt, which meant a lot because she didn't trust many.

"I'm going to walk you to class. Hopefully, Ms. Remi doesn't give me any shit since I missed class."

"Just turn in your definition and she may give you a little lenience."

Laughter erupted from both of their mouths and caused heads to turn. Lenience was not a character trait of Ms. Remi's, at least not one they'd ever seen.

"You'll meet me at my house, right?" she asked again, wanting to make sure his answer hadn't changed. Reassurance was important to her, and though it may get annoying, she couldn't help it.

"Yes, Mikayla," Jeremiah reassured her as gently as possible as they stood in front of her classroom.

"Okay. Oh, wait. I don't have your number."

Shaking his head with a slight grin on his face, Jeremiah unlocked his phone before handing it to Mikayla. She smirked as she dialed herself before returning his phone. Without another word, Jeremiah walked off, heading for his class.

The rest of the day went by slowly for Mikayla as she anticipated Jeremiah meeting her at her house. She thought of all the ways they could avoid Riley, who she knew would kill her for allowing Jeremiah back into the house without her permission once again. By the time she made it home, her nerves were less shaky, and she had it all figured out.

Mikayla sat on the living room sofa, leg shaking in anticipation, as she waited for Jeremiah to arrive. She hadn't been home a full five minutes but couldn't help wondering what was taking him so long. She removed her cell from her pocket, contemplating whether she should text him. She didn't think asking when she could expect him would hurt. Her thumb tapped against the phone as she bit her bottom lip, going back and forth with what she should do. As she had made up her mind to say fuck it and send the text, there was a knock at the door.

Mikayla leaped from her seat as if she'd sat on a bed full of nails and rushed to the front door. She checked the peephole, ecstatic and relieved to see Jeremiah on the other side of the door.

"Riley isn't here, is she?" She could hear the nervousness in his tone, and if the situation weren't as serious as it was, she would have laughed at him. Granted, the last time he was in their home and Riley was there too, it was not a friendly visit. So she could understand his hesitancy, but whether Riley was home or not, she was going to help him.

"No. Now follow me. Let me show you where you'll be hiding out." Mikayla took his hand as he kicked the door shut. She led him upstairs, opening the door to her bedroom.

Jeremiah looked around the room, which was painted a lighter shade of gray than their living room. Mikayla's walls had many photos on them, primarily cartoon-style images of black women. There was a white desk in the corner of her room with a small bookshelf next to it.

"You're gonna have to hide out in my closet." She took the couple of steps and opened the double doors to what he knew would be her closet.

Jeremiah was impressed with its size. The walk-in closet contained shelves and plenty of floor space. Though it wasn't the comfort of his own home and bed, at least the area would give him wiggle room. It was definitely bigger than a cardboard box.

"There are blankets in there, and I'll bring you some dinner after Riley gets home and cooks. Oh, I can bring you a few snacks to have. Um, we eat dinner at the table, so while I'm down there, you have free range of my bedroom. I use the bathroom across the hall because Riley has her own, but I'll need to make sure the coast is clear before you go in there."

"I got it. I'll be good. Thanks for even doing this, Mikayla. I won't be any trouble at all."

"No problem."

Mikayla chilled with Jeremiah until about ten minutes before Riley was due to arrive.

"Hey," Riley greeted her with her brow furrowed because she hadn't expected Mikayla to be sitting in the living room when she arrived.

"Hey." Mikayla offered a soft smile to her cousin. She knew Riley was looking at her sideways because she rarely met her at the door when she came home, but she couldn't risk Riley deciding to do something she hardly ever did, which was come to her bedroom.

"What's up?" Riley asked as she took a seat next to her cousin. She knew something was up with Mikayla and decided to ask rather than wonder.

"Well, you were right. I spoke with Jeremiah today, and we decided to be friends. I'm glad that friendship is the route we decided to take."

"See? I told you. I'm glad it worked out for you two. He seems like a good kid. That brother of his is still up for debate, but he seems like he was raised right."

"You know his brother is helping raise him, right?"

"That's also up for debate." Riley rolled her eyes.

"His brother is fine, huh?" Mikayla nudged her.

"He was until he opened his mouth."

"You met your match and can't take it."

"Are you hungry? I've been craving enchiladas all day, so that's what I'm making." Riley smoothly changed the subject. Mikayla knew her too well, and rather than admit her little cousin was right, she deflected.

Mikayla laughed before agreeing with her cousin's choice for dinner. She knew Jeremiah would enjoy them because Riley's enchiladas were always good. She learned how to make them from her ex's mother, and she had perfected the recipe like she'd grown up cooking them every day.

"Yes, do you need me to do anything?"

"Just grab the ingredients and set the table. I'm going to change out of these clothes."

Riley headed to her bedroom and Mikayla to the kitchen. She sent a text to Jeremiah, letting him know to keep quiet because her cousin was heading upstairs, before busying herself with grabbing the items Riley needed to make dinner.

"How was school today outside of you and Jeremiah officially becoming friends?" Riley asked as she sat across from Mikayla, with her right elbow on the table and fork in the air. She watched as Mikayla chewed and then swallowed to prepare to answer the question. She really wanted to ask if Mikayla had run into any of the little shits who tried to violate her, but she didn't want to be pushy.

"Nothing much. It was a typical day." She shrugged before taking another bite of food.

"Well, nothing interesting happened to me today, either."

"I mean, I did see one of the guys in passing."

"What did he say to you?" Riley put her fork down and gave Mikayla her undivided attention. If he or any of them got out of line, it would take the strength of ten men to get Riley off their asses.

"Nothing. He looked at me but didn't say anything. The look he gave me, though, was almost like he felt bad."

"Girl, do not fall for that. Fuck him and his fake remorse on his ugly-ass face."

Mikayla covered her mouth to prevent her food from spilling out as she choked back a laugh. "You don't even know what he looks like."

"He ugly, his friends ugly, his mama and daddy ugly. Anybody who pulls some shit like he did does not have a cute bone in their body."

"I guess that makes sense." Mikayla shrugged. She knew she wouldn't be able to argue anything different with Riley, so she didn't try.

"It absolutely does. And they are still getting their asses whooped. Our people will be coming out here. We're waiting for things to die down a little bit, but they catching a beatdown."

"Did you tell them what happened?" Mikayla knew she hadn't done anything wrong, but the thought of her cousins knowing how she came close to being violated did something to her. Besides, she knew her family had always pegged her as a fast little girl. She couldn't say that her actions hadn't made the assumption seem true. It hurt that no one in her family other than Riley cared enough to understand why she took to men or craved male attention. She was still trying to understand it herself, but it felt good to have someone care enough to try to figure it out with her when she was open enough to do so.

"No, that's your business to tell. Plus, you know Li'l June and they love to fight. All I had to say was that some high school boys tried you, and they were ready to drive down here." She laughed.

"Yes, if Li'l June can't do nothing else, he can fight," Mikayla added.

"Hey, you're sure you're holding up okay?"

"I have my moments, but for the most part I feel okay," she told her honestly.

"Well, I'm always here if you need me."

"I know, and I appreciate you so much, Riley."

"I love you, stinka." Riley smiled at her cousin. Mikayla was such a beautiful young lady, and she would stick by her no matter what, all while reminding her of the beauty she possessed.

"I'll put the food away," Mikayla volunteered. If Riley did it, she wouldn't be able to make Jeremiah a plate.

"What are you smiling at?" Riley asked, giving her a skeptical look.

"Oh, nothing." She shook it off. She hadn't noticed she was smiling. Oddly, the thought of Jeremiah did that to her. She was also happy that, up until now, she had kept her cool, knowing she was basically harboring her new bestie turned fugitive.

"If you say so. I'm about to go start my nightly routine. But afterward do you want to watch a movie?"

"Will I hurt your feelings if I pass? I have an assignment I want to knock out and then catch up on my favorite YouTube couple. Rain check?" Mikayla gave her a sweet smile, although the disappointed look on Riley's face made her feel bad.

"I guess," Riley groaned. "I need to catch up with a couple of my shows anyway." She stood from the table and began making her exit. "Holler if you need me," she told her.

"Will do." Mikayla waited until she was sure Riley was locked away in her bedroom before grabbing a paper plate and piling enchiladas, rice, and beans onto it. She set the plate aside and then put away the rest of the food. After grabbing a soda and water for Jeremiah, she went to her bedroom.

When Mikayla entered her room, she headed straight for the closet. She thought Jeremiah would have taken advantage of her bed, knowing she and Riley were downstairs and wouldn't bother him, but instead, he opted for the floor in her closet.

"Hey." She looked at him lying on his back and scrolling through his phone with his head resting on the pillow she'd given him.

"Took you long enough. I was up here starving," he teased as he sat up then took the plate from her.

"You want to eat in here? You could go sit at my desk or on my bed."

"I'm cool here unless you're too good to chill on the floor with me."

"Not at all." She smiled before taking a seat Indian style across from him.

"Your cousin cooked this?" he asked, his mouth full.

"Yep." She smiled, proud that he was enjoying the meal.

"Man, this tastes like something straight out of a restaurant," he told her, smacking his lips.

"She learned how to cook it from a Hispanic woman. It's one of my favorite meals for her to make."

"Ay, can you tell me what happened that day? I mean, if you're comfortable talking about it." Jeremiah looked up from his plate.

"I'm not sure. I was heading to class, and they cornered me. Then we heard someone coming down the hall—that someone was you—and they pushed me into the bathroom. They tried to say a rumor is what made them think I'd be easy." She shrugged as she felt tears fill her eyes. She was tired of reliving the moment, but she felt comfortable letting Jeremiah know.

"They still gotta catch a fade with me. That was some bitch-ass shit." His tone changed, anger dripping from it, and she couldn't help feeling like he was taking the situation personally.

"You don't have to do anything. My cousins are coming down from the Bay Area, and they do not play."

"Their get back and mine is different."

"Why?" she wanted to know.

"Because that was some bitch-ass shit they pulled, and since you're my best friend now, I definitely gotta come to your aid."

"You already did that, though." She chuckled, trying to lighten the mood.

"Yeah, but not good enough," he spoke somberly.

"What are you not saying, Jeremiah?"

She placed her hand on his calf, and this time, he didn't flinch at her touch. He knew there was nothing sexual behind it and it was only a gesture to let him know he could trust her with whatever was bothering him. Hell, she was hiding him in her bedroom to keep him from jail. He had no reason to think she wasn't trustworthy.

"When I was eleven, I watched two men rape my mother." The admission tightened his chest.

Mikayla's hand flew to her mouth. This was the last thing she expected to hear from him. She watched as sorrow overcame him. She could see how his eyes lowered and his lips turned down-ward. There was even a slight change in his skin tone. He appeared darker at that moment. As she looked at him, she tried to think of a question to change the subject even though she wanted him to elaborate. So instead of trying to find words that clearly weren't going to come to her, she sat silently and waited for him to choose what would come next.

"Two dudes she thought were cool did it. At the time, my brother was locked up, and I was the man of the house and couldn't protect her. After that day, I vowed to never watch another man violate a woman and not speak up."

"Is your mother okay?"

"Yeah. I mean, I think so. She doesn't show any signs of not being okay. Other than getting rid of me."

"What do you mean she got rid of you?"

"I started getting in trouble. She claimed I became too much, so she sent me to live with my brother. He moved out here to stay out of trouble. He was in the streets heavy back home."

"Sounds like my mom. She believed people over me, and I ended up here with Riley. Honestly, I like living with Riley way better than with my mom, so it worked out."

"Yeah, living with my brother isn't so bad. It actually makes me feel like a grown man and shit." He chuckled.

"I know. There do seem to be fewer rules when you're living with an adult who isn't much older than you." She laughed.

"Ay, thank you. I know we're just starting to bond, and I may be going away. It's fucking us up."

"No, it's not. Plus, you're not going to jail."

"I hope not, but the chances are very likely. I know somebody saw us, and one of my friends got caught. Eventually, they'll put the pieces together. Hopefully, I'm far enough away when they do."

"What did you do?"

"Some dumb car shit. I don't want to tell you much because the less you know, the better."

Mikayla wanted to reassure him that he could tell her everything and there wouldn't be enough threats or torture that would get her to reveal his secrets. But since he said that knowing less was for her own good, she would accept that.

They stayed up talking until their eyes were too heavy to keep open, not knowing it would be some time before they would have another night like this one.

Loud banging on the door caused Mikayla to stir in her sleep. She placed the pillow on her head, frustrated because she couldn't understand why Riley had the television so loud.

"Somebody was knocking on your door like the damn police," Jeremiah grumbled, poking his head through the small opening of the closet door.

His words lingered in the air for a few moments before they both realized what he had just said. Mikayla jolted up in bed as the closet door flew open with Jeremiah standing there, fear written all over his face.

"There's no reason for the police to show up here. Riley has a tendency to have the TV loud. I'm going to check it out." Mikayla's eyes glanced at the clock on her nightstand. The time caused a lump to form in her throat: 7:55 a.m. on a Saturday. There was no way Riley had the TV up that loud, or on for that matter.

"Hold the fuck on!" Riley's voice echoed through the hall.

Mikayla stopped in her tracks and looked at Jeremiah, who now looked like he was ready to shit bricks. She tried to force a reassuring smile, but even she wasn't sure what was going on.

"I'm going to go check it out. Stay here. I doubt it's the police, but if it is, I'll yell a safe word, like 'You,' and you can hide or go out the window. I doubt it's the police, though, because no one knows you're here."

Without waiting for a reply, Mikayla rushed out of her bedroom. She'd barely made it to the second-to-last stair as Riley snatched the front door open, pissed.

"Where is my brother?" Jermaine stormed into the house, practically knocking Riley over.

"Excuse you?" Riley turned toward him, and if looks could kill, he'd be dead on impact.

"My brother. Where is he? Jeremiah!" Jermaine's baritone voice carried through the entire house. He was definitely loud enough for Jeremiah to hear him even with Mikayla's bedroom door closed and him hiding in her closet.

"First of all, your brother is not here. Secondly, if he were, you do not barge yo' tall ass in my house. You truly do not have any fucking manners, and I am about to lose my religion."

"Fuck all that. I know he's here because I tracked his phone to this location."

"Well, something is wrong with your tracker because he is not here!"

"What you got my brother into?" Jermaine turned toward Mikayla, his face contorted in anger.

"You don't get to speak to her! Get the fuck out of my house." Protectively, Riley stepped in front of Mikayla, who stood unsure of what to do.

"I'm not going anywhere without my brother."

"How many times do I have to say he is not—"

"I'm right here." Jeremiah's voice cut Riley off. Each of them turned toward the top of the stairs where he stood, but the only person he cared to look at was Mikayla. Dejected was the only way to describe the look he had in his eyes before he mouthed an apology to her.

"Bro, what the fuck?"

"Yeah, what the fuck?" Riley questioned with her hands on her hips as she turned to face the two teens.

Jeremiah took the steps two at a time, stopping right in front of his brother. "Bro, calm down. Ain't no need to talk to either one of them like that."

"What the hell you doing here?"

"I said it was okay," Mikayla spoke up. She refused to allow Jeremiah to be the only one catching heat, especially for something she told him was okay to do.

"Mikayla." Riley's tone wasn't one of disappointment. It was of exhaustion.

"You really trying to act like you ain't know he was here?" Jermaine spoke, releasing a light chuckle. There was nothing funny about what was going on. However, it was necessary to help calm the anger brewing inside of him.

"What you trying to say?" Riley was extremely sick of his shit.

"Jeremiah Stately." Shock registered on everyone's faces as their attention was directed toward the front door, where two police officers stood, hands on their weapons, looking directly at Jeremiah.

"What y'all want with him?" Now it was Jermaine who had taken a protective stance in front of his sibling.

"Sir, we need you to step out of the way. We have a warrant for his arrest."

"For what? Let me see the warrant."

"Yes, let us see the warrant 'cause I know damn well my address isn't on it for y'all to just be walking into my house." Riley looked the two male officers up and down. One was white and the other black. Though she was pissed at their intrusion and the entire situation, she was grateful they hadn't come in ready to kill, especially since she had no clue why they even wanted Jeremiah.

"He's a suspect in a carjacking. Unless you want us to force him out of the home, I suggest you move out of the way and he make his way toward us."

"He's not going nowhere with you. Unless he's under arrest, I'll drive him down there as a suspect not guilty in my eyes," Jermaine protested, still remaining in front of his brother.

It all happened so fast, the rushing of the officers, one to restrain Jermaine and the other toward Jeremiah. It took everything in Riley not to help the men, but she had to hold a hysterical Mikayla back.

"I'm going, damn. Just let my brother go!" Jeremiah yelled. Though afraid, he remained calm, fully prepared to cooperate.

"Fuck off me!" Jermaine yelled as he snatched away from the officer.

"Mikayla, I'll be okay. Bro, I'll be fine."

"Don't say shit, Jeremiah. Every time they say something to you, say, 'Lawyer.'"

"Okay." Jeremiah kept his head held high as he was escorted out and toward the police car.

"This shit is your fault." Jermaine's cold eyes landed on Mikayla right as he slammed the door.

Chapter 6

"Mikayla, what did I tell you?" Riley could no longer hold back her frustration.

"He needed me, Riley, and when I didn't even know I needed him, he was there for me." Tears fell from Mikayla's eyes like a leaking faucet. Her heart was broken as a million thoughts ran through her mind. She knew Riley was upset with her, but she couldn't help wondering about Jeremiah. She knew he was tough, but even the toughest guy didn't want to go to jail. She hated that neither of them thought to get rid of his phone. Then Jermaine wouldn't have found him, and he surely wouldn't have led the police to her home. Mikayla placed both hands on her head as she began pacing the floor. Riley's complaining sounded muffled as she did her best to tune her out. Her only concern right now was Jeremiah.

"He doesn't deserve to go to jail," she cried as she stopped pacing and turned to look at her cousin with tear-filled eyes.

"They didn't pick him up for nothing," Riley said as gently as possible, placing her hand on her shoulder.

"Black boys get harassed by police every day. I said he didn't deserve to go to jail. We have to help him." Mikayla laid her head on her cousin's shoulder, silently praying that Jeremiah was okay. She didn't want to think about how life would be without him.

"Why didn't you come to me? I probably could have helped him. I'm not sure what I can do now."

"You were just pissed at me for having him over. There's no way that I would've thought to bring this to you. I can already tell you think he's trouble." She wiped her eyes to no avail as the tears kept coming.

Riley looked at her cousin as she tried to figure out what she could say without sounding insensitive. Mikayla was right. She probably would've told her that Jeremiah was cool and all, but he wasn't their problem. But seeing him be pulled out of her home in cuffs and how distraught Mikayla was, she wasn't so sure of that notion anymore. Jeremiah was currently feeling like their problem. She could see he was troubled but not enough to have someone turn their back on him. Hell, as much as she couldn't stand his brother, she admired how hard he went for him. It was how hard she went for Mikayla, if not harder at times.

Riley walked over to Mikayla and wrapped her arm around her shoulders.

"What do you want to do? What can I do to help?" That question seemed to have shocked Mikayla's tears away. Hell, she was surprised at how easily the questions came from her mouth.

"I don't know. I've never been through anything like this. All I care about is him being okay. Can you just make sure he's okay?" Mikayla sobbed. She thought she might have been done crying, but that was obviously far from the truth. She'd more than likely be crying until she heard from him and knew he was okay.

"I'll do my best. I don't know anything about them. I don't know if his brother will tell me anything if I am able to get in contact with him."

"I understand."

Riley took a deep breath as she felt crushed for her cousin. Mikayla's emotions were always up and down. Not only that, but she spent more time shutting Riley out than she had letting her in, so on the strength of that alone, she would do her best to find out what she could to bring Mikayla peace, even if it was only a little bit.

"I need you to be honest with me." Riley placed a hand on each of Mikayla's shoulders, forcing her to make eye contact. Despite Mikayla's blurred vision from the tears, Riley needed this connection when she asked this question.

Nodding, Mikayla waited for the question.

"Do you know what he did to get himself arrested?" A pregnant pause made Riley give Mikayla a look demanding she not lie.

"He said there was a carjacking."

"A what?"

"He didn't do anything. He was with his friends and—"

"Come on, you expect me to believe that?"

"Can you just make sure he's okay?" She knew Jeremiah being wanted for a carjacking was not helping her case about him at all. But their cousins in the Bay Area had done and were doing things way worse than this, and Riley would ride for them until the wheels fell off. She even enabled them some, given that she had called them to come and beat Levi's, Daniel's, and Jason's asses. It would be hypocritical for her to feel one way about Jeremiah and not their cousins.

"I'll do what I can, but this conversation isn't over."

Mikayla released the breath she didn't know she had been holding when Riley agreed to see what she could do. Although she would worry about Jeremiah until she heard from him, she was glad her cousin promised to try to check on him at least. "Okay," Mikayla conceded as she got up and headed toward her bedroom.

Riley watched her take the stairs slowly, head down, shoulders slouched, and spirit broken.

"Where the hell do I even start?" Riley mumbled as she headed toward the small office space in their home. She sat at the computer and Googled the local police station. She didn't deal with cops enough to know the number by heart, and even after making the call for Jeremiah, she didn't plan to use it again unless absolutely necessary.

"Shit, my phone." She patted the pocketless sides of her pajama pants, realizing her cell was still in her bedroom. She wouldn't be able to make the call without it. She rushed up the stairs two at a time, grabbing her phone before making her way back to the office. Riley dialed the number to the police station and was surprised the phone rang six times before someone picked up. She doubted crime had them too busy to answer immediately and assumed they didn't care enough to respond immediately.

"District six, how can I help you?" There was an evident attitude present in the tone of the woman who answered the phone.

Explains the six rings. "Hi, I wanted to check if you have someone in custody."

"Name?"

"Jeremiah Stately."

"Hold on, please."

Before she could verbally agree, the *Jeopardy!* theme song was playing in her ear. It was not that tune exactly, yet boring just the same.

"He's here."

"Can you tell me what he's been charged with, please?"

"Who are you?"

"I'm his older sister. Is that information you can give me?"

"You'll need to check back in a few hours. He's not showing up in our system yet."

"Okay. Thank you." Riley was disappointed, but it hadn't been that long since the cops left her home with Jeremiah in tow.

If Riley had another question, she wouldn't have the chance to ask, because the line went dead. She sat back in the office chair, wondering how she would find out how she could get any further news on Jeremiah. There was only one person who could tell her more of what she wanted to know, but the way he showed his ass not too long ago, she doubted he would provide her with any information. Besides, she had no clue how to get in contact with him.

"It's worth a shot," she said to herself as the revelation that everyone was on social media came to mind. She sat forward in the chair and typed Facebook in the search engine. Logging into her account, she immediately searched Jeremiah's name. She hoped he wasn't one of those people who made an outrageous profile name. She searched his page until she came across his brother's profile picture. She went to open his page and found herself slightly disappointed that he wasn't as open as Jeremiah, who unfortunately had more incriminating things on his page than she would have liked to see, like photos of him with a bunch of knuckleheads showing guns tucked in their pants and holding up gang signs. Even though Jeremiah hadn't been holding a gun or twisting his fingers in awkward positions to broadcast whatever clique he was a part of, he was still in the photo with them. As protective as Jermaine had shown himself to be, she was surprised he hadn't made Jeremiah take down some of the bullshit he had posted. Maybe he had. Jeremiah not listening was more of a possibility than Jermaine not advising the removal of the bullshit. Raising Mikayla was not for the weak, and apparently that also seemed to apply when it came to Jeremiah.

Riley looked at the few photos Jermaine had public and found herself unintentionally lusting after him. Unintentional because now wasn't the time to have thoughts of his juicy lips wrapped around her areolas, but she was. Nor was she supposed to think about how secure she would feel having him on top of her, deep stroking her in the missionary position. But she was. Especially since his attitude toward her and Mikayla had been shitty from the beginning. He was an asshole. A fine as hell asshole, though.

"Let me get this over with," she mumbled as she opened the option to send him a message. It was simple.

Please let us know how Jeremiah is and if there is anything we can do to help. Here's my number: (510) 555-3233.

She sent the message, and almost instantly she noticed the read receipt, so she waited, curious as to how he would respond and fully prepared to cuss him out if his response was anything short of appreciative.

All right.

That was his reply. She waited because surely he had more than that to say. But after 120 seconds, it was apparent that he didn't.

Riley logged off the computer, then sat back in the chair. Her mind wandered. She had no solid information to provide Mikayla, and that was disappointing. With Jermaine's generic-ass reply, she doubted he would be any help.

The loud vibration of her phone on the desk pulled her from her thoughts. Seeing a number she didn't recognize made her hesitant to answer. With everything going on, she felt that they were not exempt from any further bullshit. Still, her gut told her that it might be a call worth taking, so she did.

"Hello," she answered politely. Though hesitancy flowed through her, revealing it wasn't an option.

"Yeah."

"Um, for you to have dialed me, you sure are coming at me like I owe you something. Who is this?" The hesitancy and politeness flew out the window due to the rudeness the baritone voice on the other end of the line possessed.

"You asked me to call you, right?" Jermaine spoke like he was not in the mood to be bothered because he truly was not.

"Listen, I'm going to give you a pass and not cuss you out because I know you're going through something. But I am so over your rude and fucked-up-ass attitude toward me and my cousin, who you don't even know. You've been an asshole since we met you, and all we're trying to do is make sure Jeremiah is okay." Riley's chest heaved up and down as she tried to calm her nerves. Jermaine was a piece of work.

"Y'all trying to check on him, yet it's mighty funny how the police knew exactly where to find him."

Riley removed the phone from her ear and looked at it as if a bug crawled out. She was disgusted by his accusation. When she thought he couldn't get any more obnoxious, he proved her wrong.

"What you're implying is fucked up. I had no idea your brother was even here, and my cousin cared about him so much she defied my wishes to make sure he was good. You should take a look at yourself to figure out how the police tracked him to my house. If you found his phone, maybe they did too. But I guarantee they didn't find him courtesy of anyone here. We ain't no snitches."

Riley ended the call, then placed her phone back onto the desk. As fine as Jermaine was, he was not worth the headache. Riley rolled her eyes as her phone began to vibrate with what she assumed was Jermaine's number. She only debated for half a second before deciding to take the call.

"Yeah." She hit him with the same greeting he gave her minutes ago.

Chuckling, Jermaine admitted, "I deserved that."

"And then some."

"Look, my bad. It's been a rough few weeks with my brother, and then this shit happens to be the icing on the cake."

"I get it. But it still doesn't give you the right to be an asshole."

He chuckled again.

"You've laughed twice. I wasn't sure that was something you could do."

"You wanted to know how my brother is doing?"

"That's the only reason I reached out."

"I doubt it. But uh, he's good. He goes to court on Monday. Since it's Saturday, he has to stay in there. I was able to talk to him. He wanted me to get in contact with your cousin and let her know he was cool."

"Crazy how close they've grown in such a short time."

"Yeah." Jermaine's tone sounded as if he was accusing the teens of being to each other what they weren't.

"They aren't romantically involved. Your brother is a decent kid, and both have assured me they're only friends. Since I can tell when Mikayla is lying, I know it's true. And since my cousin put her freedom on the line harboring your little fugitive, I'ma need you to show her a lot more respect."

"I ain't even say shit."

"You implied some bullshit."

"A'ight." Jermaine chuckled again. Oddly he was enjoying the conversation they were having although it wasn't one about them. They were speaking in a cordial manner that strangely flowed way easier than when they were in person.

"What time is his court hearing Monday?"

"I was told to be there around eight a.m."

"If you don't mind, can we—"

"Ay, I gotta take this call. It's a lawyer. But Monday's good." Now it was Jermaine ending the call, not allowing another word from her. Now all she had to do was figure out how to keep Mikayla calm until Monday arrived.

Chapter 7

"Did you talk to Mikayla?"

The call had barely connected before Jeremiah blurted out his question. Jermaine was slightly offended that his brother was overly concerned with someone outside of their household and immediate family, given that he and their mother had been going through it ever since he hadn't come home the night before. Knowing Jeremiah was okay gave them some relief. Having Jeremiah behind bars, however, overpowered that relief with worry.

"No, I didn't."

"Bruh, I asked you to check on her. Damn, man, you couldn't do that for me?"

It took everything in Jermaine not to abandon the call. His brother was now being ungrateful, and it pissed him off.

"If yo' hothead ass would've let me finish, you would know that I spoke to her cousin and not her."

"Okay. Thanks. Was she good?"

"Bro." Jermaine could no longer hide his irritation. It wasn't that he was jealous or even cared that much about Jeremiah's concern for Mikayla. It was that Jeremiah only seemed to be concerned about Mikayla. He was the one calling lawyers, calming their mother, and feeling like a failure because he was supposed to be the one taking care of him. Jeremiah was his responsibility, and he was doing a shitty job, even though he was also doing his best.

"My bad, bro. She was just so fucked up when they took me. I can't get the look she had out of my head."

"She ain't the type to try to hurt herself or nothing like that, is she?" Jermaine wondered out loud. With the explanation his brother supplied, his resentment toward Mikayla eased up slightly.

"Honestly, I don't know. She doesn't seem like it. We're still getting to know each other."

"You on this hype about somebody you don't even know?"

"She's special. After that shit in the bathroom at the school, I felt the need to protect her. We're nothing more than friends. I almost look at her like a little cousin or sister."

"Well, you can't protect her from there. Fuck was you thinking? Know what? Never mind. She was straight, her cousin said." Jermaine was trying to be sensitive to what his brother was going through, but he'd be lying if he said he wasn't irritated and disappointed. Not only that, but he was unsure of why Mikayla was his concern when he was the one facing some serious time.

"Good. If they decide to keep me, can you make sure Mikayla has the address to write me?"

"She won't need it 'cause you're getting out. They don't hold innocent men."

"Right, right. Ay, so how's Mom? I know you talked to her."

"She's being Ma, ready to take a flight down here, but I convinced her to wait."

"I'll call her after we hang up if I get a chance."

"How are you holding up?"

"I'm straight. This is only a minor setback for a major comeback." Jeremiah sounded confident with his words, yet the aching in his chest when he spoke them told him he wasn't so sure. He held the phone's receiver with his right hand and stood with his back against the wall as he looked around the room. A few inmates were hanging around waiting for their turn on the phone, while others were in there to ear hustle. Keeping his back to the wall was a protective stance his brother told him about when they would discuss his time in prison. Although he didn't care to have anyone in his business, he hoped that what he just said to Jermaine let the few people in the room know he wouldn't be letting jail change him.

Jermaine smiled, listening to his brother use words he used when they were both younger and something hadn't gone their way. It was a motto their father had taught him, and when shit happened, it was the motto he remembered as motivation to pick himself back up and keep going.

"That's definitely the way to look at it. I found you a lawyer. She should be coming to see you soon. If not by tomorrow, then hours before your court appearance."

"She cute?"

"Man, if you don't carry yo' ass on . . ." Jermaine laughed.

"Shit, I'm serious. I've only been here a few hours, and already I miss seeing females on the feminine side. There's one in here who works the front, and she ain't no kinda type of mine." The disappointment in Jeremiah's tone brought about more laughter from Jermaine. It was laughter he welcomed under the circumstances, because where his brother was and where he could end up were far from laughing matters.

"Shouldn't be looking anyway since you so worried about Mikayla," he teased.

"Bro, she's like a sister to me."

"How, when you've only known the girl for two seconds?"

"Because I said so. Anyway, you think I'ma get out on Monday?"

"I don't know. What they're accusing you of is serious."

"I know." His admission left the two of them speechless. They were lost in their own thoughts until the operator informed them that there was only sixty seconds left on the call.

"Thanks, bro. I'll call you tomorrow or something." Jeremiah tried to sound like he was okay, but Jermaine could tell he was disappointed their call had to end. So was he.

"A'ight. But if you get ahold of the phone again, after you call Mom, you can call me back."

"All right."

"Thirty seconds," the automated system announced.

"Keep yo' head up," was the last thing Jermaine said before the call went dead.

Placing his phone on the coffee table in front of him, Jermaine put his feet on the bottom rail of the table with his legs slightly apart and knees bent as he rested his elbows on his thighs and placed his face in his hands. To say he was stressed was an understatement.

"Fuck, man." His head shot up as he leaned back on the couch. He couldn't relax, and he wouldn't until his brother was home. As he slouched on the sofa, placing his hands behind his head, he couldn't help but wonder where he went wrong as a big brother.

"But why do you have to go?" 12-year-old Jeremiah asked as he stared up at his brother, tears welling in his eyes that he refused to let fall because big boys didn't cry.

"Because I have to, Mouse. I made a mistake, and I have to correct it."

"When I make mistakes, I just say sorry. I don't have to leave you or Mom. So why you gotta go?"

"Because the kind of mistake I made takes more than an apology."

"How long are you gonna be gone?"

"It'll be for a little while, but it'll go by fast. As long as you do what you're supposed to do around here, it'll seem like hardly any time passed when you finally see me again. This is only a little setback for a major comeback." He smiled, hoping to reassure Jeremiah, but the look on his face said he still wasn't convinced.

"Will I be able to call you?"

"No, I'll have to call you, and I promise to call you a couple times each week."

"Okay." Jeremiah's shoulders sank, his head hung low, and the parts of his eyes that Jermaine could see remained moist.

"Don't be mad at me, all right? This is the first and last time I'll leave you and Mom. I need you to be the man and take care of things here until I come back. All right?" Jermaine placed his hand on the top of his little brother's head, forcing him to make eye contact with him. It pained him to hurt his brother, and seeing how hurt Jeremiah was made him regret fucking up. He had, though, and he couldn't take it back. Now he had to go do his time because he committed the crime. Because he didn't want Jeremiah more afraid than he was already hurt, he and his mother decided it was best that he didn't know that Jermaine's new *home would be Folsom Prison for at least three years.*

"All right." Jeremiah's arms wrapped around him so swiftly that the act caught him by surprise. It only took a few seconds for the shock to wear off, and he returned the hug. He hugged him as tightly as he could without hurting him and did his best to embed the feeling in his memory because it would be a long time before they embraced this way again.

The memory of the day Jermaine had to turn himself into prison reminded him of the day things had also begun to go downhill for Jeremiah. Jermaine hadn't been gone a full ninety days before Jeremiah began acting out. It started with little things in school, petty things that got him warnings because none of his actions reflected the kid the teachers knew. Maybe if his repercussions had been harsher, the kid they knew might have shown back up instead of the kid no one knew.

He couldn't just blame the teachers, though. He and his mother were also to blame. She made excuses for Jeremiah, and Jermaine felt so much guilt for not being there that he didn't remind Jeremiah who the fuck he was and that, no matter what, he would and could still put his foot up Jeremiah's ass. Jermaine's not doing so only assisted in the shitload of events that led Jeremiah to spiral out of control. It led their mother to call and practically beg Jermaine to take him in because she feared he'd end up dead or in jail. His mother had succeeded in making sure neither happened because she gave the responsibility to Jermaine. And Jermaine allowed to happen what she didn't want for him.

"Fuck, man. Shit!" That was all he could say. Those were the only words to express himself. His frustration. His aching heart. Words were all he had, though not many until he could help his brother get home. Monday couldn't come fast enough.

"Mr. Stately, I understand that your grades are good and that you've never been in any serious trouble with the law. However, you have associated yourself with well-known menaces to society. These young men you call your friends have been involved in a number of fights, as well as carjacking around the city. Your association with them, represented by the tattoo on your calf, makes me assume you have been present for some if not all of their acts of crime. Because of this, bail is revoked, and you will be remanded until your next court date."

The gavel's sound echoed in Jeremiah's ear as the sounds of everything else around him seemed to be drowned out.

"Your Honor," he heard his lawyer plead.

He looked at her, seeing her mouth move but not hearing any of her words. It was the same when he looked over to the judge. His heart raced. His hands became moist, and his mouth felt like it had been stuffed with cotton balls. The judge hadn't given him permission to sit down, but if he didn't, he was going to pass out. He could feel it. The room was all of a sudden getting hot, and his legs were starting to feel weak, so he sat and stared off into space. It wasn't until his lawyer practically shook him that he came to again.

"Jeremiah. Don't worry about today's verdict. You will not spend as long as you think in jail. I promise you." Landra McCullough, his attorney, assured him.

He nodded, then turned around in his chair in search of his brother. Though he had fucked up royally and knew Jermaine was beyond pissed at him, seeing his face was the only way he was going to feel any sort of comfort or hope at the moment. When they locked eyes, Jermaine mouthed for him to call ASAP, and he agreed.

"I'm going to speak with your brother, and then I'll be back to visit you in the morning," Landra advised him as the bailiff prepared to take him back to the juvenile facility.

Jeremiah's face was slack with defeat. The metal clamping around his wrists was a reminder of how serious a situation he was in. Not being able to bond out caused a sickening feeling to bubble in his stomach. Vomiting on the spot would've been a bit much, so he held his composure as best he could. His eyes pleaded with his lawyer for some answers, yet she had none. All Jeremiah could do was nod his head as he was taken out of the courtroom.

"The judge sounded like he decided to keep my brother based on assumptions rather than actual facts," Jermaine spoke as soon as Landra was only a few inches away from him.

"I think it's a scare tactic. He wants him to understand how much trouble hanging with the wrong crowd can get him in. I do have a question for you."

"What's up?"

"Did you know about the tattoo?"

"Man, hell nah. If I had, he would have gotten that shit covered up right after I broke my foot off in his ass," Jermaine said honestly.

"I'll find a way to say it was peer pressure or a cry for help because that may be the biggest thing biting him in the ass. I'm going to visit with him in the morning and try to come up with a new strategy. Still, I believe we have a shot of getting him out at the next court appearance."

"That's a month from now."

"I'm aware. If we can get it pushed up, I will. Your brother is a tough kid. He'll come out of this stronger than ever."

"I hear you. Thanks again."

"Anytime, and if you ever want to discuss his case over dinner, it'll be my treat." She smiled flirtatiously at him.

"I hear you." Jermaine wasn't turning her down. He also wasn't accepting the invitation. Getting with his brother's lawyer was the last thing on his mind. Besides, if they didn't work out, it could ruin things for Jeremiah.

"Okay, well, I'll be in touch." She smiled, then walked away, sure to sway her hips a bit extra just in case he was watching.

Of course he was watching. He was a man, and she was gorgeous. She looked like Tatyana Ali, and he could appreciate that. Once he could no longer see the bouncing of her cheeks, he turned on his heels and headed out of the courthouse.

"Hey, Ma," Jermaine said as soon as the call connected. He tried to sound like his usual self, but he had a multitude of emotions coursing through him and felt like he'd explode at any moment. Just hearing his mother's voice on the other end of the phone had him fighting to keep them at bay.

"Hey, baby, how are you?" she asked, and he could hear her choking back emotions as well. It was crazy how such a simple question could make a person want to spill all their worries and a fistful of tears.

If he thought his confession wouldn't have made his mother look at him differently, he probably would have answered her honestly. He may have even cried a river and spilled every worry he had to her. But he couldn't. He wasn't in a space where he could show weakness. He was the man of the family, and she and his brother counted on him. He also didn't want her to feel like she made a mistake giving him custody of Jeremiah, though she probably did feel that way and wouldn't say it. And though he was unsure of where things were headed with his case, he was going to do his best to remain optimistic.

"I'm doing as good as I can be given the situation. I'ma be good, though, because you and Pops raised us to handle tough situations with our heads high. So Jeremiah is going to be good as well."

"I know you will, baby. I just hate that you have to deal with any of this."

"Me too, Ma. I hate you're dealing with having a child locked up again," he said honestly. Jeremiah was supposed to be different from him, and even though he was showing his brother a better route to take, somehow he still ended up on the wrong road.

"What are they saying? Do you need money?" The questions left his mother's lips quickly, overwhelming Jermaine. He'd called to give her an update, but he was still processing watching his brother be cuffed and carried away a second time.

"His bail was denied. The lawyer is going to try again, though. I think the judge wanted to teach him a lesson more than anything, so he's gotta sit in there a little longer," he said, feeling defeated. This was his brother's first offense, and though the allegations he was being charged with were serious, he hoped the judge would have some leniency since he wasn't a kid who had run-ins with the law.

"How long was he running around with the kids who got him in trouble?" she questioned.

"I'm not sure, but Jeremiah knows right from wrong."

"I know. I thought by moving away he would find a better crowd to be around, different from the group he was with here."

Although she meant well, Jermaine could not help feeling her words were a dig at him, and it took everything in him not to say something out of line to her. She sent Jeremiah to live with him not long after he had been released from prison, with no regard for him having to reacclimate himself to society. He became a free man and a parent damn near overnight.

"I can't choose his friends for him," he told her.

"I know, baby. As much as I don't want to be a young grandmother, a call about Jeremiah having a baby on the way would've been much better than being told my baby was locked up." His mother was good for going from supportive to condescending.

"All right, Ma, I'll tell him to call you. I gotta go handle a few things."

"Okay, baby, I love you," she told him before ending the call.

Jermaine took a deep breath to calm his nerves. As much as he loved his mother, conversations with her could be exhausting. She had said one thing he agreed with, though: Jeremiah having a baby on the way would have been much easier to handle than his current predicament.

"Damn," he whispered as he thought of Mikayla and how wrong he was about her. Now he only wished that she had come into Jeremiah's life sooner, and maybe things would be different.

"Nah, his ass is responsible for him." He spoke out loud. Ever since he could remember, excuses had been made for Jeremiah, and the reality was that his brother knew right from wrong. There was no one to blame other than Jeremiah.

Retrieving his phone from the coffee table, where he'd placed it when he ended the call with his mother, Jermaine scrolled through his recent calls until he got to Riley's number. After their last call, he was optimistic that she'd answer. The call hadn't ended on the best of terms, but it also hadn't ended on the worst. Besides, he knew she wanted to know how Jeremiah was doing, for Mikayla if not for herself. Jermaine tapped the number, placing it on speaker, almost shocked that she answered on the second ring.

"Is he okay?" The uncertainty in her tone almost made him think it was Mikayla who answered the phone. But the sultriness of it, which only a grown woman could possess, let him know it was her.

"He's good. He'll be in there for a little while."

"That's gonna crush Mikayla," Riley said, speaking more in general than directly to him.

"Yeah, he wasn't too happy with the verdict either."

"Is there anything we can do to help?"

"Give Mikayla the address to write him. That's all I can suggest right now."

"I can do that. And he's welcome to call her. I'll make sure she has money on her phone."

"That's cool. I'll reimburse whatever he charges up."

"Not necessary."

Jermaine was a bit shocked by her reply. If she could see his slightly widened eyes, Riley would assume she'd said something wrong. But she hadn't. His silence came from being appreciative. It seemed since he'd taken Jeremiah in, he'd been in this thing alone with no help. Yet, the small gesture to cover Jeremiah's and Mikayla's phone charges was enough to not make him fight her on it.

Riley removed the phone from her ear to make sure the call was still connected. "Hello," she said.

"Yeah. My bad. Um, well, I'll keep you updated."

"I appreciate that. Wish we could have made his appearance, but maybe next time."

"Yeah, next time. Thanks again for looking out for my brother."

"I owed him." She smiled, and though he couldn't see it, her tone told him the corners of her plump lips were spread. Her face was embedded in his memory, and just the thought of her smiling pleased him.

"All right, tell your cousin be straight and to keep her head up."

"Will do. Thanks again. He'll be hearing from her soon."

"Yeah. I'm texting the address now. Have a good night."

"Oooh, you too."

Jermaine chuckled, knowing she was caught a bit off guard by his politeness because he had yet to show he was capable of such a thing until now. Jermaine ended the call satisfied that one thing went well today.

Chapter 8

Mikayla's elbow rested on her desk as her chin sat in the palm of her hand while she stared toward the classroom door. She hated knowing that no matter how long she stared, the one person she wanted to see walk through the door would not be doing so anytime soon.

"Hey, Mikayla." The slight nudge given to her by her classmate caught her off guard, and her elbow slipped, making her head dip slightly as her palm was involuntarily moved from beneath her chin. Frustrated, she looked at her classmate, ready to tear into her because she was not in the mood for any class pranks or stunts. Shayla shrugged before nodding toward the front of the room, letting her know the teacher wanted her attention. Guilt washed over Mikayla, and she hoped Shayla felt it from the remorseful expression on her face.

"Mikayla, is there something more important you need to be doing, or are you ready to participate?" Ms. Remi asked. She looked at Mikayla, and for the first time, Mikayla saw just how fed up her teacher was with her. Ms. Remi did not play about students respecting her and paying attention in class. Mikayla, usually one of the top students, hadn't had the luxury of being scolded by her. Today she was finding out what it felt like to be the center of Ms. Remi's irritation.

Mikayla swallowed the lump in her throat. "No. I'm ready to participate." Her clipped tone caused a few oohs from her classmates, and Mikayla rolled her eyes toward the ceiling.

"Obviously not. You can excuse yourself to Mr. Feng's office, and maybe tomorrow you'll be ready to learn." Ms. Remi folded her arms across her chest and shifted her body weight to her right as she stared at Mikayla, daring her to protest her order.

Unwilling to beg her teacher to allow her to stay somewhere she did not care to be at the moment anyway, Mikayla snatched her backpack from the floor, stuffed her notebook and pencil inside, then stormed out the door, heading directly for the office.

Mikayla walked past the receptionist, who was too busy with her phone to notice, and headed straight for Mr. Feng's office. She wasn't sure if he was inside, but since she'd never been sent to the office for being a disruptive student, she did not know the proper protocol and let herself in the room.

"Ms. Triumph, how can I help you?" Mr. Feng pushed away from his desk with a face full of confusion as she plopped down on the chair across from him.

"Ms. Remi sent me in here." She shrugged.

"What do you need?" His brows furrowed as he took in her demeanor. She was slouched in the chair, and her shoulders were droopy. Her hair was in a high ponytail, she wore a baggy graphic tee and oversized sweatpants, and she looked anything but the model student he knew she was.

"She said I needed to come in here because I wasn't participating in class." She shrugged again, and as the words left her mouth, she felt her stomach turn. She'd never been an issue in class, so the realization of why she was here made her feel a way. However, she couldn't find the strength to care enough to come out of this funk she was in.

"That isn't like you," Mr. Feng said as he stood and came around his desk, taking a seat on it in front of her.

Mikayla was unsure of how to respond to the obvious. She wasn't going to beg Mr. Feng to understand her plight, nor would she try to explain what she was going through. How did you describe heartbreak anyway? One minute she would feel sick to her stomach. Another, she was angry. Then there would be days she felt fine. And other days, she'd be moving about, completing a task, without remembering even doing it. Life was on autopilot, and then life was like hanging out of a hot-air balloon. There were too many emotions Mikayla was facing, and she'd feel them all until Jeremiah was free, because whether he or any of them liked it or not, she wouldn't feel like herself until things improved for Jeremiah. Hopefully, the improvement was freedom.

"Mr. Feng, can I ask you something?"

"Sure." Mr. Feng relaxed, one foot planted on the floor while the other dangled off the desk. His hands were clasped in front of him on his lap as he looked at her, giving her his undivided attention.

"Do you care about all of the students at this school?"

"Of course I do."

"Well, why aren't you trying to help Jeremiah? You could write a character reference letter or say how he doesn't deserve to have his future thrown away from being behind bars, but you haven't done it."

Mr. Feng's face turned its usual beet red when he was nervous and caught off guard. Although he cared for all his students, Jeremiah included, he believed that everyone had to pay consequences for their actions.

"I try not to get involved in legal matters outside of the school, Ms. Triumph. We also have a mission statement we follow here at the school—"

"Yes, and it tells us to do our best and have each other's backs. We are one union, one school, one body, and we represent family. But you're saying it's okay to turn your back on Jeremiah when our mission tells us to do the opposite. I'm not sure how that makes sense in this case, Mr. Feng." Mikayla was feeling herself, and when it came to taking up for her friend, she would find no issue with doing so. She wasn't sure if Mr. Feng's word would make a significant change, but it would mean one more person coming to Jeremiah's aid, and he needed all the support he could get.

"Uh, I'm going to give you a pass for your next class. Please do your best to focus on your goals. You do not want to allow this semester to slip away from you when graduation is right around the corner. If you can do as your teachers require for the rest of the day, we can avoid a meeting with your cousin."

Mikayla chuckled. It was the only thing she could do to keep herself from exploding. She stood from the chair with the same attitude she'd left Ms. Remi's classroom with. When she made it to the hallway, it took everything in her to not head for the exit. Mr. Feng saying they would keep Riley out of his office today if she was not sent to his office anymore was enough to send her to her next class. Riley was already a bit overbearing, so a call from the principal would possibly take her over the top.

Mikayla went to her classes and participated as much as she felt comfortable. Every answered question was forced. Her mouth would feel dry right after, but she got through it, and knowing Jeremiah would be proud of her for pushing through gave her the push she needed. She was also thankful the rest of the day went by quickly.

I'm home.

Mikayla sent the text to Riley. She asked her to do so today, and she wasn't sure why, but to help her not be so worried, she did as was asked.

"Good, we've been waiting for you."

Mikayla frowned, hearing Riley's voice coming toward her. She didn't expect her cousin to be home and felt herself slightly becoming annoyed because she wasn't sure of the reason for the text if Riley was going to meet her there.

"Here." Riley wore a huge grin on her face as she passed the phone to Mikayla.

Mikayla looked at Riley, questioning who was on the other end of the phone as she took the receiver hesitantly. However, she would have to figure it out on her own because Riley turned her head and shrugged like she hadn't been holding a conversation with the person before Mikayla walked through the door.

"Hello?" Mikayla's voice was timid as she waited for the person on the other end to speak.

"What's up, bestie?" Jeremiah's cheerful voice hit Mikayla's ears like a beautiful melody. And the smile across her face was so wide her cheeks hurt.

"Jeremiah," she sang into the phone as she dropped her backpack and walked up to Riley, giving her a hug.

"Oh, you big happy," Riley teased when Mikayla removed her arms from around her. "You sure the two of you are just friends?" Riley asked with a raised brow.

"Ugh, yes. We're only friends." Mikayla frowned.

Riley was happy to see Mikayla so lit up, because when she left their home this morning, she could sense Mikayla's mood being off. It was usually off most days, but today seemed different. Mikayla didn't even try to force herself to look unbothered, which Riley knew she'd done a time or two when talking about her day or Jeremiah.

"Best friend, you will not believe what happened to me today," she said lively as she took a seat on the sofa, removing her shoes and then tucking her feet underneath her butt. "In class today . . ." Mikayla started, then looked up at Riley, silently signaling for her to give them some privacy. She wanted Jeremiah to know how Ms. Remi played her today but not enough to say it in front of her cousin, who would nag her to death.

"I'm the one paying the phone bills around here. The rent, too, but I gotta head out." Riley sucked her teeth before rolling her eyes and heading to the kitchen to start dinner.

"What happened?" Jeremiah asked, fully invested in whatever story Mikayla was about to tell him because he'd take the drama behind McClane High over the drama in the juvenile hall.

"Ms. Remi put me out of her classroom."

"No." Jeremiah was genuinely shocked because Mikayla and Ms. Remi seemed to have a decent relationship. Mikayla had never given her a reason to put her out of class.

"Yep. She was upset because I didn't answer her as fast as expected. Like, I have a lot going on, and she mad I didn't respond to her as fast as she expected." Mikayla scoffed before rolling her eyes.

"Or she just expected you to do what you've always done in her class: pay attention and answer the questions quickly like a *Jeopardy!* contestant. And what you going through? Because my situation bet' not be the reason you acting crazy."

"Well, I can't help it. I care about you being away."

"I care too. Doesn't mean you get to take this harder than me. Mikayla, I'm starting to sound like a broken record, as many times as I've told you the same thing."

Mikayla felt tears form in her eyes but knew it would only make the call between her and Jeremiah tense, as well as leave him worried about her. She hated how she was supposed to be strong for him and was slowly ripping at the seams. Now that she had him in hers, life without Jeremiah didn't seem logical.

"You're right. I'm sorry. How're things going in there?"

"It's going. I don't bother nobody, and nobody bothers me. I've actually been helping a few cats with their schoolwork. There's a program here to help get a diploma or GED. I haven't enrolled in the program because I don't plan to graduate from here—"

"You won't," she quickly cut in.

"Nah, I won't. But it's cool helping out in the classrooms. Makes me wish I'd done more of this when I had the chance."

"You'll get a chance."

"So who been asking about the boy? You find any girls who want to be my pen pal yet?"

"Uh, no. I am not going around school recruiting your little fan base."

"You know it's okay to share me, right?" he teased.

"Oh, trust, I welcome the person willing to take on my headache."

"All right, look, I have to go. I'll check back in soon. Make sure you write me, too."

"I will."

"And don't get kicked out of class anymore. Have a good night, and tell Riley I said thanks for taking my call."

"Okay, bye," she said right before the line went dead. Mikayla's heart sank to her stomach. Talking with Jeremiah brought her a feeling of normalcy, and then the call ended, reminding her they no longer had the freedom to explore their friendship.

Mikayla could smell the aroma coming from the kitchen. As always, Riley was throwing down. She just wasn't hungry. She was only feeling the ache of loss. Mikayla rose from the sofa and headed to her bedroom, lying on her stomach, burying her face into the pillow, and finally letting her tears flow.

"Mikayla?" Riley gently called out to her. She had her plate in hand and usually would have a fit about them eating in their rooms, but when she walked into the living room and saw Mikayla missing, she knew if she did not bring the food to Mikayla, then her cousin would not eat. She left the plate on Mikayla's desk and hoped the smell would be enough to get her to eat.

The weekend came and went, and Mikayla was doing her best to get through the week. Being in the comfort of her home made the days feel a little better. Some days she wondered how she could get back to the girl wandering the halls before becoming friends with Jeremiah. The upside of it all was she knew eventually she would get back to her.

She rushed upstairs and placed her backpack on the floor and had been on her way to sulk on her bed when papers on her desk caught her eye. Mikayla hurriedly opened the letter on her desk. She didn't care about Riley entering her bedroom when she wasn't home since it was to drop off a letter from Jeremiah. She smiled as soon as she looked at the words, "What's up, bestie," in his neat handwriting. Mikayla's heart fluttered, and she hugged the letter to her chest briefly before opening it up fully and reading.

Mikayla, the days in here are long, but they also go by fast as hell. I guess it's having a routine and a list of things to do all day, every day, before the lights go out. The good part about all that is that it leaves me hardly no time to dwell on the small shit. Something you should not be doing as well. A quick rundown of my day is we get up at 5:30 a.m. and handle hygiene. Well, at least I do. There's some nasty-ass dudes up in here. You know I'm staying clear of that crowd. Anyway, after that, we go eat. Then there's

*classes. You already know I'm a tutor. Then
I kick some ass in basketball. We can't lift
weights and stuff, but this six-pack is still on
the six, so I'm good.*

"Mikayla, telephone!" Riley's voice echoed through the house. Placing the letter down, Mikayla followed Riley's voice downstairs.

"You holding up all right?" Riley asked as Mikayla looked at her anxiously, fighting the urge to snatch the phone from Riley's ear. "All right, Jeremiah, let me give this girl the phone before I knock her into next week." Jeremiah's laughter could be heard before Riley gave her the phone.

"It wasn't that funny," Mikayla said with an attitude as soon as her ear hit the phone, halting his laughter.

"It was because, knowing Riley, she probably could knock you into next week. You get my letter?"

"I did. I was reading it until I was rudely interrupted,"

"You can go back to reading. I can call somebody else."

"No, you cannot." Mikayla walked over to the sofa and took a seat, tucking her feet underneath her butt. Sitting this way had become routine when on calls with Jeremiah.

"I really wasn't talking about nothing. Only giving you a quick rundown on what I be doing around here. Guess what?"

"What?"

"Man, tell me why I almost got in trouble for contraband."

"Jeremiah, what? No, that is not okay."

"Damn, let me finish before you start thinking the worst." He spoke as if he were hurt, then quickly chuckled because he didn't want Mikayla getting all down. Then the call would be spent trying to cheer her up, and he hadn't called to do that.

"You know my ex, Christy. This girl sent photos in lingerie, like a dummy. I told her in the letter she could send me pictures. I thought she was smart enough to know not that kind."

"Wow, does she know the guards look at your mail?"

"Yeah, she does, which is why she dropped to my bottom five. She's cool to talk to for the time being, but we'll never be in a relationship again. She too far gone." Jeremiah shook his head like Mikayla could see him.

"See, I told you you have bad taste in women. Promise I can pick out my future sister-in-law or your next serious girlfriend because if the choice becomes yours, we're all doomed." Mikayla laughed.

"Hell nah. I can pick my own chick. Besides, I treat all women with respect and accordingly. Christy will never be my girlfriend again because she's no longer girlfriend material. I won't disrespect her, but I will be making it known that we can only be cool. Or friends with benefits."

"Ugh, TMI."

"You have one minute left," the automated system cut in.

"Dang, it doesn't even feel like we were talking that long," Mikayla whined.

"I'll try to call back tonight. If not, I'll be speaking with you soon. All right?"

"Okay." Before Mikayla could say goodbye or tell him to stay tough, the call ended. Hearing Jeremiah's voice was always appreciated, but it could also bring her spirits down. At the moment, however, she was feeling okay.

Chapter 9

"Mikayla, another one of your teachers contacted me about your behavior in school. This is the third time this week." Riley spoke gently as she took a seat at the foot of Mikayla's bed. She looked at her younger cousin, feeling bad for her. Mikayla's agony was overly present as she lay in bed buried underneath the covers.

"I'm not even bothering anyone, so what behavior could they be talking or concerned about?" she grumbled, rolling over so that her back was now toward Riley. After last week, she made sure to answer a question when Ms. Remi asked and hadn't been sent to Mr. Feng's office, so she wasn't sure what more the teachers wanted from her.

"You know that's not what they mean. You're letting your grades slip. Your class participation has been nonexistent unless you're practically forced. This is your last year of high school. You have to stay on top of your work."

"Fine."

"I'm not leaving. You think 'fine' is going to suffice, but it isn't. I thought Jeremiah gave you a pep talk when the two of y'all spoke," Riley said, referring to the phone call Jeremiah and Mikayla had a week ago.

"He did, but it didn't change much. He's in there. I'm out here, and it sucks." Mikayla threw the covers from over her and rolled back over so that Riley could see her face. And as expected, Mikayla's eyes were puffy. Tears had become second nature, and as tired as Riley was of seeing her cousin in such a state, she remained as gentle as possible when she wanted to tell her to snap the fuck out of it on many occasions. It was why she appreciated when Jeremiah took the words out of her mouth.

"Well, I have something to tell you that may finally put a smile on your face. If this doesn't work, then I may have to send you off until I get my Mikayla back. I'll take the snotty-attitude teenager over this one any day," she teased.

"Oh, I can still get an attitude. Fast."

"Oh, yeah, she's still in there. Never mind, put the cover back over your head," she joked, and both she and Mikayla laughed.

"She laughs. While you remember how to do so, allow me to enlighten you with the good news I came in here to tell." She watched as Mikayla sat up, providing her undivided attention. "We are going to visit Jeremiah in the morning."

Shock that transitioned to a smile were the expressions displayed by Mikayla at the conclusion of Riley's words. Still, it seemed to take a moment for it to fully register. Riley knew the exact moment it did because Mikayla was no longer sitting up at the head of her bed. She was practically in her lap with her arms tightly wrapped around Riley's neck.

"Are you serious?"

"Yes, and can you not yell in my ear?"

"I'm sorry. I just didn't expect it. I can't believe you're going to take me to visit him in jail."

"Well, I am under one condition." She gently removed Mikayla's arms from around her neck so that they could make eye contact and she could feel the seriousness of her next words.

"Anything," Mikayla quickly agreed, slightly bouncing on the bed.

"After this visit, I don't want any more calls from your teachers about your lack of participation nor any more of your grades dropping. In fact, you need to bring your grades up."

"I promise."

"Damn, all I had to do was get you a visit, and this slump you've been in for the past three weeks would have ended?"

"No. I mean, I'm still going to be sad and in a little slump, but I was going to get my shit together when it comes to school anyway. I hate bad grades, plus I promised Jeremiah."

Genuine. That was the best word she could think of to describe the smile spread across Mikayla's face. It was the first genuine smile that Riley noticed in weeks. Even the excitement present seconds ago hadn't reached her eyes like the smile currently on her face. Over the past few weeks, all of the smiles she'd seen on Mikayla seemed forced or minimal. Even the calls she took from Jeremiah only provided a short-lived piece of joy that seemed to not have mattered once the call concluded.

"Wow, so me stressing over you screwing up your senior year had no effect on your choice to get your shit together?" Riley faked being hurt. She placed her hand over her heart while pouting.

"Believe it or not, you were included in my decision. You've done a lot for me, so I also don't want to let you down."

Appreciation. *Does she finally get what I've sacrificed?* Riley couldn't remember a time when Mikayla acknowledged wanting to please her. Not that she wanted or needed that kind of acknowledgment from her. However, it was and would always be welcomed.

"I appreciate that. I only want you happy."

"I know. Thanks. What time do we have to be up in the morning?"

"Five a.m., and honestly, I'm not glad about it." It wasn't that she wasn't a morning person. She just wasn't one on the weekends. Saturday and Sunday were the days she slept in.

"I'm sure you aren't. I really appreciate you." Mikayla leaned forward, wrapping her arms around Riley.

Feeling herself become emotional, Riley hugged her back tightly before being the first to pull back. She was definitely going to cry when she made it to her bedroom.

Riley furtively shook her head as she watched Mikayla's leg bounce nervously. She wanted to laugh at how her cousin was acting but refrained. This was only Mikayla's second time visiting someone in jail, a first at a juvenile facility. For Riley, jail visits weren't foreign. She'd visited men when she was straight up out of high school—her uncle and father. Although it was a place she could do without visiting, she would always make the trip for someone she deemed worthy. Today, that was Jeremiah.

This trip wasn't just for Mikayla. It was for her too. She wanted to see how he was doing. The updates Mikayla gave via the letters they wrote one another and the phone calls were always good ones, which she was happy about, but she'd known enough incarcerated men to know it wasn't always good.

"Next!"

Mikayla's head shot up in the direction of the loud guard. He gave her an impatient look, which prompted her to look at Riley for clarification.

"We're next, Mikayla. It's okay," Riley assured her, taking her by the hand and being the first of them to go through the second security check. Each time, Riley volunteered to go first because she wanted to show Mikayla there was nothing to worry about. She also wanted to check the temperature of the guards patting down visitors. Although she didn't anticipate the guards using their power to get their feels on because they were patted down by women, she couldn't put anything past them either. Thankfully this pat down was just as smooth as the first for her and Mikayla.

"You still nervous?" Riley asked as the guard allowed them back. They were standing on the opposite side of the waiting room. Once those doors opened, Mikayla and Jeremiah would be reunited. Only for a few hours, but she knew those hours would mean a lot to them.

"Yes. I've never been to a juvie jail, and although Jeremiah and I have grown really close, I'm still kind of nervous to see him."

"Are you still feeling him?" Riley asked with a raised brow. She didn't want her cousin going through all this with Jeremiah in hopes that it would make him feel obligated to take it there with her on a romantic level, especially when he already made it clear that he only wanted her as a friend. Hell, the term "little sister" had even been thrown around a few times.

"Oh, girl, no. We really have a brother-and-sister relationship. I mean, I never had a brother, but I'm assuming that's what we got. Or maybe best friends. Either way, I don't like him like that anymore. Besides, he likes his girls a little too dumb for me. If you heard some of the stories, you wouldn't be able to stop shaking your head. That's how I was. He does have some juicy stories, though, so I don't stop him from telling me. His ex-girlfriend Christy is wild, or dumb. I'll say she's both, actually," she chuckled.

"Okay, that over answered my question." Riley chuckled as well.

Mikayla looked at her as if she wanted to say something else, but the loud clanking of doors halted her words.

"Step back, please," the male guard, who looked like the dad from *Family Matters,* said as the doors began to open. Mikayla gasped as the heavy doors began to open sooner than she and the other people waiting around expected. Her eyes widened as she watched a frail woman barely escape being pinned behind the door.

"Fat bastard," the woman yelled before lifting her middle finger. She stepped back a little farther, seemingly not trusting that things were all clear. Mikayla nudged Riley, and the smirk on her face let her know her cousin saw what happened as well.

"These guards do not care. I would've let the door smash me, and we would be paid," Riley whispered in her ear.

Mikayla laughed, "You would do something like that."

"Hell yeah. We aren't prisoners, so they have to still treat us with respect. The lawsuit I would have brought to this place, had that been me, would have everyone from the warden to the janitor singing a different tune," she said as they walked through the door.

Riley spotted him first. As soon as they entered the room, it was like her eyes automatically wandered to the back of his head. She didn't want to let Mikayla, who was looking around swiftly, know that she had spotted the table because she didn't want to seem more anxious than her cousin.

"There he goes." Mikayla's excitement was clear as she practically threw Riley's hand down. She had held it entering the room but apparently didn't need it anymore.

"His brother is here." Mikayla's eyes landed on Jermaine, which slightly altered her excitement. With a pleading look in her eyes, she turned to Riley. "Please be nice. I don't want to get kicked out of here, especially on the first visit."

"Girl, I know how to conduct myself. If he don't start nothin', it won't be nothing."

"Come on." Mikayla took her hand again and started their walk toward the back of the visiting room, where the men were sitting. Mikayla was annoyed they had to walk through so many gawking eyes. Other girls and women were in the visiting room, but she and Riley seemed to turn all the heads they passed, the male guards included. As they grew closer to the table, Jermaine did a not-so-subtle nod toward them, prompting Jeremiah to turn their way.

As soon as he laid his eyes on Mikayla, he smiled so wide the corners of his mouth appeared to be only inches away from his ears. Mikayla's smile mirrored his. When they stopped a few feet in front of the table, Jeremiah finally stood, embracing Mikayla so swiftly it caught her off guard. Riley's heart swelled. Their embrace was far from romantic and only proved they had a bond she hoped to never see break.

"What's up, Riley? Thanks for bringing her," Jeremiah greeted her once he and Mikayla separated, walking to her with open arms for a hug that she openly accepted.

"No problem. I was hoping you could talk some sense into her." She winked.

"Riley," Mikayla whined.

"Let's sit down." Jeremiah grabbed Mikayla's hand, having her take the seat next to him, leaving Riley next to Jermaine.

"Hey." She greeted him first. It wasn't a dry greeting, but it also wasn't full of enthusiasm.

"What's up?" Now Jermaine's reply was too regular for her liking. As always, he acted as if he didn't care to be bothered with her.

"Bro." Jermaine looked at Jeremiah, who called himself checking his brother by kicking him underneath the table with a frown.

"My bad." Jeremiah chuckled, aware that his brother had gotten the point. "Riley, what did you need me to get on Mikayla about?"

"Wow, we haven't been here a minute, and y'all are ready to start in on me?" Mikayla frowned, folding her arms across her chest.

"She's right. I'll tell you later," Riley responded.

That was all the two teens needed as they turned toward one another and began catching up. They became so engrossed in conversation with each other that Riley's and Jermaine's presence went unnoticed. Riley wished she had been able to bring her cell. Then she at least wouldn't have been so bored. Granted, she didn't expect the visit to go any different had it only been the three of them, but having a whole other body next to her, who was also being ignored, ignoring her existence, was irritating to say the least. Especially when she was fighting the attraction she felt toward him.

"Bro, I'm hungry. Can you grab us something from over there?" Jeremiah asked.

"Riley, me too," Mikayla joined in.

"Yeah," was all Jermaine said before he stood.

"Sorry about my brother."

"You do not have to apologize for him." Riley stood and headed toward the vending machines, ending up behind Jermaine.

"You didn't have to get up. I planned to grab enough for everybody."

"And I was supposed to know that because you've been so talkative?"

"You ain't say shit to me either."

"Because since the day I met you, you've been an asshole. I promised Mikayla I wouldn't get us kicked out of here from cussing you out, so I decided only to speak when spoken to." She shrugged.

"Guess I deserve that." He chuckled.

"Definitely do." Riley's confirmation left an uncomfortable silence between them. It wasn't until the line moved that Jermaine decided to speak again.

"What y'all want? I already know what my brother likes. What about you and Mikayla?"

It may have not seemed like much, but Riley appreciated him using Mikayla's name rather than calling her "your cousin." It meant he was trying to recognize her as a person in his brother's life.

"I can grab our stuff."

"Man, I'm trying to be nice here. You gon' let me buy y'all stuff?"

Riley shook her head, ready to continue to be difficult because he really did not deserve any kind of slack, but it was becoming evident that he was different. So his definition of trying was not what she was used to.

"Sure," she agreed, then chose a couple items she and Mikayla liked.

"Look, my bad, man. This shit with my brother has me fucked up. I been going through it with his little ass for the longest, but this shit takes the cake."

"I get it. My raising Mikayla hasn't been a cake-walk either."

"Oh, word." He smiled, and though she knew he was being funny based on their initial meeting and what he assumed he knew about Mikayla, she chuckled, finding humor because they both knew his assumption had been wrong as hell.

"He seems like a good kid. Just got caught up with the wrong crowd."

"Yeah, him and the wrong crowd have met one too many times. I think he may have learned his lesson this time, though."

"It's just you and your brother?" she asked, unafraid of continuing small talk since he finally decided to open up a little.

"Yeah, out here. Our mom lives in Nevada. I moved down here first, and then a couple of years later, I had Jeremiah."

"That sounds similar to our story, although our family, the small one we have, lives only a few hours away. Mikayla came to stay with me, and it's pretty much been just us. I'm actually happy she's built a relationship with your brother." Both Riley's and Jermaine's eyes wandered to the teens, who were still smiling and talking so carefree.

"Yeah, me too. So far, he's made it clear he doesn't want to disappoint her, like he ain't been hittin' my ass over the head every chance he gets. But keeping her happy motivates him to do better, so I'll take it. Shit, weird how he feels like that and she ain't even his girl. He really looks at her like a little sister and hasn't known her but a popcorn minute."

Riley laughed at his old-school saying and almost let him know he was showing his age. "That's the same thing I said to her last night." She paused as the revelation of what she was about to admit next hit her. "We have more in common than one would have thought."

"Seems that way," he agreed in his common nonchalant attitude. This time she didn't get offended.

"Sure you don't want anything else?" Jermaine asked once they made it to the window to pay. Because the vending machines were out of order, the facility set up a small shopping space with a guard as the cashier. It was their way to allow the visitors to still make purchases.

"No, that's enough. We'll probably grab something later."

Jermaine nodded, then proceeded to pay for their items. He carried them all to the table. Instinctively they all waited for Jeremiah to choose what items he wanted first, even though he'd told them they could choose. They all had the same reason for waiting: wanting to provide Jeremiah with a choice. They could easily get up and spend money, while he couldn't do the same.

"Riley, what was it like growing up?" Jeremiah asked. The visit was coming to an end soon, and he and Mikayla had been so caught up in each other while Jermaine and Riley watched on. The smiles on their faces as they watched them interact let him know they weren't miserable. However, he would bet his freedom they were bored.

"Um, it was cool. I fought a lot because someone was always trying me. They always got a rude awakening, too. I came up wrestling and slap boxing with my boy cousins, so when females tried me, they learned the hard way." She shrugged.

"I can see it. You don't take no shit." Jeremiah nodded in approval. "My brother used to be knockin' dudes out," he volunteered.

"Damn, who said I wanted my business out there?" Jermaine mugged his brother.

"Oh, relax. Women like men who can handle themselves. Sometimes knowing how to put a person in their place screams, 'Big dick energy,'" Riley said.

"I knew it," Mikayla said through a cough. She was not so subtle with that comment but tried playing it off, hiding behind a cough.

"Knew what?" Riley feigned innocence. She knew with an attitude like his, Jermaine had to have been knocking dudes out, causing havoc and breaking hearts.

"Nothing." Mikayla smiled sweetly.

"How was your brother toward the ladies, since he was making dudes fear him?" Riley asked Jeremiah like Jermaine wasn't right there and couldn't speak for himself.

"Don't know, only seen him have one real girl-friend. He treated her good from what I saw. Since we moved down here though, girls don't seem to like him," Jeremiah teased, and he, Mikayla, and even Riley laughed.

"You a damn liar, and y'all can stop talking about me like I ain't here."

"It's probably his attitude that keeps women away," Riley stated matter-of-factly, causing Mikayla and Jeremiah to chuckle.

"Guarantee it ain't that. You talking like you want to find out." Jermaine gave her a challenging look, and Riley felt her cheeks heat up.

"Uh, no." She rolled her eyes, sitting back in her seat.

Knowing her cousin, Mikayla could see how flustered Jermaine's comment made her. And the only time a guy could get her like that was if she was attracted to him. She looked from Riley to Jermaine and smirked. They definitely would look good together, and although Jermaine acted like a grinch most of the time, she was sure he was feeling her cousin too. He'd be crazy not to.

"Y'all, I want to celebrate when I get out of here. Can be anything—a trip, a gift, a party," Jeremiah spoke up, breaking the silence before it got any more awkward.

"Ooh, that sounds fun," Mikayla chimed in.

"Man, if I were in your shoes, a celebration would be the last thing I received after getting out of juvie," Riley said.

"I was, and I got a crazy-ass teen for my gift," Jermaine said as he ruffled Jeremiah's barely kempt hair.

"Yeah, they don't make them from this kind of cloth no more," Riley teased.

"Visitors, you have five minutes. Inmates, say your goodbyes," a guard yelled, instantly shifting the mood. However, this was the most Jeremiah and even Mikayla had laughed and smiled since he'd been gone, so he refused to let it ruin the rest of their day.

"Thank you again for bringing her," Jeremiah said to Riley as they hugged.

"No problem. If necessary, we'll be back, but hopefully it won't come to that."

"It won't. He's getting out." Even knowing his release wasn't guaranteed, Mikayla chimed in so confidently that everyone believed it. No one wanted to admit that it was better to believe that what Mikayla affirmed was true, so instead, Jeremiah turned his attention to his brother.

"Thanks for coming through, bro."

"It's nothin'. I got you." They embraced in a brotherly hug before Jeremiah turned his attention back to Mikayla.

"Make sure you take yo' ass to school and show out. You are too smart to have dummy grades. You fuck up in school and it's a wrap on our friendship. I don't hang with females who are dummies."

"Nah, you just like airheads, which isn't a far cry from dumb," she teased. "Don't worry about me. I got this. My grades will be back in tip-top shape before the month ends. Besides, all my teachers like me, so they aren't even that bad because they all know I've been dealing with something. They've cut me a lot of slack," she stated matter-of-factly.

"Well, you done going through it, so put yo' actions where yo' mouth is and get it together."

"I will."

Riley shook her head at how easily Mikayla complied. If only she had this kind of power over her cousin.

"Final lineup call!"

"All right, y'all, I gotta go. I'll call everyone later."
Jeremiah gave out more hugs before heading to
the line, leaving with his head held high. Riley,
Mikayla, and Jermaine watched until he was on
the other side of the door and they couldn't see
him anymore.

"Y'all got plans when you leave here?" Jermaine
surprised them with his question, breaking the
uncomfortable silence.

"Just grabbing food," Riley informed him.

"Oh, all right."

"You can come with us, huh, Riley?" Mikayla
offered.

"Ye . . .yeah, that's fine. I can pay you back for
what you got us earlier."

"Nah, that's not necessary. I have a few things to
do as far as work, so maybe next time."

"Okay." Riley was shocked at the disappointment
she felt at him turning down the chance to enjoy a
meal with them.

"Is it okay if I call you? To talk about my brother
and shit?" For the first time since she met him,
Jermaine appeared bashful, and it was sexy as hell
to her.

"Yes, that's fine."

Jermaine nodded, unsure of what else to say but
positive that he would be reaching out.

Chapter 10

"This girl better be happy I love her," Riley groaned as she placed her AirPods in her ears before scrolling through her contacts list until she reached Jermaine's name. She tried to shake the flutters she felt just seeing his name, but they had taken over and probably wouldn't go away until after their call ended. They hadn't spoken really since the visit, and though all ended well, she wanted to avoid him because she hated how the visit made her see another side of him, making him more attractive. Well, of course he was handsome. Fine as hell if she had to use better words to describe him. But their first meeting didn't go well, the second either. So being skeptical of his moody ass wasn't wrong.

"What's up?" His voice came through, and Riley stopped in the middle of the aisle to squeeze her thighs together.

This mean-ass man should not have me feeling a way, she thought as she willed herself to find her voice.

"Hey, how are you? Um, this is Riley." She hurried out the last part. Asking how he was then assuming he'd know it was her had her slapping herself on the forehead.

"I know who this is," he clarified sexily, and her thighs clamped together again. If he kept sounding the way he sounded, she wasn't sure she'd make it out of the grocery store with the items she came for. She'd need to run home to take care of the surge he sent through her body.

"Uh, okay, well, I was just calling to see how things were going with Jeremiah. And if you guys needed anything."

"Bro's court date. I'm sure he'll want y'all there." He caught himself from giving her a task for himself since she cared enough to ask what he needed. Thing was, the task would be R-rated, and though she had a mouth on her, he doubted she could handle him.

"Of course we'll be there."

"That's what's up."

"Did you think we wouldn't?" She wasn't sure why she cared to know. She just wanted to.

"Nah, I figured you would."

Riley smiled. It felt good that he was beginning to recognize Mikayla's and now her loyalty to his younger brother.

"Well, I guess we'll see you in a few days."

"You could see me sooner," he said, and Riley gasped, causing Jermaine to chuckle. "Nah, I'll see y'all at court. Thanks for calling and checking on us."

"You're welcome." Riley felt her cheeks heat up as she ended the call. "I do not like that man," she vowed, putting her phone inside her purse and focusing back on the items on her grocery list.

Jermaine's heart swelled when he noticed Riley and Mikayla walk through the doors of the court-house. It took a moment for them to spot him up front, but once his and Riley's eyes connected, he smiled, and she did the same. It had been almost a month since they last saw one another, but only days since he spoke to her about today. Oddly, after that call he found himself looking forward to her showing up. Of course, he wasn't happy about the circumstances, but seeing her face again, especially after knowing his subtle flirting had caught her off guard, he wanted to see her face.

He felt they were slowly building their own bond, and he was glad that after he'd acted an ass on multiple occasions, she was open to getting to know him. Asking how he was and if he needed anything let him know a door was open between them that he wasn't looking to have closed. The same feisty attitude he thought he hated about her he actually enjoyed. The more they became acquainted, the more he understood why she didn't take no shit. And he also understood her having to have a tough exterior to lead by example for Mikayla. No, she wasn't raising her to be cold and heartless. She only wanted her to be a strong, independent young woman who knew what she wanted. Talking to Riley helped him recognize that he was doing his best regardless of the choices Jeremiah made. They were both thrown into parental roles when all their lives they only knew how to be a sibling or cousin. If becoming a parent didn't come with a manual, then there sure as hell wasn't one for them.

Jermaine kept his eyes on them as they made their way to him. He badly wanted to wrap his hands around Riley, who was looking good as hell in a navy blue pencil skirt, which was one with her hips, and a white button-up shirt with blue polka dots, which accentuated her round breasts. Her hair was pulled up into a top-knot bun, and minimal makeup adorned her face. Riley was looking breathtakingly beautiful.

"Hey, is he first?" Mikayla asked as she moved from his embrace.

"Nah, he's third. Three is a lucky number where we come from, so today should be a good day." Though full of fear for what was to come, Jermaine still tried to remain optimistic. That was why he was glad to have Mikayla and Riley in the courtroom with him. He and Jeremiah needed all the positive energy they could get.

"That's good to know. With luck and my un-wavering prayers, today will be a good day," Riley assured him as she smiled at Jermaine.

"Hey, Jermaine."

His name being called by a soft voice pulled his attention from the girls and made Riley's heart skip a beat. Within seconds she had multiple thoughts crossing her mind, one being, *I know he didn't invite us and his bitch.* Yet when that thought hit, she immediately threw it away. Jermaine wasn't hers and probably would never be, and she wasn't there for him anyway. Today was about Jeremiah. She had no business feeling even a tinge of jealousy even though she was.

"Hey, what's up?" He didn't smile, nor did he frown. Riley's attraction to him and the jealousy she felt made her feel that his demeanor was one of a man who'd just been caught.

Stop it, Riley, she mentally scolded herself as she looked toward the witness stand, trying her best not to appease her curiosity by turning to see who the woman behind her was.

"I just came from seeing your brother. I went over a couple things with him. Is it okay if we step to the side so I can run it all by you?"

"That's not necessary. You can tell me right here. This is Mikayla, Jermaine's best friend, and her big cousin, Riley. You can talk in front of them. They are here to support him."

Jermaine's unorthodox introduction was all Riley needed to turn around. Riley felt her eyes expand and silently prayed no one noticed, especially the woman she was staring at. Riley was not and never would be the girl who compared herself to another or became insecure behind another woman. What she would do and had always done was give props where they were due, and today would be no different. If Jermaine was attracted to this woman in any way, she completely understood why. She was gorgeous, from her flawless brown skin to her badass Coke-bottle shape.

"Hi, I'm Riley." She extended her hand, and the woman before her did the same, except there wasn't an ounce of humbleness in the quick gaze she gave Riley. It was one of smugness or irritation. She couldn't really describe it. Maybe she was tripping.

"Landra McCullough," she quickly introduced herself as she removed her hand and turned her attention back toward Jermaine. "Okay, well, we only have a few moments. I know he doesn't plan to testify against any of the guys, but I plan to present all the evidence they have as substantial. Even though Jeremiah was in the vicinity, none of that proves his guilt. Even if he were hanging with the guilty parties, that doesn't mean he's also guilty. What he has going for him is that he has never been arrested before."

"Do what you gotta do, and bail won't be an issue if it comes to that," Jermaine assured her.
Jermaine knew his brother wouldn't snitch, and
although he wouldn't judge him if he did, he
wouldn't be the one to ask him to do so. He was a
changed man, but the codes of the streets still re-
sided within him, and he didn't want to be labeled
a snitch nor be associated with one, so he would
respect his brother's decision. Having done time
before, he knew jail was harder for a snitch, and
if things did not work in his brother's favor, he'd
rather he be known as a stand-up young man than
the kid who told on his homeboys.

"I'm sure it won't be. You have me on retainer,
and I ain't cheap." She winked before walking off,
making sure her hips left him something to think
about. Neither Riley nor Mikayla missed the not-
so-subtle flirting on her end, giving each other a
knowing look before sitting. Their seats hadn't had
a chance to warm before the bailiff spoke.

"All rise. The Honorable Judge Dyer presiding."

Mikayla reached for Riley's hand as her nerves
began to go haywire. This was a lot for a teenage
girl to take, and it was even harder for her because
she'd already been through so much, especially
with young men. She practically squeezed Riley's
hand when the judge walked in and took his
seat. He did not look like an easygoing man at all.
Though he didn't look a day over 50, the hard look

on his face made him appear as if life had turned him hard. If his looks were even a small reflection of his insides, Jeremiah was probably in trouble.

"You may be seated," he directed.

The first two cases left Riley, Jermaine, and Mikayla feeling very doubtful that things would work out for Jeremiah. The judge practically threw the law in the face of every defendant he saw, including a member of Jeremiah's gang. The judge hadn't taken it easy on the kid, sentencing him to five years. Although the boy had priors, he would be well into his twenties before he was a free man, and it frightened Jermaine. He could only hope that the judge did not take the saying "You are who you hang with" seriously when it came to his brother.

"Case number 2652. Jeremiah Stately," the bailiff announced. Jeremiah walked into the courtroom looking very handsome even under the circumstances. Jermaine did great with the attire he chose for his brother: a white button-up, gray slacks, and white dress shoes. His hair had been cut, and Mikayla wondered how that was possible since he was in jail.

"Mr. Stately, you are being charged with intent of auto theft, intent to steal property, and endangering bystanders. There looks to have been a charge of battery removed as the plaintiff admitted you were not physical with him. Still, you are looking at serious charges."

Jeremiah's face scrunched as he turned to look at his lawyer. He hadn't been told about the battery charges being dropped.

Landra smiled before leaning closer to him. "This is a good thing. If you didn't attack the victim, it'll make it hard for them to prove you were there at all. Or that you were there to do everything the DA is accusing you of with that minor detail. It may sound off, but that's big news for us. Just watch." Landra gave him a reassuring nod before sitting back in her seat, giving her attention to the front of the room.

Everything she said sounded good, but Jeremiah's nerves were still kicking his ass. He swallowed the lump in his throat as he clasped his hands together in front of him, imagining one hand being Mikayla's providing him strength.

Mikayla, on the other hand, was doing her best not to fall apart, understanding that each charge being read was years off of Jeremiah's freedom. She also felt bad because she hated that people in the courtroom would think he was a bad person. She wiped a lone tear, fighting the urge to release the flood and sob. She would have let out a full-blown sob had she not cared about getting removed from the courtroom.

"Mr. Stately, how do you plead?"

"Not guilty, Your Honor."

No sooner than Jeremiah entered his plea did the district attorney begin his case.

"Your Honor, and people of the court, I understand this man's plea of not guilty. However, he's known to run with the 619 gang. Why should we believe he was not with them during this crime? He's cut classes according to his school record, though he's never been to jail. He has been reprimanded by the school authorities for fighting. And his mother sent him to be raised by his brother, who has a criminal record as well. Does this sound like an innocent young man?"

Jeremiah, a teenager who held a 3.0 GPA, had never been to jail, and was raised by his older brother, was made out to be this delinquent with no home training or an empathetic bone in his body. After each breath the DA took, Mikayla wanted to yell and tell him to go to hell. She'd never wanted to cuss somebody out so badly. She hated that she assumed the DA would cut him any kind of slack. With her fist balled tightly, Mikayla's leg shook violently as she tried to remain calm, but tears streamed down her face.

"It's okay. It's still going to be okay," Riley soothed her as she gently pulled a crying Mikayla's head onto her shoulder. When Mikayla's head was down, she could finally get a good look at Jermaine. His jaw was tense, and veins protruded from his forehead. There was no question that he was pissed. Riley hadn't been privy to Jeremiah's past, but even so, it was just that. However, life had taught her that the past could come back to bite you in the ass. She only hoped that wouldn't be the case for Jeremiah. She'd grown to like the person he showed her he was with their interactions and felt he was being genuine. Because of this, she, too, felt the DA was being extremely unreasonable in the descriptions he placed upon Jeremiah and the crew he ran with.

Riley had heard about the 619 boys and how they were a bunch of terrorizers. Still, she hated for someone of another race to talk down on her people. Maybe they were badasses or fuckups, but they were the badasses and fuckups of a strong community who would always see the potential for them to display black boy joy and not the menaces they were made out to be. She hated how the system was set up for them to fail.

"Your Honor, nothing the district attorney has said proves that my client is guilty. This is clearly a situation of being in the wrong place at the wrong time. My client has decent grades and has pending college applications to schools he has a great chance of getting into. The minor infractions back in his hometown that Mr. Heredia speaks of have never led to a conviction or even a slap on the wrist. Is he guilty of possibly hanging with the wrong crowd? Maybe. But based on the young man who sits before us and has also had multiple character letters sent to this courtroom, Your Honor, none of what the prosecutor says describes him."

"How do you explain the many coincidences surrounding your client and the 619 gang?" the district attorney asked, his lips pulled together in a thin line as he looked at Landra like this question had won him the case.

"Please explain, Ms. McCullough," the judge advised.

"As exactly what they are—mere coincidences. What actual proof is there that my client committed any crime?" Landra gave her undivided attention to the DA, whose face turned beet red. She knew she had made a point he wasn't quite prepared to prove. In fact, the entire case against Jeremiah was circumstantial. However, if the DA was going against any other attorney, Jeremiah may have been fucked. But Jermaine had done his research and hired her, the best fucking attorney in town, so what little evidence they did have meant nothing going against her.

"Your Honor, we are asking my client be released on bail until his next court hearing. He isn't a flight risk, and this time out of school is harming the opportunities he has that will help him become a pillar of society sooner rather than later. "

"Your Honor, we ask that Mr. Stately remain in custody. He and his gang are savages."

"Excuse me, please refrain from derogatory name-calling," the judge scolded him. His deep baritone expressed he would not ask twice, and from the way the DA's Adam's apple bounced when he swallowed, he knew the judge wasn't joking.

"Now I have listened to the argument from both parties, and though both have made appealing arguments, there are still some facts that need to be proven from both parties. However, based on letters from Mr. Stately's community and support system and his not having any priors, I do not see him as a flight risk and grant him release on his own recognizance."

"Your Honor!" The DA practically shouted his disapproval.

"Mr. Heredia, you have thirty days to prove why this young man should be in custody."

"Sorry, Your Honor."

"Now, Mr. Stately, this release does not mean you have free reign. You go to school and stay out of trouble. If I see you before the next court date, I will not be so lenient. The defendant is to be released immediately. Court adjourned."

The judge hit his gavel, and Riley, Jermaine, and Mikayla finally released the breath they had been holding. No one wanted to shout in joy more than Mikayla, but she refrained. Instead, the tears that fell from her eyes now were happy tears. Jeremiah turned around and flashed the three of them an award-winning smile, then turned back around, where the bailiff was standing in front of him.

"Wait, why is that cop taking him?" Mikayla asked in a panic.

"It's okay. They have to process him out," Riley assured her, rubbing her back to calm her down.

"Let's go out front," Jermaine suggested as Landra headed their way. Jermaine waited until they were outside of the courtroom to speak with her.

"You really worth that high-ass rate you charge. Thank you."

"Well, there's still one more court date ahead. But the next one will be the last one." She smiled, and Riley couldn't help noticing how straight and white her teeth were.

Probably paid for 'em, she thought as she placed her attention elsewhere.

"So what's next?" Mikayla asked, anxious to know why Jeremiah hadn't walked out of the courtroom.

"He should be out shortly. We have to meet him on the next floor. Jermaine, you have to sign a parental document."

"All right." They all followed Landra to the area of the court where Jeremiah would be released.

Mikayla's heart thumped due to nerves the entire walk. Riley couldn't help become slightly annoyed by Landra and her hand touching Jermaine's shoulder one too many times. At this point, it had nothing to do with her feeling Jermaine. It was Landra acting as if she and Mikayla weren't even there. Thankfully the walk to the release area hadn't been a long one. Neither was the wait for Jeremiah. As soon as the doors opened, Jermaine was on him. Mikayla wanted to run to him, but Riley held her back, knowing the brothers needed and deserved their moment first. However, Jermaine's first words shocked the hell out of them all.

"Bro, you do some stupid shit to end up back here and I'm done with yo' ass for good, hear me?" he told him as he pulled him into his chest, hugging him tightly. Everything about the scolding and embrace made Riley look at him in another light. He became sexier to her at that moment.

"I promise, bro. I ain't coming back here."

"Bet' not. I meant what I said." Jermaine released Jeremiah, and they gave each other one last look of assurance that they meant exactly what they said.

Jeremiah looked around his brother and lit up like a Christmas tree at the sight of Mikayla. Like a romance flick, the two rushed into each other's arms, embracing so lovingly that the only thing missing was a French kiss. Still, Riley and Jermaine were happy for the two to be reunited outside of the juvenile walls.

Chapter 11

"You almost ready?" Jeremiah asked his brother, who stood in front of the full-length mirror in his bedroom, checking over his attire. He was dressed in Polo from head to toe. The weather was sixty-five degrees, which provided the right temperature for the navy and white crew-neck sweater and blue jeans.

"First off, don't rush me. I don't ask how high when Mikayla says jump," he teased.

"Man, you tripping. I don't move like that when it comes to her. I'm just ready to get out of the house and eat. I'm never taking real food for granted again."

"Yeah, sure. You've been out of jail all of three weeks, and I bet you can tell me more about that girl than you know about yourself." Jermaine laughed. "And from what I've witnessed, if you're not where she wants you when she wants you, she gon' have a fit, and the last thing you're trying to do is hurt her feelings."

"It's wrong for me to not want to see her hurt?"

"Not at all, bro. I just really wonder how you can keep up with this brother-and-sister act when clearly there are some feelings there. Gotta be, 'cause you jump through more hoops than a circus act."

"I really don't look at her romantically."

"Then what is it?" Jermaine asked honestly, curious why Jeremiah had such strong feelings about protecting and loving Mikayla in such a short amount of time.

"I guess it's because in many ways we're similar, and I get to be to her someone I wanted and needed." Jeremiah's eyes moved to the floor when he said that. He wasn't sure if his brother caught on to what he meant.

"I wanna ask you something," Jermaine said, regaining Jeremiah's eyes on him. He didn't want to ruin the mood or put a damper on his spirits before they headed out to go and do whatever Mikayla had planned, but he had a question weighing on him since Jeremiah was released from jail.

"Yeah, what's up?"

"Why were you hanging with those dudes? I know you been kicking it with them for a minute, and though I wasn't happy about it, you seemed to stay out of the way of dumb shit until you didn't. I've known you to make some crazy decisions, but being a follower isn't one of 'em. We don't rock like that."

Jeremiah looked at his brother and thought about his answer. He knew if he lied, Jermaine would see right through it. But he also knew the truth could hurt his brother's feelings, and that wasn't what he wanted to do. The old him, before getting locked up, wouldn't have cared what Jermaine felt. But after being locked up and his brother holding him down, his feelings toward hurting his brother were different. He also knew that being honest was the best way to restore their relationship, and that was something he wanted.

"Truthfully, because they made me feel wanted. Needed. They gave me a brotherhood I had been longing for since the day you left me alone with Mom. They made me feel like they had my back, and I was invincible when I was with them. There was never a question of if they had my back. I got a brotherhood that I didn't feel inside these walls."

His words were like a stab to Jermaine's heart. He knew that things changed the day he left. But he didn't think it was that deep or didn't want to believe it to be that deep.

"Damn, bro. You know when I left Mom's house, it wasn't because I was trying to get up out of there and away from y'all. I had to leave. I went to jail." Although he was sure Jeremiah figured out where he went those years ago, shame had stopped him from talking about it. So to admit it now felt like removing a weight from his shoulders.

"I know that, but you didn't come back. You moved out here. You had a choice to come back and didn't. And Mama said you didn't come back to us 'cause you weren't about to let my fuckups send you back to jail." Now Jeremiah was the one removing a heavy load. He resented his mother and brother the day she told him that.

"She really said that shit?" Jermaine was disgusted.

"Yeah, that's why she and I still have a little shaky relationship."

"Man, I never said no shit like that. I moved out here because I wanted a fresh start. Being in prison taught me a lot and made me realize a lot. My decision to not come back home had nothing to do with you. Mom was wrong for lying like that, but she also felt a way because I didn't move back. I'm not making an excuse for her, 'cause that's fucked up, but don't hold it against her too much." Although angry with the lie their mother told, Jermaine was still going to protect her.

"I'm not. It is what it is," he said, then shrugged.

"Ay, I apologize if you feel or felt abandoned in any way. There's not anything I wouldn't do for you. And though it may have felt like you gained some brothers with your crew, you have a real one right here. Blood means more than made bonds to me. If ever you feel like I'm not being the big brother you need, holler at me. Don't go looking for it somewhere else because, I promise you, a thousand men can't hold a candle to one of me." Jermaine smirked, easing the tension although he was serious.

Chuckling, Jeremiah nodded before he extended his hand, and the two embraced in a brotherly hug. "I hear you, bro." And he did. Those words from Jermaine meant more to him than his brother would ever know. Even though Jermaine had done the ultimate by taking him in and then having his back when he fucked up, his words still meant something. The saying "Actions speak louder than words" would always be a good one, but what people forgot to mention was that telling then showing is equally important. Jeremiah wanted his brother to tell him what it was and then show him. His gang had done that, said they'd have his back, and did when he had beef. Said they'd help him get money and did when he was down to his last few dollars. None of what they promised stood on doing good. But they proved what they said each time, and that had been good enough for him.

Mikayla had been another person to say something and follow through with action. It was obviously different with her, and that helped Jeremiah see that the brotherhood he had with the 619 boys was conditional.

"A'ight, let's roll out. Before you get in trouble."

"Bro, you like to make fun of me with Mikayla, but you can't front like you don't want to be around Riley's fine ass. I know you feeling her."

"Man, me and her are cordial on the strength of y'all." He said what he had been trying to convince himself of silently over the last few days. He did not want to admit that he liked Riley, nor that he thought about making love to her on more than one occasion. He couldn't take it there with her, though, and tried to convince himself of that because if things didn't work out with them, he didn't want it to affect Mikayla and Jeremiah's relationship.

"Yeah, keep telling yourself that, bro."

Jermaine opted to not reply. Instead, he headed out of his room and to the kitchen, where his car keys were with Jeremiah not far behind him.

"You were gonna leave me? I definitely know you like Riley now," he teased as his brother turned up the radio and headed toward their destination.

Mikayla moved frantically around the house, making sure everything was in place. She convinced Riley to let her throw Jeremiah a small welcome home gathering and had been obsessing over everything being perfect ever since. A few of their peers from school were in the garage where the party was being held because Riley refused to let some unruly teenagers fuck up the inside of her house.

"Why are you fluffing pillows if y'all are going to be down there?" Riley asked as she watched Mikayla put the pillow back on the sofa.

"Because I'm nervous. And I have no idea why," Mikayla replied honestly as she plopped down on the couch. Riley made her way over and took a seat next to her.

"He's going to appreciate this. I honestly think he would appreciate anything you choose to do for him. I want to ask you something again."

"No, I do not like him as a boyfriend, for the hundredth time." Mikayla rolled her eyes before flashing Riley a smile. She understood her cousin's hesitancy to believe her when she said Jeremiah was just a friend, but that was truly all he was. And it was exactly what she needed.

"It's just so . . . not weird, but unexpected and fresh. Like, I love this new bond for you, but I'm also kind of jealous."

"Really?" Mikayla frowned in disbelief. That was the last thing she expected to hear Riley say. They weren't the closest mainly because Mikayla kept a wall up, and Riley at times would be buried in so much work she had no time to think about it. Still, she didn't think a friendship with someone would have her feeling a way.

"Yeah, I mean, I've been trying to get through to you since you moved in, and although I notice you changing some for the better, it sucks that I wasn't a part of it."

"But you were. You are. I may not say it, but I take note. Do you think I'd be doing so well in school if it weren't for you? I know you have this success because you graduated and did what you had to do. That motivates me. It's just Jeremiah and I have a lot in common, and he did save me from the boys at school and . . ." She paused, trying to think of how to say what it was she was going to admit out loud for the first time.

"Every male I've come across always wanted something from me. None of them ever made me feel protected, and if they did, it was only momentarily to get something they wanted out of me. Jeremiah hasn't, and though I know he's capable of it, I feel deeply in my soul that he's different. I finally have a guy in my life who wants what's best for me and wants to protect me. His friendship may help me with a future relationship, like, show me how a guy is supposed to treat a girl because my dad didn't."

"Whew," Riley breathed out. Mikayla had just provided a mouthful of things to unpack, and she knew it would take more than tonight to do so. She opened her mouth, ready to at least acknowledge the level of maturity she was seeing in her cousin, only for the doorbell to ring.

"They're here." Mikayla practically leaped from the sofa toward the front door.

"Mikayla, wait." Riley paused any further movement from her. "I know your dad may not have shown you much, but you don't need a man to show you how you want to be loved. The only manual that can tell you about being loved properly is the one you draw out for yourself. Learn your love language by understanding what feels good to you and what makes you happy, and you express that to the man who deserves you. You'll know who deserves you by what he's willing to do for you. All right?"

"All right." Mikayla gave Riley the warmest smile, and she knew her little cousin got it and was growing up.

"G'on and answer the door now. I know you're dying to," Riley told her before releasing a light chuckle as she watched Mikayla practically skip to the door.

"What's up?" Jeremiah's voice sounded through the house as Mikayla stepped back and allowed him inside. Riley watched them embrace this time without a hint of romanticism involved and didn't take her eyes off them until Jermaine stepped into her view.

Jermaine was a sight to see—not just for sore eyes, but for all kinds. Hell, she'd wish sight on the blind even for a few minutes to see the fine-ass brother before her.

"What's up?" He did a simple nod toward her, and she felt a way. She knew they had made progress. She wasn't delusional, so how he reduced her to a simple nod and "what's up" had her confused.

"Hey," she replied to him before standing to greet Jeremiah.

"Riley, I thought you were cooking. I don't smell no food, and I am starving," Jeremiah groaned.

"Boy, I didn't promise you a meal."

"Man." The disappointed look on his face made the girls laugh.

"Boy, come on," Mikayla grabbed him by the hand, leading the way toward the garage door with Jermaine and Riley on their heels. As soon as she opened the door, "Surprise! Welcome home!" echoed throughout.

"This is for me? Ay, y'all dope for this! Riley, thank you, 'cause I know how you are about your spot."

"It's nothing. Go have fun and eat. It's good down there as long as no one ate it all."

"I'm beating some ass if they did." Taking Mikayla by the hand, Jeremiah pulled her into the garage.

"You can go down there and chaperone if you want."

"And where are you going? I ain't the one throwing his ass a party," Jermaine told her.

"After I grab a plate, I plan to sit on my back patio. I can see them from there."

"You want some company? 'Cause I'm not babysitting their asses."

"Sure." Riley smiled before going into the garage with Jermaine behind her to grab food. The party had officially begun as the DJ played music and the kids were on their feet dancing.

"Um, who is that boy Mikayla is dancing with?" Riley asked Jeremiah, who stood in front of the table like he was guarding the chicken wings.

"He's a dude from school. He coo', plus he knows better than to be disrespectful. Mikayla is good, Riley."

She nodded and went back to making her plate. After she and Jermaine loaded up, they headed out to Riley's back patio.

"This is dope." Jermaine admired the setup. There were plush lounge chairs and tiki torches lit. The patio decor was a whole vibe, perfect for a date if they had been on one.

"Thank you. I made sure to set it up so that even on cold nights like this one I could come out here and relax without freezing."

"You laid all this out?" Jermaine asked, impressed.

"Yup. Interior design was my thing for a while. But because that's not big out this way, I never made a career out of it. I'd have to live in Los Angeles or somewhere to see any real money for interior design."

"I feel it. Thanks again for all the love you show my brother. Throwing him a party is dope 'cause I sure as hell wouldn't have these little badasses at my house."

"That's why it's only a few, and they are in the garage. I did it for both him and Mikayla, but I guarantee this is a one and done kind of thing. I'm still not even sure how she talked me into it."

"So you're wrapped around her finger too."

"Guess you could say that." She shrugged and watched as Jermaine dug into his pocket.

"You mind if I smoke?" he asked, fine with going to smoke in his car if she said no.

"Only if you are sharing." The devious grin she gave him turned him on and had him adjusting himself in his seat.

"I got you." He began rolling up the blunt, and Riley did her best to avoid focusing on his lips when he licked the blunt to seal it. "Since this is your spot, you can have it first." He lit the blunt and passed it to her.

It had been a while since she smoked, and she hoped she didn't look like an amateur as she placed the perfectly rolled blunt between her full lips. She was also happy she hadn't put on any lipstick or thick gloss because sharing wouldn't have been appealing. Both left stains behind that even she didn't care for. She took a nice-sized inhale and held it for three seconds before releasing the smoke. She tried her best to hold in the cough she felt arising but couldn't.

"Ay, you all right?" Jermaine popped up and patted her back. The coughing fit didn't last but a moment, but it still worried him.

"Yes, it's just been a while, and this is some intense shit."

"Oh, yeah, I should have warned you I don't smoke nothing but the best."

"I see." She took the blunt back to her lips and held in her laughter at the shocked expression on his face. She was sure he thought she was done, but she was a big girl and refused to let him believe she couldn't hang. This time when she hit the blunt, she released the smoke like a pro, and there was no coughing. However, she was now feeling good off those two puffs and passed it to Jermaine. She now was good for the time being.

"Can I ask you something? Are you single?" She hadn't waited for him to say it was okay to ask her question. Weed courage had her, and she was going to ask regardless. If he answered, he answered. If not, she'd later get the answer from Jeremiah.

"I am. Why you want to know?" He smirked.

Shrugging her shoulders, she told him, "I was curious."

"You?"

"I am. Now why are you asking?"

"Maybe because I want to take you out."

Riley leaned forward in her seat, wanting to be sure she heard him correctly. No, he wasn't sitting far from her at all, but getting closer to understand him better wouldn't hurt. "You what?"

"Want to take you out."

"Like on a date?"

"Yeah, man. So what's up? You gon' let me take you out?"

"You gon' act like you were raised right?" she teased.

"Damn, I haven't redeemed myself by now?"

"You been doing all right."

"Then what's up?"

"Where you taking me?"

"You'll see. Be ready tomorrow night."

She smirked.

Chapter 12

"Dave & Buster's?" Riley asked as Jermaine helped her out of his car.

"Yes, word around town is that this is one of your favorite spots." He looked down at her and winked. He wasn't that much taller than her since she had on wedged heels, which was one of the reasons she was slightly perturbed about the location he chose for their date.

"It is, but I am not dressed for this place." She pouted some as she looked down at her outfit. She wore a black knee-length skirt, a black, white, and gray button-down blouse, which she tied at her midsection, and the black-and-white wedge heels, which were comfortable but not how she'd like for here. When she came to Dave & Buster's, tennis shoes were always a must.

"No one told you to try to be cute."

"I don't have to try to do that at all," she told him. "Anyway, the outfit is fine. It's just not as comfortable as I'd like it to be when I kick your ass on these games."

"Okay, so I can throw all that chivalry shit out when we start playing these games, 'cause I was going to let you win, seeing that is the right thing to do, but since you're talking reckless, it's on," he promised as he held the door open for her to walk inside.

"Oh, I am very competitive. That's probably why Mikayla told you I enjoy coming here. She's itching to hear about the beatdown I'm going to give you."

"All right. Well, you mind if we eat first? It sounds like I'm going to need the fuel to keep up."

"Don't tell me you're scared now."

"Not at all. Which do you prefer, table or booth?"

"Booth."

Riley followed him to a corner booth in the back of the eating area, taking a seat across from him. Usually, she would have sat next to her date, but she decided she wanted to look into his eyes when they spoke.

"You've changed," she told him, bringing his attention from the menu.

Jermaine's brow furrowed as her words not only caught him by surprise but confused him as well. "How so?"

"Well, not literally. I mean, from when I first met you. You were such a cynical asshole, and now you're not. Like you've actually become or shown me a guy I could see myself dating."

"Hmm, ain't that the pot calling the kettle black."

"I am not, nor have I ever been, a cynical asshole."

"No, you were mean as fuck, though."

"Not mean. Protective."

"I can dig that. Now back to this you could see yourself dating me."

"I'm here, ain't I?"

"Nah, the way you said it sounds like we'll have more than this one. Probably on some exclusive shit."

"I did not mean for it to sound that serious."

"It's cool. I might feel similar." He smiled, and she could have sworn she saw hearts in front of her, almost like in a cartoon when hearts flew from a character's eyes. The waitress walked up and, taking their order, halted their conversation for a bit.

"How's everything going with Jeremiah since being home?" She opted for a safe topic.

"It's been cool. We've finally come to a solid understanding, and he released some things he'd been holding in, and it's definitely helped with us moving forward."

"Mikayla and I had a conversation realer than any we've had in the past too. Seems like they are positively rubbing off on each other."

"They are. But enough about them. It's just you and me for a reason. Tired of them little delinquents." He chuckled.

"Um, only one of them is a delinquent, and it's not the one I'm raising."

"Maybe, but she's still a troublemaker. Anyone who can get my brother to jump through hoops has to have something wrong with them."

Riley laughed because, for Mikayla, Jeremiah did jump through hoops. For it, she appreciated him more than he could imagine.

They continued to make small talk as they ate, and once they finished, Riley was ready to make good on her promise of beating him in the arcade games.

"Okay, let's play *Connect 4* first," Riley suggested as they made their way to the arcade floor. This was a game she had been a beast at since before she could remember. No way could Jermaine beat her at this game. She also chose it as a way to set the tone. He was about to enter an evening of losing.

"All right, bet." Jermaine rubbed his hands together like he knew something she didn't know as they made their way to the game. "Best out of three," Jermaine said, wanting to put some odds in his favor.

"Sure," she agreed, taking the first shot. Her ball landed in the center, right where she wanted it. It was a strategy that always worked.

Jermaine chuckled at the amateur move, because who didn't know that starting in the center was a sure way to win? And that she did, quickly. Riley beat him in fewer than ten moves.

"That's one." She smiled from ear to ear. The excitement on her face let him know that her level of competitiveness was much deeper than he thought.

"Yup, that was only one. Loser gets first shot," he said, shooting the ball, and it landed to the left of the center circle. Riley was almost thrown off by his move but held it together. The winner came down to who would make the last shot, and in their case, it was the one who took the first shot.

"Lucky win," she told him as she shrugged as if it didn't mean anything.

"All right, if my win was so lucky, make sure you don't aim for the middle," he said, letting her know he knew her strategy.

Never one to back down from a challenge, Riley aimed for the end of the board, making her shot land in the left corner. Jermaine nodded, impressed by her bravery, before taking a shot of his own. Back and forth they went until Riley's shot killed the game. She won, and though he wasn't happy about losing, he respected having a worthy opponent. After a few more rounds of games and Jermaine racking up tickets to get prizes for Riley, they shut the place down.

"Time sure does fly when you're having fun," she said as he opened the car door for her.

"The night doesn't have to end. Mikayla is straight with my brother at your house. Mine is free if you're cool with coming to kick it there with me."

Riley thought about what she should do. This was their first date, and it would be her first time at his home. Ideally, she would have liked to see it on some casual thing first, but the opportunity was being presented now as a nightcap, she was sure. Her mind was telling her to decline the offer, but her body and urge to be with him a little longer told her to go for it.

"Sure." She smiled, hoping it masked the nervousness she felt. She absolutely felt safe with him. It was that she wasn't trying to give the wrong impression.

Hell, we're grown, so it is what it is. I need this night, she told herself as she sat back and listened to Musiq Soulchild coming from the car speakers.

Riley looked at Jermaine's home, impressed. It was a nice-sized condo with a two-car garage below them. "Your place is nice." She admired how big and spacious the front room was. She loved open spaces in homes.

"Thank you. Still have some decorating to do, but this spot is definitely better than our last place."

Before purchasing this condo, Jermaine and Jeremiah lived in a tiny two-bedroom apartment. He had always wanted to own where he rested his head, a house preferably, but did not want to buy a home until he found a woman to start a family with. He looked at this condo as an investment. Either Jeremiah could have it later, or he would make good money renting it out.

"I mean, you have stuff on the walls, so you've started somewhere." She gave him credit. She hadn't had high expectations for him in the sense that his home would be decked out and decorated like he'd hired an interior designer. If it had been, she would have been surprised.

"I'm going to grab us something to drink," he told her as she went to take a seat on the black leather sofa.

Riley wasn't a fan of leather couches, but this one was very comfortable. In fact, it was comfortable enough for her to take a nap had she not been more interested in spending more time with Jermaine.

A bottle of wine and two wineglasses were what he returned with. He placed everything on the end table near her before filling both their glasses and taking a seat next to her. Riley looked at him, and the intensity he stared back at her with gave her chills. In a good way.

"Why are you looking at me like that?"

"'Cause, man, you're beautiful as fuck."

"Thank you." She blushed.

"For real, why are you single? Who's dumb enough not to hold on to you?"

"I just haven't had the time, I guess. Busy working and trying to raise a teenager. I left dating on the backburner. And honestly, I wasn't feeling bringing some guy around Mikayla." She hated to feel that way, like Mikayla may flirt with a guy or he may get the wrong idea about her. She hated that things in Mikayla's past that were far from her fault had affected who she brought around or if she even wanted to date anyone until she knew her cousin was healed.

Mikayla had come a long way, but she would be crazy to think that one person had helped her overcome years of trauma seemingly overnight.

"What about you? Why are you single?"

"I was in a situation not too long ago. Our goals didn't align, so I called it quits." He shrugged as if what he said wasn't a big deal, but for her, it was a red flag. What kind of goals did he have that did not align with a woman's? The only thing she could think of would be being committed. And if that were the case, she needed to know, because a booty call she was not. Tonight possibly, but not for the long haul.

"Can I ask what kind of goals?"

Jermaine nodded with a smirk on his face, fully aware what his words had her assuming. "I want kids one day, a big house, a family. And she didn't. She's about her career and traveling the world and not messing up her figure. Kids aren't in the cards for her, but they are for me, so there was no reason for either of us to continue wasting time."

"Wow."

"What? You thought I was gon' be on some bull-shit, huh?"

"I mean, you look like you're still enjoying the bachelor life."

"You're the first woman I've brought to this house since we've moved here. If I'm on some bachelor shit, then I have the rules messed up."

"It doesn't have to be about a woman. It could be for all the reasons your ex doesn't want a family."

"What about you? You see yourself as a wife and mom one day?"

"Absolutely. I don't think I want a girl though. Whew, knowing how we change as teenagers may have me underneath somebody's jail. I want a son."

"Shit, they ain't no ballpark either. Or did you forget about my brother kicking it with the wrong crowd and getting locked up?"

"Yeah, I guess you're right. We ain't raising our kids, so I still want some of my own." She laughed and Jermaine did too.

"That's what's up." Silence suddenly engulfed them, like they didn't know what to say next.

"Did it just get awkward?" She spoke in a teasing manner but meant it, because the room seemed a bit too tense.

"I mean, it could go that route, but we won't let it. What else you want to know?"

"What do you want from me?"

"What do you mean?"

"Like, is this casual or possibly going some-where?"

"To be honest, I'm feeling you. That's gotta be obvious, and the more I get to know you, the more I want you around for a bit."

"Well, the way Mikayla and Jermaine seem to be glued to the hip, I don't think we have a choice but to be around each other."

"This don't have anything to do with them. Take them out of the equation, and I'll still feel the same way. I mean, we may have started a connection because of them, but what I'm hoping to build is something special of our own."

Damn, she thought. *He is damn smooth.* She put her head down to hide the smile creeping, but he caught it. Her skin had flushed with red, and he noticed.

Jermaine felt like he had been open with his intentions. His interest was clear as well. He had done enough talking. He put his wineglass down, taking hers as well and placing it next to his, then took her by the chin, lifting her head to gaze into her eyes. He was hesitant at first, but then she licked her lips, and there were no more reservations.

He leaned in and kissed her with as much sensuality and passion that he could muster. She reciprocated, so much so that she found herself moving to his lap, straddling him. At first, she was only kissing and sitting, but then her hips started to move like they had a mind of their own.

"Ay, we may need to slow down."

"We don't have to."

"You sure?"

"Positive." She was, too. Her body was on fire, and she hadn't craved a man this hard in a long time that she could remember.

"Riley, I'm telling you now, once you let me in, I'm not letting you go."

"Then don't," she said into his mouth before intensifying their kiss.

Chapter 13

Riley took Jermaine's hand as he assisted her out of the car. She smiled, appreciating the gentleman he was, because had someone asked her a few months back if he had a gentlemanly bone in his body, she would have laughed in their face. Mikayla stood next to her and Jeremiah to her right as they made their way toward the entrance of their destination. They were excited to be enjoying a night out together. To the blind eye, it looked like a double date. However, only two people fell into that category, and that was Riley and Jermaine. Jeremiah and Mikayla cherished their bond too much to be anything other than the friends they were.

"Wow, I haven't been to a carnival in forever," Mikayla exclaimed as they exited Jermaine's car.

"Heck, me too," Riley said, realizing that she too was mighty young the last time she had been.

"That's crazy. They have this fair every year, and me and bro probably have only missed one. We really only come for the food and the bit—the food."

"The who?" Riley teased as she cut her eyes at Jermaine.

"Damn, bro, that's what you on?"

"Ay, y'all relationship new and shit. I mean, it's weird seeing y'all together and not fight."

"I know, right?" Mikayla laughed as they walked up to the entrance line.

"Well, I ain't come here to do nothing but make sure Riley has a good time. Mikayla, I hope Jeremiah's pockets are long enough for you, because since y'all wanna be some little haters, forget that ride pass."

"Hell nah. I left my wallet at home 'cause you said you had us." Jeremiah frowned, ready to cuss his brother out.

"Well, I didn't. Riley taught me never to depend on a wallet other than my own, not even hers." Mikayla smiled, proud the lesson from her cousin stuck and was apparently useful.

"I know that's right." Riley lifted her hand for Mikayla to connect, and she happily obliged.

"Man, you're not about to pay for me. I'll walk home for my wallet before I accept some shit like that."

"You see how sensitive he is, Riley, but I was supposed to take it on the chin when he tried to throw me under the bus," Jermaine teased as they made their way to the ticket booth window.

Jeremiah wanted to say something else smart but decided against it, as his brother paid for the biggest package on the menu and handed him a few $100 bills just in case. He laughed as they slapped hands and embraced in a brotherly hug.

"Okay, can we go now? I want to get on at least three rides before eating," Mikayla said, bouncing from one foot to the other. Her childlike excitement made Riley smile.

"Come on." Jeremiah took Mikayla by the hand and began pulling her toward the rides.

The first one they headed to was a roller coaster called the Wicked Twister. It was a ride that twisted as it went up and the same as it came down. Just looking at it made Riley's stomach turn. But she wouldn't be the one to punk out. If she happened to throw up on Jermaine, then she just threw up. She'd make it up to him later.

"I feel your hand shaking. You sure you want to get on?"

"I mean, I am nervous, but I'm not about to let these little shit talkers try to one up us."

"This why I like yo' ass so much. Your competitiveness. I know with you on my side we can fuck some shit up."

"Especially if it's about them."

Jermaine halted his steps just for a moment. Her words hadn't caught him off guard per se, but they meant something to him. She'd said "them."

He knew she would go to bat for Mikayla and had even shown ultimate support for Jeremiah, but the way she said "them" made Jermaine a part of an exclusive package, and he appreciated it more than she would ever know. She made it final with those few words. As much as they moved him, he was too player to show it right now, so he moved his feet, gently pulling Riley along and ending up right behind Jeremiah and Mikayla.

"Ooh, this is about to be so much fun. Riley, do not scream, okay?" Mikayla turned to her with pleading eyes.

"Um, you do not get to tell me how to react."

"We shouldn't sit by them," Mikayla said seriously.

"Man, what you not telling us?" Jeremiah asked, amused with how Mikayla was acting toward her cousin.

"When she's scared and screams, she sounds just like a howling cat."

Jermaine and Jeremiah broke into full-blown laughter. They were laughing so hard that tears formed in their eyes. It was at that moment Riley found another likeness between the brothers, one she didn't care for currently. They laughed exactly alike.

"Really, Mikayla?"

"Well, you do. I'm sorry."

"It's okay, baby. We don't have to sit by them." Jermaine, still laughing, tried to show support, but the fact that he was still tickled did not work in his favor.

"Nope, we're sitting right behind them, and if you don't quit laughing at me, you will be going home without me." She pushed past them, being the first to show the ride attendant her wristband.

"I hope she does scream. I got my phone ready to record that shit," Jermaine said to his brother and Mikayla, who both snickered. Jermaine was more controlled this time because going home alone was not something he was trying to do.

Riley hadn't heard Jeremiah's comment as she was too busy lost in her thoughts, telling herself not to scream. She wasn't even sure she'd be afraid on the roller coaster. Screaming hadn't even been a thought. She had been more worried about vomiting until Mikayla had to open her big mouth.

"Come on, baby, it's cool." Jermaine kissed her cheek before taking her hand.

She wanted to keep the attitude she had with the three of them, but that would only ruin the rest of the evening, so she tucked in her pride and forced a confident smile to spread through her lips as she took Jermaine's hand and followed him to the seat behind Mikayla and Jeremiah.

"You good?" he asked, looking at her.

She was expressionless as she nodded and told him, "Yeah, I'm fine."

The ride operator walked the aisle, checking to ensure everyone was secure in their seats. When Riley heard the click of the metal, she took a deep breath, and before she could fully exhale, they were going up. She kept her lips pressed together tightly. The ride began to move, going backward then quickly forward and up, and she felt a lump the size of a tennis ball form in her throat. It may have been a slight exaggeration, but there was definitely something big there. Another click, and she gripped Jermaine's hand tighter. Before she could brace herself more, the coaster dropped, and so did her heart, which felt like it passed through her ribcage right into her stomach.

Riley still did her best to hold it together, but the ride seemed to have gotten faster. And before she knew it, she lost control and screamed. Not for long though. She immediately released Jermaine's hand to cover her mouth, muffling the sound that he and everyone around them heard. To the untrained ear, it was just a sound. No one knew it came from a ride passenger. To the people Mikayla exposed her to, a howling cat sound from Riley's mouth was what they heard.

"Oh, shit, you were right," Jeremiah exclaimed before bursting into a fit of laughter that had Riley ready to slap him.

She turned to Jermaine, who was red from fighting the urge to laugh. At least he was showing some form of loyalty, unlike her cousin. The ride went up and down twice more, then ended, and she couldn't get off fast enough.

"All right, what ride is next?" Mikayla asked, adrenaline still pumping.

"Wherever y'all want to go, but we will not be going. This is where we separate," Riley said, snuggling closer to Jermaine.

"Aw, Riley, your scream wasn't even that bad," Jeremiah said, doing his best to keep a straight face.

"I'm putting ex-lax in your food the next time I cook for you," Riley teased.

"Nah, man, don't play, especially when you know I love your cooking. We can separate shit. Or I will forget how to laugh. Matter of fact, what the fuck is a laugh anyway?" Jeremiah became serious but was hilarious to the other three.

"Y'all g'on and have fun. We will meet up with you later, but call my phone if you need to," Jermaine told them.

Mikayla hugged Riley, thanking her before she and Jeremiah took off.

"You good?" he asked her.

"I am. Even though she sold me out, I'm so happy she's happy. It's been so long since I've seen her like this." Her voice cracked.

"It's okay to get a little emotional. You did a great job with her."

"I'm still working on her." She smiled.

"All right, let's go have some older folks' fun."

"Yes, I always wanted a huge bear from the carnival, and you can spend all night on a game until you win me one." She provided a sweet smile.

"Maybe. We about to do some other shit first. Like eat. I'm hungry."

"Me too. I made sure to save my appetite just to pig out here. Now are we going for corndogs or tri-tip?"

"I'm a grown man. A corndog not about to do shit for my belly."

"Tri-tip it is then."

They made their way through the throng of people, making mental notes of the areas they wanted to visit after they ate.

"Look at them." Riley pointed toward Jeremiah and Mikayla, who were in line waiting to get on the Kamikaze, a ride she absolutely would not get on.

"All these people and you were able to spot them. My kinda girl, for real." He pulled her closer, kissing her on top of her head. They began walking again, making it to the food stand in no time.

"People are at this carnival as if it's the last night."

"Yeah, it's crazy. Long as no shit pops off, it's cool, I guess."

"There are so many food options. The tri-tip sandwich sounded good before I saw all these places."

"I know. They got stuff I've only seen on the Food Network *Carnival Eats* show. And I always said I would try something because that shit be looking good."

"I never would have taken you for a man who watches the Food Network."

"You judging?"

"Not at all. Let's try everything you've wanted to try and then some. We get one of each and share. Let's think of it as a wine tasting but with food."

"All right, I'm with that, but we'll start with the shortest line first." Jermaine led them to All About Meatballs. The menu looked solid, and the line wasn't long. "What do you want to try first?" he asked, leaving the choice up to her.

"Let's do the Turkey Cheesy Explosion."

"That shit gon' fuck my stomach up. Too much dairy in one bite."

"Well, you pick."

When they made it to the window, he ordered what Riley wanted and something he wanted to try. For over an hour, that was what they did: order and eat, order and eat. By the time they finished, they were stuffed.

"We need to walk to make room for dessert," Jermaine said, happy with most of the foods they tried.

"I got the itis. I'm ready to sleep."

"I thought you wanted me to win you a huge bear."

"Oh, I do. We can walk." She stood from the bench, ready to move because they weren't leaving without her bear. "Okay, so what game are we going to?" Riley asked, excited to see him in action for her.

"Right here. I haven't tested out this throwing arm in a minute, but it's in me not on me, so this should be easy." He led her to the football-throwing game. The object of the game was to throw the ball through the circle. The more bull's-eyes he made, the bigger the gift.

Jermaine placed a $50 bill on the counter and told the attendant to keep the balls coming until he won the biggest stuffed animal on the board.

His first throw was shifty, literally. The ball wobbled from his hand to the back of the wall, missing the hole he was aiming at. So was the second. Jermaine set the ball down and stretched his arms, pulling the right across his chest, holding it in between his left elbow and forearm, before doing the same on the opposite side. Then he clasped his fingers and stretched his arms in front of him. He shook his arms, then picked the ball back up. He threw it, and it went straight through its target, not hitting the sides or anything.

Riley was impressed. His stretch routine had turned things around for him, and he was kicking ass. Ball after ball he didn't miss his target, winning her a huge, beautiful tie-dyed stuffed bear after throwing fifteen balls consecutively.

"You want to get on some rides now?"

"No, now I want to beat you in some games. Let me win you a bear, baby," she teased, leaning in to kiss his cheek.

"Man, all you can do for me is rub my shoulders when we get to the house."

"That's all you want?"

"Nah." He winked suggestively. "Ain't that Mikayla?" he asked, noticing her standing off to the side alone.

"It is," Riley acknowledged, and she wasted no time heading in the direction of her cousin. She looked upset standing there alone, and Riley needed to know why, especially when she was supposed to be with Jeremiah.

"Mikayla," Riley spoke her name loudly, gaining her attention.

She watched as Mikayla mouthed, "Shit," before turning all the way toward her.

"Why are you over here alone? Are you okay?"

"Yeah. I'm fine. Jeremiah will be right back." She hoped he would. At least, that was what he'd told her five minutes ago. To her, "right back" meant within a minute, so he was already long overdue.

She had begged him not to go over to the group of guys who were beckoning him their way. She had a bad feeling about it. But he told her things would be much worse if he didn't go. Reluctantly, she stopped giving him a hard time and watched him walk off toward members of the 619 gang.

"Where is he?" Jermaine asked, and the look on his face told her she couldn't tell him the truth. Jeremiah was supposed to be as far away from gang affiliation as possible. Not only that, but Jermaine would make it known that his brother could not be around them, and she knew the gang members wouldn't handle that well.

"Talking to some girl from school." She lied so effortlessly and felt bad about it, but if she told the truth, Jeremiah would never forgive nor trust her again. If he wasn't back soon, though, she would have to break his trust, because she was worried.

"You okay?" Riley asked as Jermaine turned his head. He wouldn't get in between that especially because of their relationship title. Mikayla shouldn't be in her feelings about Jeremiah talking to anyone else.

"Oh, yeah. I don't care about that," she said honestly. What had her so disturbed about his absence was that he was talking to some of the members of the gang he knew better than to be around.

"Okay, well, we'll wait with you."

"You don't have to."

"Ay, what y'all doing over here?" Jeremiah asked, seemingly appearing out of nowhere.

Mikayla gave him a look she hoped he could read, letting him know not to snitch on himself.

"We saw her standing here alone."

"She was in my view the whole time, Riley. She was good. Plus, I went to get her this." He smiled, handing Mikayla a stuffed basketball.

"Thank you."

"All right, y'all ready? Mikayla and I did everything there was to do here," he said honestly, and they had. They had run around the entire park like the two teens full of energy they were.

"Yes, let's get my funnel cake and we can go," Riley spoke up.

Together they walked toward the dessert stand, talking about the rides Mikayla and Jeremiah got on and cracking jokes on Jermaine for winning Riley a bear that was practically bigger than her. The evening was perfect, minus the mild heart attack Jeremiah gave Mikayla. Both women hoped to have more nights like this because the Stately brothers had definitely grown on them.

During the car ride home, Jeremiah was lost in thought. Tech had basically called him a snitch even though there was no paperwork to prove it. Then he brandished a weapon Jeremiah had no clue how he got through the metal detectors.

"Yo' ass gon' make sure our niggas behind bars is good, or you ain't gon' be good. You feel me?" Tech had asked, lifting his shirt to show the gun.

Jeremiah had kept a poker face the entire time, but he was scared shitless. He knew they would have had no problem beating his ass right there or even jumping him, but if he'd shown fear, then he would have received just that, because fear would equate to guilt.

Mikayla nudging him pulled his attention to her and from the window he was staring aimlessly out of. Her brows rose, silently questioning what was wrong with him. Shaking his head, Jeremiah forced a smile and mouthed, "I'm good," before removing his phone to show her a funny video he saw on the internet. The laughter the video brought was distraction enough to keep her from asking any other questions.

Chapter 14

"You sure Riley cooked?" Jeremiah asked as he and Mikayla stepped off the bus. They were headed to her house because he promised to sit over there with her while Riley worked and then ran some errands with Jermaine.

"There's leftovers. She said she was cooking again tonight, but that's all I know. Anyway, I don't know why you had to come home with me today anyway," she said, stopping to turn toward Jeremiah, who bent down to tie his shoes.

"Damn, you don't want me at the house?"

"It's not that. It's just that after coming home by myself since forever, all of a sudden I can't now because you're in my life."

"Yep, because before I came into your life, some fuck boys tried you."

"And now that my cousins came from the Bay and kicked their asses, they know better. I haven't had a problem since. They even go the opposite way when they see me in the hall," she said, then snickered.

"Man, fuck all that. You still safest with me," he told her, standing and dusting off his clothes. The sounds of screeching tires coming toward them pulled their attention toward the street.

"Fuck, man," Jeremiah mumbled as he immediately recognized the dark blue Buick LeSabre that pulled up on them. He knew from the aggression of the driver that this was not going to be a pleasant meeting. There was tension from the day at the carnival even though they tried to slow play him.

"Ay, we need to holler at you," a member known as T-Man said, walking up on Jeremiah with three of their homies behind him. They were some of the most ruthless in the gang, the ones who only got their hands dirty when it was time to punish someone.

"What's up?" Jeremiah asked, head held high. He wasn't afraid at all and made sure to show it in his body language. If he did have any fear, he still wouldn't show it because weakness wasn't allowed among them. Besides, they were a brotherhood, so he had no reason to worry. Yes, there was tension, but what bond didn't have friction from time to time? T-Man hadn't been present when Tech and a few of the other guys threatened him at the carnival, but he was sure he'd heard about it. It sucked because it only took one person to plant the seed that Jeremiah wasn't a real one for the rest of the crew to believe it.

"What's going on with that case?" T-Man's skepticism was present in his body language. He stood a few inches away from Jeremiah, kept his arms near his sides, and hadn't presented him with a brotherly hug as he usually would when they crossed paths.

"What you mean?"

"Why you out but my KJ still in?"

"My lawyer got me out. I'm not sure what's going on with KJ. We were separated," he told them honestly. He hadn't gotten that out to Tech because it was apparent his mind was already made up about who Jeremiah was. He chose to stand his ground by not showing fear and avoiding arguing for the sake of not wanting to cause a bigger scene with a gang of black men standing around in 619 attire.

"That shit sound funny. But look, KJ been down with us much longer than you, and as you know, newbies gotta earn their stripes. You need to take the charge."

"Take the charge? My lawyer said that's unnecessary. They don't have enough on me to convict me of anything."

"But you were there, so you can take that shit. What it sounds like is it's between you and KJ and you saying fuck, bro."

"Nah, y'all saying fuck me. It's not my fault my lawyer can get me off. He shouldn't have a public defender anyway—"

Before he could finish his sentence, he was hit in the mouth, hard. It stunned him a bit, but he quickly pulled himself together. He swung, connecting with T-Man's jaw, and that was the only hit he remembered connecting. Jeremiah fought like his life depended on it, but with six fists hitting his body, he was more concerned with protecting himself than throwing punches back.

Mikayla's screams pierced his ears, and that gave him the motivation he needed to fight back. On the ground, he uncovered himself from the fetal position and grabbed the first foot he saw coming toward him. He twisted it as hard as he could, bringing down the body of the person it belonged to.

"Stop! Stop! Get off him!" Mikayla screamed, horrified. She wanted to jump in and help him, but she was being held back. No matter how much she wiggled and pulled away, she was no match for the big, burly dude holding her.

"You kids, stop that shit before I call the police!" someone driving a navy blue Mazda yelled from their window. Mikayla was thankful for the stranger as those words seemed to have stopped the beating Jeremiah was getting.

"Make sure you take that charge, pussy!" One more kick was sent to his abdomen before they rushed off.

Mikayla rushed to his side with tears streaming down her face. As she tried her best to check on Jeremiah through blurred vision, his face was noticeably bloody given all the red she saw.

"Jeremiah," she cried, gently tugging on him.

"I'm good, Mikayla. Just help me up," he spoke through fat lips. She did as he asked, feeling her heart break as he groaned with each movement.

"I can call for help."

"No, let's just get to your house." He mustered up all the strength he could to stand. He knew this was taking a toll on Mikayla, and he probably looked worse than he felt, so he pulled himself together for her sake at least.

"Mikayla, stop crying, please."

"I can't. I'm so angry and hurt. And I wanted to help you, but some fat ass kept holding me back."

"It's okay. You're helping me by getting me to your house and being strong, all right?"

"I wish I told your brother and Riley when we saw this at the carnival," she fussed.

"There was no reason to, and please let me do the talking when they ask what happened."

"Are you going to tell the truth?"

"Mikayla."

"No, Jeremiah, if we had said something—"

"This still would have happened."

"But—"

"I don't want to talk about it no more." His tone was final, and though it hurt her, she respected his wishes. With his arm wrapped across her shoulders and hers around his waist, she used all her strength to hold him up as he limped to her house. The short walk had never felt so long. They both were relieved when she inserted her key and unlocked the door.

"You want to go lie down? I can help you up the stairs," Mikayla said as Jeremiah practically fell onto the sofa.

"Nah, I'ma stay right here. Jermaine will buy Riley a new couch if I get too much blood on it." He tried laughing, but it hurt too bad.

"Damn the couch. She'll be fine. I'm going to grab you something cold for your face."

"How bad is it?" He moved like he was going to stand, only to be forced back down from the pain.

"It'll heal, conceited ass. Let me go grab the ice." She walked off to the kitchen, where she grabbed a frozen bag of peas before sending a text to Riley, telling her that she and Jermaine needed to hurry up and get there. Jeremiah's eye looked as if it were closing, and he kept holding his side like his ribs may have been broken. All sorts of things were going through her mind, like wondering if he had internal bleeding, if his eye would remain swollen shut, and the scariest thing—how much worse he may have gotten beaten if the stranger hadn't come threatening to call the cops.

"Here." She handed the bag of peas to him, then headed to the bathroom for a warm towel and the first-aid kit. He flinched with each touch and even cussed a few times as the peroxide burned the scrapes on his arm.

The sound of laughter coming from the opposite side of the house froze Jeremiah and Mikayla. Riley and Jermaine had made it, and the two of them knew it was about to get real. The mama and papa bear in them would not take Jeremiah's ass whopping lightly, especially once they saw the damage the gang members had caused.

"Let me talk, Mikayla," he mumbled through fat lips. Even with putting the frozen vegetables and warm towel on his face, Jeremiah still looked like a milder realistic version of Martin Lawrence when he got his ass beat in boxing.

"Hey, y'all, I decided not to cook," Riley yelled as she made her way into the living room with Jermaine on her heels.

"Man, hell naw." Jermaine was the first to notice his brother holding the bag over his eye, his ripped shirt, and the bloodstains splattered on him. He rushed to his brother, damn near knocking Mikayla out of the way as he knelt down, tears stinging his eyes. "Who the fuck did this to you, bro?" He quickly moved his hands from Jeremiah's legs when he noticed him flinch at his touch.

"What happened? Should I call 911? Mikayla, why didn't you call us? Are you hurt too?" Riley asked frantically, looking from one teen to the other.

"I texted you to come home. I'm sorry. It happened so fast. I just needed to get him here," she said as she stood off to the side, arms folded as a form of comfort while tears streamed down her face.

"Who the fuck did this? Was this the little niggas who were messing with you?" Jermaine asked Mikayla.

"No."

"Nah, bro, this is all me. Some people weren't happy that I'm a free man. Temporarily."

Riley wanted to call Jermaine out on his insinuation but didn't because it could have been true, and her explanation of things wasn't making things any better.

"The 619 dudes?" Jermaine stood aggressively, and the look in his eyes told that he was two seconds from fucking some shit up.

Knowing his brother, Jeremiah was positive he had his gun somewhere close. So instead of giving a straight answer, he put his head down. If he voiced confirmation, no one would be able to stop Jermaine from rushing out of Riley's front door.

"Was it them?" his voice boomed, echoing off the walls of the house, frightening both Mikayla and Riley. Knowing Mikayla had a thing with men raising their voices, Jeremiah immediately looked to see how she was. She was visibly shaken up, but she stayed, and he knew it was for him.

"Bro, relax."

"Fuck you mean, relax? Have you seen yourself? I'm about to go turn some shit up. Tell me who did this shit, and I'm not playing, Mouse."

Riley watched in horror as he paced the floor. Jermaine was like a caged pit bull.

"I'm not telling you because it's not worth it, bro. Niggas couldn't see me one-on-one, so they had to jump me, and I know I beat someone's ass."

"You did," Mikayla assured them all quickly. If the situation weren't so serious, her response would have been comical.

"That's coo' and all, but you know how we roll. They jumped you, so it's time to see me. Whoever thought you was alone thought wrong."

"Jermaine." Riley walked up to him, placing her hand on his shoulder. He turned to look at her, fire still burning in his eyes, but she knew his anger wasn't directed toward her. "Baby, come here, please." She took his hand, and before he could protest, she pulled him toward the kitchen.

"Sit down."

"Riley, not right now."

"Jermaine, sit down. Please?"

She asked this time, still firmly, though she added pleading eyes into the mix, which worked. He sat. She used her legs to pry his open a bit farther, standing in between them. She placed a hand on each side of his face before leaning down to kiss his lips. She needed him to feel her loving energy. She knew it wouldn't put out his raging fire but hoped it would tame it a bit.

"I know you're upset, and you have every right to be, but you can't go and do something you'll later regret. Not saying you'll regret getting even. You will regret the consequences. They are kids. If it were some grown-ass men who jumped him, then I have your bail money. But they are kids. You can't go back to your old ways for them."

"I'm going back to my old ways for my brother. They tried him 'cause they obviously don't know who the fuck I am. I can let 'em know, though, proudly."

Jermaine was being extremely stubborn, and this was a side of him she hadn't seen. There was no reason to, and if ever she crossed this area of his personality, she only cared for it to be because he didn't want to lose her.

"Will you listen to me, please? Let's get him to the hospital to check him out. You have to think about how much he needs you. He still has a case pending. If you go out and get into trouble too, then what? Yes, y'all have us, but for the longest you've only had each other. No way can I override that."

Selfless. That was the first thought that came to Jermaine when he looked into her eyes when she was done speaking.

"You trying to have me fall hard as fuck, ain't you?" He pulled her closer to him, wrapping his arms around her waist.

"I mean, that wouldn't be so bad, would it?"

"Not at all. You just stopped me from catching multiple bodies. Some shit like that isn't good enough for an ass whopping, as repercussions for something like that can only be marked in blood. They fucked my brother up." His voice cracked, and she wrapped her arms around his neck, holding as tightly as possible without hurting him.

"I know, so let's get him checked out. Everything else we can figure out later."

"We gotta figure out what to tell the hospital now. They are gonna call the cops when they see him."

"Let me handle that part. Let's just go make sure he's not hurt beyond what we can see."

"Thank you." Jermaine eased her back so that he could stand, and once he did, he cupped her chin, bringing his lips to hers for a passionate kiss. He had already fallen hard.

Chapter 15

Jermaine watched a sleeping Jeremiah as he stood at his open bedroom door. His heart broke as he looked at his brother's bruised face. Yes, it was healing. However, the evidence of a good ass whooping just a few days ago was very present. When they took Jeremiah to the hospital that evening, he was kept overnight to clean his wounds and assist him with his fractured ribs. Luckily, he had no internal bleeding from all the kicks to his abdomen, where there were footprints left as proof that they wanted him to remember that ass kicking.

"Why are you staring at me like you're watching your baby sleep or something?" Jeremiah mumbled, slowly waking from his medicated slumber.

"'Cause I am. You are my first child and all," he teased, finally walking completely into the bedroom.

"You can head on with that shit. I ain't nobody's baby, not even Mama's." He tried laughing, but the simple act hurt, causing him to hold his bandaged side.

"You gon' always be our baby. Now quit laughing at your own lame-ass jokes before you wind up back in the hospital."

"If there's one place other than jail I don't want to be, it's the hospital. I can't stand that place. Granted, the shit they gave me there was way better than the meds they sent me home on. I can't even yawn without it hurting."

"It'll get better."

"Maybe."

"What you mean, maybe? The doctors said within a couple of weeks you should be fully healed."

"That's not what I mean." He moved slowly, sitting up a bit more so that the words he was getting ready to speak would match his body language, as much of it as he could, given the circumstances. "I think I should just take the charge. I talked to Ms. McCullough, and she said I would be looking at eighteen months max."

"Man, hell nah, you not doing that shit. I don't know why you even fixed your mouth to say some shit like that."

"Hear me out."

"I was listening until you started talking crazy."

"But it's not crazy. The only way to prove I'm not a snitch is to just take the charge. Besides, if I don't, they might try something worse than jumping me. Or come after you, Mikayla, Riley."

"You're not taking no time for them or for us. They will be straight. And if you're scared—"

"I ain't scared. I'm only trying to avoid more problems and trouble for you. You gotta keep cleaning my shit up."

"And I'll keep doing it ten times over if I have to. You're worried about the wrong shit. I'm not letting nobody hurt you, and I ain't letting you take nobody's time. You told me you ain't do the shit, so you not doing time for it."

"But I was there. I took an oath with them, and part of it is having their back and doing stuff I may not always be comfortable with."

"For you to be so smart, you sound dumb as fuck. If you're worried about doing some time because you were there, then you did more than enough. I guess you forgot about how you did over thirty days in juvie and the ass whopping they gave you a few days ago. You worried about a punk-ass oath, but what about the brotherhood you told me you were searching for when you went to hang with them? A real brother wouldn't have you out here bad like this." He stood and left the room. Their conversation hadn't gone anywhere near what he'd thought, and before he said anything that would disrupt their relationship, he walked away.

"I can't stand that he's always right," Jeremiah mumbled as soon as his brother slammed his door as he left the room. Still sitting in his upright position, he threw his head back as thoughts of all he'd been through flooded his mind. He had never lost a fight and probably wouldn't have lost that one had they not jumped him.

Either way, he was bound to wind up in some shit behind the 619 boys. What he hadn't anticipated was them turning their backs on him. He was starting to feel like who he truly was to them: a pawn. He had to have been. Otherwise, why would they deem it okay for him to take a charge rather than accepting that the other member got caught and needed to man up and take whatever came to him from his own faults? Instead, they wanted him to take it all and lose his freedom and future for someone who already was a lost cause. He was beginning to feel stupid for ever getting involved with them because their true colors were showing bright as day.

Grabbing his phone off the nightstand, he scrolled to Mikayla's number. Though everything his brother said resonated, he was still considering taking the charge, if for nothing other than to keep him safe and out of any further drama. But before doing so, he needed to speak with his best friend. He knew what she would tell him to do. Still, he needed to hear her say it. She was going to have a fit for him even thinking such a thing, but she would hear him out and understand.

"Hey, is everything okay? Your nap should have lasted much longer," Mikayla said into his ear.

"You were supposed to say hello and wait for me to respond."

"Whatever. What's up? What's wrong?"

"Why does there have to be something wrong?"

"Because there is, so tell me."

"I told Jermaine that I was thinking about taking the charges," he told her. There was an expected moment of silence before he heard her blow her breath into the phone like she was irritated.

"And of course, he told you that was not happening. Which it is not."

"I honestly don't know what I'm going to do yet. If I did go that route, you'd understand why, wouldn't you?"

"You are not going to get me to agree nor say that it would be okay for you to do that because it's not. I am one hundred percent against it. However, I would understand why you did *if* you did, but since you are not, there is no need for that kind of understanding."

"They may try to start some shit with my brother. Even you or Riley could end up in the middle of this bullshit," he said solemnly.

"I'm not worried about that. My cousins from the Bay Area will come out here and turn shit all the way up if they mess with me and Riley. They are punks. Took three of them to fight you."

"You know you done got real tough since you've started hanging with me," he told her before releasing a light chuckle. Anything deeper than that would have him in a tremendous amount of pain.

"Not tough. Confident maybe, because I've never been scared nor a punk. Anyway, you wanted my advice, and I say you are not taking the charge for anybody."

"That's not advice. It's telling me what to do."

"Same difference. Now that we've gotten that out of the way, I've got something to tell you."

"What? And don't try telling me about no crush you got. I am not trying to hear how fine Marcus is."

"Well, I don't think Marcus is fine anymore, and it's about Riley and your brother. She's been smiling and walking differently. I think they did it," she said all giddy.

"Man, you late. My brother been hit."

"Ugh."

"What? I ain't said nothing no different than you."

"You actually did. You made it sound gross. I made it sound like a romance novel. Now I don't want to talk about it anymore. I'll come over with Riley when she heads that way. Okay, if you got any girls coming to play nurse, tell them your sister is on the way and to clear the attitude or hit the door."

"You don't run nothing. I'll see you when you get here. Ask Riley to stop and grab me some Cane's, please."

"I'll think about it. See you later." She ended the call before he could say anything slick.

After placing his phone on his nightstand, he thought about what his decision would be, and he wasn't taking shit. If they wanted to go to war behind it, then so be it. He knew he was going to have to watch his back, and he absolutely would not get caught slipping again. Since Jermaine was very adamant about him not taking the charge, he hoped he was ready to purchase another car or allow him to drive his because there was no way he would be going back to walking and catching the bus. He hadn't been a part of the gang long, but he had gotten to know them well enough to know that if he didn't do what they asked, their problems were far from over.

Chapter 16

"Are you sure you're okay?" Riley asked as she stared at Jermaine through sad eyes.

"Yeah, I'm good," he said in a clipped tone.

Riley rolled her eyes before taking a deep breath to calm her nerves. It was obvious something was wrong with him, but if he didn't want to talk about it, she knew not to force it. He would have to say something to her.

"My day went well. Thanks for asking."

"Good."

"Wow," she huffed, folding her arms across her chest and sitting back in her seat. Deciding to let him be in a mood, Riley almost wanted to tell him to turn the car around and take her home, but she held out hope that the evening would turn around.

"Are you planning to have a good time or is this because you think it'll appease me?"

"A good time."

Riley blew out a frustrated breath and kicked herself for even saying anything again, because she was obviously stirring the pot rather than simmering it down.

Now here they were sitting in Ruth's Chris, and the only time he had spoken was to place his order. Even that had been barely audible. He was sulking, and she hated it.

"I just need a minute, Riley, damn." He hated that he had come at her this way, but the silence he ached for during the car ride she hadn't caught on to. Even with his giving her short answers she still hadn't gotten the hint.

Riley released an angry chuckle before she slammed her napkin down, stood, and stormed to the ladies' restroom. If he needed a minute, he could take it by himself. He was lucky that she hadn't driven because she would have walked right out of the restaurant. She understood he was dealing with something, mainly issues surrounding his brother, but she would not be disrespected in the process.

When she entered the bathroom, she headed straight for the mirror. She didn't need to pee. She only needed a moment to gather herself before she made things worse by cussing him out. As she looked at herself in the mirror, she felt a little slighted. She was looking damn good, and it hadn't been enough to distract him for even a moment. The navy blue midi body-con dress she wore hugged every curve she had to offer. Her ass looked extra round, her breasts were sitting high, and her legs looked amazing. She was more than a snack tonight. She was an entire meal, and her man seemed not to have noticed. She had even done her makeup very minimally like he liked it. He said too much hid her beauty. She was giving him everything he couldn't resist, and that was exactly what he was doing: resisting or ignoring. Either way, it hurt.

"He's going to have to get it together, or we will be taking our food to go," she mumbled before retrieving her phone from her purse.

Are y'all okay? She sent a text to Mikayla to check on her and Jeremiah. She was also worried about him, and if Jermaine took the time to ask, he would know that.

We're good, Riley.

That was good enough for her. Now it was time to go and face the music. She refused to be holed up in the bathroom and hoped that there was a positive change in Jermaine's energy when she got back to the table.

"Here goes nothing," she said as she smoothed her dress down, washed her hands, then exited the bathroom.

As if he could feel her coming, he lifted his head from his phone, and their eyes connected. Jermaine produced a small smile, hoping it showed her that he had gotten his attitude together.

"My bad, babe," he said as soon as she sat down.

"My bad" wasn't the kind of apology she was interested in, so she didn't say anything, only looked at him.

"Babe, I said I was sorry."

"Now you said you were sorry. 'My bad' was not an apology. It may have been if your attitude toward me was milder, but the way you snapped a moment ago definitely warranted something better than that."

"I can respect that. So again, I apologize. Can you forgive me?"

She rolled her eyes up toward the ceiling as she thought about whether she was going to forgive him. She knew the answer but wanted to make him sweat a little, and from the way he tapped his hand on the table, it was working.

"I mean, I guess. Since you're looking for forgiveness and all, are you willing to let me know what's going on?"

"Same shit, really. This damn case, the damn gang, my brother, all this shit is starting to pile up, and there's nothing I can do."

"Babe, you are doing a lot. Just because it's not exactly what or how you want to do or handle things does not mean you aren't trying. We all see how hard you're going for your brother."

"But it's not enough. Do you know the other night he said he wanted to take the charges so that he wouldn't have to worry about beefing with the gang or them coming after any of us?"

"Is he crazy? He's not doing that."

"Same shit I said, but it fucked me up because I feel like he doesn't think I could protect him, or y'all for that matter. As a man, that's not some shit we want to hear. Not only that, but I'm stuck between a rock and a hard place because if this weren't some kid shit, I would have handled this entire situation. I really wish I knew who these kids' brothers, uncles, or fathers are because then I could get on some shit I know would shut all this bullshit down."

"Maybe, but there are consequences for every action. You not trying to go back to a life you left, and some little knuckleheads whose nuts haven't even dropped yet should not be the ones to take you to that place." Riley extended her arm across the table so that Jermaine could take her hand. It was her way of physically offering support. Oddly, when he took her hand, she felt a disconnection rather than comfort.

"I know. That's why it hurts me to have to make this next move."

"And what move is that?" His words frightened her. Something in her soul told her she was not about to like what he was getting ready to say.

"I need to take Jeremiah and get out of town. He's concerned about some shit he shouldn't have to worry about, and since I really can't go for what I know, I have to do some shit that's totally unlike me. And that's leave town."

She could hear the beating of her heart through her ears as she slowly released her hand from his. She knew she wasn't going to like what he had to say, but damn, she wasn't expecting this. She couldn't imagine him leaving her, not even for a little while, now that they'd become an item. She'd fallen for him hard, and it seemed to be mutual, so she couldn't understand how he was so ready to up and leave.

"It won't be forever." He noticed her disposition and saw her face drop into a look of despair.

"You can't promise that, especially when you already made it sound so final. It hurts that you've even considered leaving, hurts even more that you've made it more of a choice than a consideration." She paused and took a deep breath. "I can't tell you what's best for you and your brother. I won't tell you what to do when it comes to him. I just wish it hadn't come to this."

"I want you to tell me something."

"I'm not sure how. There's a tug of war going on with my emotions right now, and the side that doesn't want to see you go is winning." She was trying not to become choked up, but it wasn't working.

"You really feeling the kid, ain't you?" He produced a sexy smirk.

Riley rolled her eyes before smiling herself. "I mean, you're all right."

Jermaine pushed his chair back so that he could stand, and Riley watched his every move, confused as to what he was doing. However, she wouldn't have to wonder long. He moved the chair to her right side and sat down, looking her in the eyes lovingly.

"I'm not trying to leave you just as much as you don't want me to go. I'll try thinking of another option, all right?"

She felt her heart fill with uncontrollable flutters. This man was everything she wanted. Now, anyway. At first, she couldn't stand him. And now she couldn't imagine life without him. She held in a smile at the thought of how that sounded, especially in such a short amount of time. She was telling Mikayla to be cautious with her feelings, and here she was feeling the same way, maybe deeper, because she had fallen for this man romantically. *Damn, what is it about these Stately men?* she wondered.

"I understand." She avoided his eyes. Her words were meant to be supportive, not express her true feelings, but there was no way she could be selfish and not support him in protecting his brother. If the shoe were on the other foot, she'd want the same support for her and Mikayla, possibly more.

"I'ma figure it out, okay? Let's enjoy our dinner and figure everything else out later." He leaned in and kissed her cheek.

"I'm fine with that." She provided a genuine smile this time as she appreciated being able to live in the moment.

For the remainder of their dinner, they laughed, joked, and drank enough to the point of feeling good but not faded. By the time the waiter brought them their bill, they both felt more optimistic about the future.

"I think I know what I'm going to do," Jermaine said as he opened the car door for Riley.

She got into the car and waited for him to walk around and get inside. She turned to face him and waited for him to tell her what decision he had made.

"I'm going to send him back home with my mom. He's not going to like it, but it'll be good for both of them. They can resolve some of the shit between the two of them, and I can keep him safe."

"Mikayla is going to be heartbroken."

"She'll be more than that if he gets hurt in these streets or winds back up in jail."

"That's true. It won't be forever, and since it's your mother's place, visiting and communication is going to be a breeze." She provided him a warm smile as she placed her hand on his thigh. She knew that sending Jeremiah off was going to be complicated.

"When do you plan to tell him? Well, them, because I'm not breaking that news to Mikayla."

"I thought we were a team." He took his eyes off the road shortly to glance at her.

"Always, baby. You know I got you. I was only playing. So where are we going? Back to your place or mine?"

"To my place, because when the haters are under the same roof as us, you like to be all quiet and shit, and I like for the neighbors to know my name."

"Oh, trust me, they know it. But we can go back to your place."

"Okay, just let them know we're not coming back to your place until morning."

"Already done," she told him as she presented her phone with a smile on her face.

"Well, Riley and Jermaine aren't coming back tonight," Mikayla said to Jeremiah as she placed her phone inside her pocket.

"Cool, because I was not looking forward to having to send Chelle home too early." He pulled glasses down from the kitchen counter.

"Yeah, me either. I mean, I don't care about Chelle going home. I'm talking about Marc." She blushed as she removed juice from the fridge.

"That nigga don't watch his hands. You don't have to worry about Riley putting him out. He gon' for sure hit the door and a couple walls, too."

"Wow, how is that fair when you and Chelle have been so on each other that for a moment I thought you were Siamese twins?"

"'Cause I can do that kinda shit. You can't. You not about to have him going back to school saying some outta-pocket shit and then I have to beat his ass."

"He isn't like that."

"All dudes are like that. We talk, especially about fine-ass girls."

"Aw, dang, I thought it was just you. Because you tell me all your business. You're the best gossiper I know outside of Riley. Well, and my cousin Tasha."

"Man, I don't do no damn gossiping. That's disrespectful, Mikayla."

"I'm joking," she said with her fingers crossed. To her, Jeremiah was a big gossiper, but to keep the peace, she took it back and wouldn't voice it again.

"That's what I thought, or homeboy was about to have to go." He took the tray filled with drinks, and she grabbed the plates and pizza. They decided to have a kickback, which technically was a double date, while Riley and Jermaine were out.

As close as they were, sometimes they needed the company of others so that they wouldn't get tired of one another. Plus, they were sick of the rumors surrounding their relationship. No one wanted to believe they were only friends. Jeremiah didn't care too much. Females were going to mess around with him regardless. But Mikayla did care. She didn't want to go the rest of high school with boys not wanting to talk to her because they assumed she was taken. It was bad enough that the beatdown her cousins put on Jason, Daniel, and Levi had made boys afraid to talk to her. Adding Jeremiah into the mix did not make it any better.

"Thanks, babe. I could have helped you, though," Marc said as he took the food from Mikayla's hand. He and Chelle had been left in the den while she and Jeremiah grabbed food and drinks.

"It's fine. We're the hosts, so there's no reason for the guests to be doing anything." Mikayla took a seat next to him, making sure her thigh was touching his. She reached forward and filled their plates with food.

"Jeremiah, you still down with the 619 boys?" Marc asked as he stuffed a slice of pizza in his mouth.

"Gang shit for life. Why you ask?" He would never show his hand or discuss what was going on with him and his ex-crew with an outsider.

"Oh, shit, 'cause I heard they wasn't fucking with you no more because you got off the case on some sneak shit." He shrugged like it was nothing, and that was when everyone in the room knew Marc was a hater. He was obviously jealous of the bond Mikayla and Jeremiah had, because he had no reason to bring up some shit like that.

"First off, I'm still going to court behind that case, and secondly you're not in the streets, so you shouldn't be discussing street shit." Pissed, Jeremiah sat forward in his seat, making direct eye contact with Marc.

"Nah, I ain't. But even I abide by the 'no snitch' code."

"What are you tryin' to say?" The question was rhetorical. He only wanted Marc to be bold enough to call him a snitch to his face so he could punch him in it.

"I'm saying your crew wouldn't be labeling you for no reason. You're not down with them no more because you snitched."

That was it. He said the word to his face with a clear indication that he felt the accusation was true. He just didn't realize he picked the wrong day to say some bullshit about something he knew nothing about. Before Mikayla, Chelle, and even Marc knew what happened, Jeremiah was on him. A good right hook to the jaw sent Marc flying back into the couch.

"Jeremiah, no," Mikayla pleaded as she grabbed his arm to stop him from swinging again.

"You taking up for him?" He turned on her, chest heaving up and down.

"Hell nah, he's just not worth it." She knew there was a lot at stake, and she refused to let a guy she brought around be the reason for her best friend getting in more trouble. "Marc, you have to go," she told him as she kept a firm grip on Jeremiah's arm.

Marc stood, holding his jaw, and he left Mikayla's home without even a small protest.

"You need ice or something for your hand?" Chelle asked, walking up and touching his shoulder. Mikayla almost forgot she was there.

"Nah, I'm about to go to sleep. I'll call you tomorrow." He didn't wait for a reply. He just left the den, heading straight for the guest room.

"So much for a chill night." Mikayla shrugged. Chelle stormed out of her home too.

Chapter 17

"You feel okay?" Mikayla leaned in and asked Jeremiah as they walked a few feet behind Riley and Jermaine.

Today was his final court date, and though his lawyer was optimistic things would be working out for the best, he was still unsure, especially since he had decided not to take the charges for the gang. Since he hadn't taken a plea deal or reached out to say he would take everything, he wouldn't put it past them to put everything on him. At this point, it was every man for himself and his word against that of his would-be codefendant and his public defender. He hated feeling unsure of the outcome, and no matter how he tried to prepare himself for a good or bad outcome, he just couldn't wrap his mind around either one.

"Yeah, just ready to get this shit over with."

"Everything is going to be fine," she reassured him, squeezing his hand. She had heard some of what his lawyer was trying to do for him and believed her when she said that this case would work out in Jeremiah's favor.

He didn't say anything, just squeezed her hand back as they entered the doors of the courthouse.

"Hey, we're going this way." They were immediately greeted by Landra upon their entrance. She had waited outside of the courtroom door for them.

"Why aren't we going in there?" Jeremiah asked.

"We will be. I want to discuss something with you and your brother first." She smiled at him. The four of them followed her until she stopped at a conference room door at the end of the hall.

"Um, I only have the authority to discuss your case with you and your brother," she said to Jeremiah once she noticed how closely Mikayla and Riley were following.

Riley released an irritated chuckle before rolling her eyes. If Landra weren't so good at her job representing Jeremiah, she would have cussed her out. Each time they had been in one another's presence, Landra acted like she and Mikayla weren't there, and when she did acknowledge them, it was short and dismissive. She understood that there may have been some sort of interest in Jermaine, but she didn't have to be rude to them because her feelings weren't being reciprocated by him.

"They can listen in. It's not like we not gonna tell them anyway," Jeremiah said, shrugging his shoulders.

"It's okay, Jeremiah. We'll wait right here," Riley said.

"You good, babe?" Jermaine asked her, knowing she was irritated by Landra. He, too, noticed how she acted toward the girls, but he wouldn't address it until she got his brother off. As much as he cared about Riley and Mikayla, he wouldn't start any drama with the woman who, besides the judge, practically held his brother's future in her hands.

"Yes. We'll go grab seats." She leaned in and kissed his lips before motioning for Mikayla to follow her back to the courtroom.

Jermaine noticed Landra's body language shift, and he held in his chuckle. That was what she got for trying to act like she could one-up a woman who, in his eyes, she couldn't compete with on her best day. He would never deny how fine Landra was and how he respected her having her shit together, but some great qualities couldn't outweigh the bad, and she was insecure. Her actions showed it by how she acted toward Riley, when she didn't know her at all, because she was interested in him. They hadn't gone on a date. He hadn't even flirted with her, so he could only imagine how she would act if he gave her the time of day on a personal level.

"What's up?" Jeremiah asked her, bringing them back to the reason they were entering the conference room.

"You won't be going to jail, but before the year is up, you'll have to provide volunteer hours at any location of your choice and pay a thousand-dollar fine. All of these things will get the time you spent in jail expunged, and you walk away a free man. If you don't take this deal, you go to trial or take the sixteen months the district attorney is trying to offer you," Landra said as she removed papers and a pen from her briefcase.

"Of course I'm going to take deal number one. I'm not a dummy. Where do I sign?" Jeremiah said excitedly. He was happy that this was all going to be behind him. Literally, as long as he did those community service hours.

"There's one catch to signing this paper," she told him, halting his movement toward the pen.

"And what's that?"

"If you sign this, you are basically saying you had nothing to do with the theft and were just in the wrong place at the wrong time. Now it's not snitching or stating that your codefendant is guilty, but it is saying you absolutely had nothing to do with anything surrounding the incident. And his lawyer can request a copy of your paperwork."

The look on Landra's face was one of slight worry. He knew it wasn't because of the deal she was able to get him. The deal was amazing, and he wasn't even sure how she pulled it off. He looked over to his brother, who had already been burning a hole in the side of his head, waiting for his reaction.

"It is what it is. I didn't snitch. The paperwork doesn't say I cooperated in any way, so I'm taking the deal." He looked his brother in the eyes. Even though they both knew to the gang that wouldn't mean much, he was sticking by his decision. He wasn't raised as a punk and refused to go out like one.

"You heard the man. Give him the pen to sign," Jermaine said. At the end of the day, he would stick by his brother—good, bad, right, or wrong. Words couldn't describe how proud of his brother he was at that moment because he was sticking to his guns, well aware of the repercussions that may follow. He also wasn't too worried because, whether Jeremiah liked it or not, he was still going to stay with their mother until things died down.

Jeremiah took the pen and signed his name on the dotted line. His heart was pumping and his palms were a bit sweaty because though it was the end of his case, it was the beginning of some new problems.

"Okay, all done. Let's go get the judge to sign off on this and you are a free man." Landra smiled at Jeremiah as she placed the paperwork back inside her briefcase before walking ahead of them toward the courtroom. Both men looked at her ass as it switched from side to side.

"She bad as hell, but she don't got nothing on Riley," Jeremiah commented.

"You been looking at my woman's ass?"

"Yeah, before she was your woman and maybe after." He laughed as he sped up his steps to avoid the punch to his arm his brother was about to give him. He reached the door of the courtroom and immediately composed himself. He took a deep breath, then walked inside, his brother right on his heels. Instead of taking a seat next to the women, he continued to the very first row and sat next to Landra. She gave him a smile of acknowledgment, then began going through her papers. He looked over his shoulder at Mikayla, who provided a thumbs-up and a reassuring smile.

"Mr. Westley, you are hereby sentenced to eighteen months in the state penitentiary." The judge speaking and the name he said pulled Jeremiah's attention back to the front of the courtroom.

He looked over to the left but was unable to put a face with the name because of the lawyer blocking his view. He was sure that it was his former 619 potna, KJ. KJ's was one of the few in his crew whose last name he knew, and that was only because they'd had a class together sophomore year before KJ dropped out. He tried not to look so pressed, but he couldn't remove his eyes from that direction until his eyes confirmed what his mind knew. He didn't have to wait long either. The bailiff seemed to appear out of nowhere, and when KJ stood to be cuffed, his identity was confirmed.

"Why are we here at the same time? That hasn't happened since the first court date," Jeremiah whispered to Landra.

"It's a scare tactic. But it doesn't matter because you've already signed your deal," she said like it was no big deal, when minutes ago she'd shown apprehension because of what may come from him signing. As with most things, he couldn't dwell on it long, as he and KJ made eye contact on his way out of the courtroom. The mug on his face told him what he already knew. The beef was on.

"Okay, we're up next." Landra stood, and he followed suit.

He couldn't understand why he felt nervous. If everything was truly as simple as him signing on the dotted line, there was no reason to feel the way he was feeling.

"Mr. Stately, do you understand what you signed today?" the judge asked him, grabbing his attention.

"I do, Your Honor."

"And you agree with the terms and the timeline set out for you?"

"I do."

"Okay. I do not want to see you back in my courtroom. You have been given a second chance, and I expect you to do great things with it."

"I will, Your Honor."

"Okay. You are dismissed. Next case, please."

Jeremiah turned to Landra with an enormous smile on his face and hugged her. She had done exactly what she said she would do, and that was get him off.

"Thank you. You really are a beast. A pretty one," he told her as they separated from their embrace.

"Thank you. Now as much as I enjoyed having you as a client, let's not end up back here, okay?"

"Oh, you don't have to worry about that."

"Well, your people are waiting for you." She nodded toward the teary eyes of Riley and Mikayla and the proud expression of Jermaine.

Jeremiah thanked her once more as he made his way to his people. She kept her eyes on them, Jermaine more so as she felt slighted that she wouldn't be seeing him again and that she clearly wasn't his type, which was odd because she was known to be every man's type. Jermaine looked back at her, mouthing his thanks before he turned to walk out of the room with his family.

"Told you everything was going to work out," Mikayla spoke excitedly.

"You did, and that expensive-ass Landra was worth every penny. She got you a deal that I didn't think would ever be available to you."

"Yeah, she's a beast. You gotta keep her on retainer."

"No, he does not need to do that. I'm sure she'll drop everything if he calls," Riley said as she passed Jermaine her car keys.

Jermaine held in his laughter with tight lips as he opened the door for her. Mikayla and Jeremiah held nothing back, laughing as they climbed into the back seat.

"So where are we going? Y'all know we have to celebrate," Mikayla said as soon as they were all inside of the car.

"I could eat. I skipped breakfast this morning. I was so nervous about how things were going to turn out."

"We told you everything would be good. But I get it. Let's go to your favorite restaurant," she suggested.

"My favorite spot to eat isn't a restaurant. It's a mom-and-pop hole-in-the-wall."

"Ay, that sounds like a plan. We haven't been to that spot in a minute," Jermaine said, knowing exactly where his brother was referring to.

"Are y'all gonna tell us?" Riley asked, looking at Jermaine.

"Nope. Just ride."

The ride was quick because it wasn't too far from the courthouse. It was far enough to do some dirt and have the chance to get away, but also quick enough for assistance if there was any needed.

"Aunt Mae's Everything." Mikayla read the sign of the place they had just parked in front of.

"Yep, and everything they cook is good as hell. You get some of everything in this place, and the prices are good," Jeremiah told her as he took her hand.

"It's crazy. As long as we've been living out here, I've never been to this place," Riley said as they walked inside. She could tell from the decor that the place had been around for a while, and from the aroma hitting her nose, she could understand why. It smelled amazing. And if the smell was any indication of what was to come, she knew she was in for a treat.

They seated themselves, taking a seat in the back, where Jeremiah had chosen a booth.

"Riley, this place really does have everything. I want the crab platter with pasta," Mikayla said as she put her menu down.

"That's good, but their soul food hit. I'm getting that." He pointed to a photo in the menu for Mikayla to view, and her mouth watered.

"I'll be eating some of your food," she easily told him.

"I'll be eating some of yours because I have to try these barbeque links," Riley said to Mikayla before turning to Jermaine. "Babe, what you getting?"

"The same thing as you because y'all not about to be digging in my plate."

"That's cold. We all are supposed to get something different so Mikayla and I can try everything since we've never been here."

"When have y'all ever been out with me and I was scared to run up a tab? You don't have to limit what you order. Try everything on this menu if you want. I'm not worried about the cost."

"Yeah, but who wants to look greedy? Duh." Mikayla sat back in her seat, looking at him as if he had lost his mind.

He shook his head. Not willing to further entertain her, he said what he said, and if she didn't take advantage of it, that was on her. Riley, however, had no issue. She ordered her barbeque and a seafood pasta she had been curious about.

"This food is so good. All of it. I hope you know you two have just started something." Riley sat back in her seat and patted her extremely full stomach.

"I see. Let me go and pay the bill, and then I'll bring the car around. You ordered the dessert to go, right?"

"Yep, and I'm waiting for boxes because I am taking the rest of this food home."

Jermaine nodded, then kissed her cheek before he stood and headed to the front. He hadn't been gone a full sixty seconds before their to-go boxes were at their table as well as Riley's desserts. Jeremiah grabbed their bags and led them out to the car, where Jermaine waited. He hadn't been able to get a parking spot right in front, so they had to walk up some. Tires screeching pulled their attention toward the street.

"It's 619, you snitch bitch." A masked figured hung from the window of the car, and although his face wasn't visible, Jeremiah had a feeling it was Tech.

Jeremiah's heart seemed to stop at that moment, and so did the rest of his limbs. Even when he saw the barrel of the gun appear from the window, he remained frozen.

Gunshots rang out, and all he could do was stand there.

Chapter 18

"Where are you going?" Riley asked, still half asleep.

"I'll be back. Go back to sleep," he told her.

There was something in the sound of his voice that worried her. It also woke her completely up. She turned on the lamp on her nightstand and sat up. When her eyes met his, she was not expecting the sight before her. He was dressed in all black, standing in his closet. She knew exactly what he kept there.

"Jermaine."

"I told you to go back to bed."

"Yeah, right. You think I'm going to get any sleep knowing that you are about to go and do something stupid?"

"Who said I was going to go do anything?" he turned to her, looking at her as if she didn't know what she was talking about.

The fact that he could wear such a straight face with the thoughts of committing a crime on his mind frightened her. "You just 'dressed in all black like *The Omen*' because you were in the mood for black? Standing at your closet with your hand in the exact place you keep your gun because you forgot something? Like, come on, Jermaine, you should know by now I am not the female you can just say anything to."

She watched as guilt washed over him. His facial expression and body language showed that she had caught him red-handed. She knew them getting shot at was going to bring out a monster in him that she didn't want to see or know. She had even tried prepping herself for what she would do the moment it happened, but as she looked at him ready to go to war all by himself, she realized there was no way she could prepare herself for this moment.

She watched him come closer to her as tears welled in her eyes. She was afraid—afraid of not being able to stop him from making a huge mistake, and even more fearful that if he did walk out his front door, she'd be left there to worry that their relationship would be over. There was no way she could stay with him knowing he was okay with taking the kind of risk he was on his way to take tonight.

Jermaine sat next to her and took her hand, and for a moment, he just looked at her. She didn't want to be the first to speak because he obviously was trying to gather his thoughts, but the longer he looked at her, the more she felt her emotions getting the best of her, good and bad.

"You realize them niggas could've killed my brother yesterday. You, Me, Mikayla too. It was one thing for them to jump him, but when they took it to the level of pulling out guns and shooting at us in a public place, I could no longer think of them niggas as kids, no matter how young they are. They wanted to play a grown-man's game, so it's time for a grown man to show them they not really trying to grow up so fast. If they're allowed to grow at all."

"I do understand. I've never been so afraid in my life for all of us, but that doesn't mean that I want you to go out there and risk your life. You're willing to go out there and risk everything, and I don't understand why."

"You do understand why. You just don't like the reason. And I get it. I'm not asking you to accept any of this."

"So what are you saying?" She frowned, not liking where their conversation was going.

"I'm saying that I know this all may be a bit much for you, so if you want to end things, then I understand."

"Are you fucking serious? Now you want to end our relationship? That's bullshit, Jermaine. I'm never going to be okay with you going out to do some dumb shit, and because of that, you want to break up?" She leaned closer to him before she pushed him with so much attitude that it forced her back against the headboard.

"Say something," she demanded as he just looked at her. She had pushed him, had tears flowing down her face, and he didn't say a thing.

"I said everything I needed to say."

"No, the fuck you didn't. Because A, you're not about to break up with me, and B, you also aren't about to go and do anything stupid. You walk out that front door, be prepared for me to be right behind you, and if you even fix your mouth to threaten a breakup with me again, then you will find yourself by yourself because that's some bullshit." She wiped her tears with the back of her hand to no avail because they kept flowing.

Jermaine placed his head in his hands and took a moment to think. She was right. He was on the verge of doing something stupid. Pushing her away, losing her would have been dumber than the bullet he was going to put in the head of one of the 619 boys. He hated being so on edge, but coming so close to losing everyone he loved sparked a fire in him that even he didn't know existed. He had been a menace back in the day, doing dumb shit without purpose. What he planned to do tonight had purpose, had reason, and it all made sense until now. Until he saw how much it would hurt her. But he was still torn. What about how much he would hurt if he'd lost either one of them? The 619 boys were just shooting, didn't care who they hit even though the purpose of the shooting was to get to Jeremiah. And that was what fucked him up, them being after his brother. If things went bad and Jeremiah had gotten shot, he'd be devastated. But he would also know in the back of his mind that his brother brought this all upon himself by joining the gang in the first place. But if Riley or Mikayla had been hit because of choices his brother made, no way would he be able to take that lightly.

And he didn't, which was why he was on his way to handle things. His plan was to do what he needed to do unnoticed and without Riley finding out. He wasn't stupid. Getting caught was a possibility. It just wasn't on his mind. He had committed crimes before, and unfortunately, he knew the act of violence was usually one crime easier to get away with. The fact that there had been no arrest made since the shooting proved it, and he knew there were people who heard them yell, "619."

Jermaine removed his hands from his face and turned his entire body toward Riley. "I'm sorry. This shit is really fucking me up." His voice trembled as he spoke. He was full of so many emotions.

"I understand, but this isn't the way."

"You know what my pops always told me?" he said, looking her in the eyes.

"No, what did he say?"

"The only way to stop a bully is to show them they can't bully you anymore. You can show 'em with your words or with action."

"I was taught that too coming up, but—"

"There ain't no buts. They have to know we not to be played with like that. You're right though. I'll find another way. One that definitely doesn't include losing you." He paused, staring intensely into her eyes because he wanted to be sure she not only heard his next words but felt them, too.

"I love you." Sincerity filled every inch of him.

His words were powerful enough to have Riley's heart thumping sporadically. At least, that was how she thought it was pumping. He leaned forward, placing his lips on hers. He had been the first one to say the words, and although it felt good to tell her, her reaction or lack thereof had him nervous. She placed a hand on each side of his face as she kissed him passionately before pulling away and looking into his eyes.

"I love you too."

"Nah, don't be saying it 'cause I said it first," he teased, smiling at her.

"You know I wouldn't do that. I do love you, which is one of the reasons I refuse to sit around while you risk so much."

"You're right. I was trippin'. Instead, what I plan to do is take him to my mom's first thing in the morning.

"Okay."

"You mad at me?"

"I was. Would have been if you had left. And Jermaine, listen, I want you to understand that I really do get where you are coming from when it comes to protecting your brother and standing your ground. I also know how decisions made with an angry mind can lead to a world of trouble. I wouldn't be a good woman if I didn't help you see all areas of your choices. If I knew you could go out there and do what you needed to do without consequences or it affecting your conscience, then I would give you my blessing because they do need to know they fucked with the wrong one. But sometimes we have to allow karma to do what she does."

"I hear you."

"Okay," she conceded. They seemed to have an understanding, as far as she could tell, so there wasn't a reason to go back and forth about it any longer.

"Since you stopped me from letting off some shots from my gun, you need to give me another place to shoot up," he told her as he winked and gave her a sexy smirk.

"I mean, I can help you with letting off a little frustration, but I ain't ready for you to shoot the club up." She had changed her voice to sound like a girl from the ghetto, and it caused him to laugh. However, his laughter ceased when she pulled her shirt above her head.

Jermaine followed her lead and removed his black hoodie, followed by his tennis shoes and sweats. He leaned forward, placing a hand on each side of her before kissing her lips.

"Mmm," he moaned, lips still on hers at the feel of Riley massaging his manhood through his boxer briefs. Just the sound of him moaning always turned Riley on, which was why she always took the opportunity to touch him in places she knew would arouse him. She broke their kiss and pushed him back slightly, putting enough space between them so that she could get his boxers down.

The way his penis sprang forward after being freed from the confines of his Polo briefs let her know that he was ready for whatever she was about to do. And though the room was dimly lit, the only light coming from the closet, she was still able to see the precum oozing from his tip, and it made her mouth water. Without any further delay, Riley gripped him with her right hand and slid her mouth over his head and down his shaft. Slowly she worked her hand and mouth, becoming wetter with each moan that left Jermaine's mouth.

"Shit, babe. You gotta stop. I'm not trying to cum yet," he told her as he had a nice grip on the top of her head. His mouth had told her to take it easy, but his movements said to keep going. She wouldn't, though. As much as she enjoyed the oral pleasure Jermaine was capable of giving her as he'd done many times, she wanted to feel him inside of her, and she also knew that he needed to be inside of her. It would help him release some of the stress he'd been under. She took one last lick around his mushroom-shaped head before she pulled back. She scooted back on the bed and waited anxiously as he climbed on top of her. Jermaine kissed her passionately as he entered her slowly.

"Uh," she moaned as he inched deeper into her slowly. His pace started as it always did, slow and steady. She was surprised that he was being so reserved when she knew a little more aggression wouldn't hurt her and could help him.

"Harder, babe," she moaned into his ear, giving him the okay to do what he needed to release his stress.

Her words were like music to his ears. Sex with Riley would always calm him. However, with everything going on over the last few months, he needed their sex to be different. He took her direction well, going harder and deeper, and even sped up his pace. With each stroke, he felt a weight being lifted. He leaned down, kissing her as he felt himself on the verge of climaxing. He stroked her three more times before pulling out and releasing on his bedroom floor.

Riley lay there with a lazy smile as he kissed her once more before going to grab towels to clean up the mess he made. She had had an orgasm, not one like he would usually give her but satisfying enough that it had her ready to put her thumb in her mouth and sleep. Tonight wasn't about her. She wanted him to release some of the tension in his body, and by the way he had gotten back into bed, wrapping his arm around her before falling to sleep and snoring loudly, it let her know he'd done just that.

"This some bullshit," Jeremiah fussed as he sat back in the passenger seat with his arms folded across his chest with a pout on his face.

"Call it what you want, but it needs to be done. It's not forever, only until this shit dies down."

"You gon' have me out here looking like a punk. And a snitch. Only guilty people run."

"You not running, and smart people leave. Did you forget you almost got shot because the people you wanted to call your friends or brothers turned on you?" He turned to look at him as they pulled up to a red light.

Instead of replying, Jeremiah looked out the window.

"Now you don't have nothing to say? You worried about looking like something when I'm worried about you still breathing. You don't want to go stay with Mom for a little bit, but you froze the fuck up. They started shooting, and you just fucking stood there. That right there tells me you not ready to be out here in the middle of this bullshit. Nah, you not a punk, but you clearly aren't built for the shit these little mothafuckas is doing either. If it hadn't been for Riley, yo' ass would be dead."

Jermaine's words hit him hard, and it took everything for him not to allow his emotions to show. The lone tear that threatened to fall from his eyes he immediately shook off before it could reveal itself. He wasn't sure if he was more hurt at the truth or because he failed in making his brother see him as a man. Their father had been gone for years. Jermaine had taken on the father-figure role when he took him in. But he wasn't his father, he was his big brother, and though the age gap was significant, he wanted to be seen as his equal, at least sometimes. But the way he failed to show up when it mattered had done the complete opposite for their relationship. He was sure of it.

"Cat got yo' tongue now?" Jermaine asked as he moved through traffic.

"Damn, bro, I get it. I fucked up. I keep fucking up. I get it, all right?"

The emotion-filled response from his brother caused him to pull to the side of the road. He unbuckled his seat belt and Jeremiah's and pulled him into a hug without hesitation. He hated to make his brother feel like he wasn't proud of him or that he felt like he was truly a fuckup. Yes, he had made many costly mistakes, but that didn't define him as a person.

"You not a fuckup. I don't think that of you. Never have, never will. You smart as hell, courageous, and got some shit in you that must've skipped me because ninety percent of the people you meet enjoy being in your presence. You made a mistake, and regardless of what you think, as your big brother, it's my job to help you clean it up. I'm riding with you until the wheels fall off. As long as there is breath in my body, you won't have to do no hard shit alone. Easy shit either. I know going to stay with Mom isn't what you want, but it won't be forever, all right? And don't ever fix your mouth to down yourself like that again. You hear me?"

It had been a while since Jermaine had shed tears, but the emotion pouring from his younger brother mixed with his own had his tears flowing from his eyes without shame. He didn't want Jeremiah to feel like less than a man because he was crying, so as his own tears fell, he didn't wipe them because he wanted to show his brother that real men cried too, and it was okay.

"Okay," he choked out. Jeremiah savored the hug from his brother a bit longer before taking a deep breath and pulling away. He knew Jermaine wouldn't be the first to break the connection because he wanted to make sure he knew he was there for him, and he did. At that moment, he knew more than any other time he showed it.

"I get it. Thank you. I'm still not trying to be with Mom too long, but I can do it because just like you got me out of jail, I know you'll get me out of this. This the last jam you'll have to get me out of, though, I promise." And he meant every word. When he got him out of this, that was it.

"All right, let's get to Mom's. I know she been watching the clock." They shared a knowing laugh.

"You sure she cool with me coming back?"

"Yeah, man, I wouldn't send you if I had even the smallest feeling she had an issue with it. I know you and Mom have some stuff with y'all. At the end of the day, you're still her son."

"She hasn't visited once. She's answered my calls but never made the trip. Don't seem like she tried to either."

"That's a conversation you have to have with her. Respectfully."

"Man, I know. Remember how easy it was to talk to her and Pops about anything?"

"It still is. You decided to quit. I get it, but I don't, because for a kid who ate dirt in front of a girl so she'd know how brave you were, I can't believe you scared of a little conversation."

"Man, I know you ain't talking. Got into a fight and came home crying. And you didn't even lose. I knew from that day, I would have hands like my big brother, but I wasn't gon' cry after winning a fight."

"I remember, and that was also the day I knew I had a real rider for a little brother. You came to the yard with a bat, ready to attack whoever did me dirty." Jermaine smiled, remembering how they always had each other and further understanding why his departure had hurt Jeremiah so much.

"Always. Ain't no obstacle too big for me to have your back ever," Jeremiah said, fighting back emotion. He was glad he and his brother were taking this ride and reconnecting more.

"Same, bro. Same." Jermaine lifted his fist, and Jeremiah met it with his own. Laughter fell from their mouths in unison as the memories replayed in their minds.

For the rest of the ride, they laughed at childhood memories, then took a call from Riley and Mikayla, and before they knew it, they had pulled in front of their childhood home. It looked better than when they lived there, thanks to Jermaine paying for remodels and upkeep.

"Told you she was watching the clock," Jermaine said as their mother stood on the front porch looking every bit of Debbie Allen's twin.

Seeing how anxious she was to see them and not laying eyes on his mother in years, Jeremiah was the first to jump out of the car. He rushed into his mother's arms and felt the love he had been missing. All his reservations were still present, but this embrace was much more important.

Jermaine gave them their moment before interrupting. "Ay, I need to get in on that," he said playfully, pushing Jeremiah out of the way. It had been even longer since he'd embraced his mother, and the feeling made him almost thankful that Jeremiah did what he did for them to end up right there.

Chapter 19

For two weeks Jeremiah had been gone, and Mikayla was going crazy. She hadn't realized how much he made a difference in her day-to-day since they met until he was no longer around. While she was sad and missing him, he seemed to be having the time of his life, not worried about her and barely answering her phone calls. She got that he was trying to become acclimated with his new but temporary life, but she couldn't believe how he was putting her, of all people, on the back burner.

Riley took a deep breath as she lifted her right hand and tapped it against Mikayla's door before letting herself in. "Hey, what are you doing?" Riley asked, walking closer to her cousin.

Mikayla looked at Riley with pouty lips, and immediately, her cousin knew what was wrong with her. "He still hasn't called you back?" She took a seat on Mikayla's desk chair.

"No. He's being such an ass. I am not the reason he had to leave, so I don't understand why I'm the one getting the cold shoulder."

"Jermaine is getting it too, believe it or not." He had told her how well things went when he dropped Jeremiah off at their mom's, but days later, when he tried to reach out to his brother, he claimed he was busy with homework or kicking it with some of his old friends and an ex-girlfriend. Then days turned into a week, and he started ignoring him altogether.

"Well, I know why he's ignoring him. He's mad at him because he expected to be there less than two weeks, and here we are, pulling up on week three that he's been gone. He thinks Jermaine is dragging his feet getting him back, especially since there have been rumors about him and the case on social media."

"Why are you just telling me this?"

"Because I said I wouldn't. But I feel like I should if it'll help get him home sooner. Even though he's being an asshole."

"I know I'm not that much older than you, but you can slow up on the cussing. And maybe he's not speaking to you because it's hard that you're here and he's there. There could be some slight jealousy."

"I hope that isn't the case. Besides, I was spilling a lot of tea to him about that little ho bag Chelle he was messing with. And we talked about some other stuff. We were fine last time we spoke, and now he's just ghosting me for no reason."

"His brother is pulling up on him soon. I would suggest we go with him, but they have to iron out what they are going through first. I'll make sure he talks to him, though. Anyway, what happened to the boy you were talking to?" Riley felt bad that they hadn't really caught up in a couple of days. She had been busy with work, talking to Jermaine, and getting into her own groove because finally Mikayla was in a better space. Aside from occasional mood swings because Jeremiah was being a little jerk, things were looking up for Mikayla.

"Oh, I cut him off. He said something disrespectful about Jeremiah, and that was it for me. Besides, he acted like he didn't understand the word 'slow.' As in, I wanted to slowly progress into a relationship *if* we found ourselves to be compatible enough for that. I realized he only wanted to rush making me his girl because he thought it meant we would have sex. Guys can be such assholes. My bad."

"I'm proud of you."

"Why?"

"Because you finally stood your ground. Guys can be assholes, but now that you know what you want and, more importantly, what you're worth, when the right guy comes along, you'll know it."

"You're right. And I'm cool off guys for a minute anyway. My best friend is acting funny, and the guy I thought I could potentially build something with turned out to be a jerk, so yeah, I'm good."

"I'm not going to argue with you on that. Books before boys."

"Speaking of, I do have a test I need to study for. Jeremiah better hope I'll speak to him when he comes out of his feelings," she said, rolling her eyes.

"How about after you study, you and I go to the mall? There's nothing like retail therapy, especially on my man's dime," she said, smiling before she winked at her.

"Oh, so you got it like that? Okay, cousin." Mikayla extended her hand for a high five.

"That man loves me, and I love him."

"I can tell. You've never looked so happy, and it's crazy because when you two first met, I knew you were going to bite his head off."

"Oh, I so was. I have to thank you and Jeremiah. I guess had it not been for y'all's friendship, we would not be together."

"You're right. So I am going to enjoy shopping on Jermaine's dime as a thank-you."

"Well, handle your studies, and I'll come get you later." She gave Mikayla a tight hug before she left her to study.

"I'm starting to regret leaving that card with you. I mean, you were doing just fine without it before we became a couple, so no reason for you to need it now," Jermaine teased.

"There was nothing wrong with you leaving your Amex. Mikayla and I really appreciate this shopping spree you're sending us on."

"I bet. You know I was joking. You can have whatever you like."

"Of course I knew you were playing. And you are absolutely appreciated. How close are you to your mother's house?"

"Like fifteen more minutes. I would have gotten here faster, but somebody drained my energy before I left."

"That's not all I drained. I expect those balls to be heavy when you get back."

"You don't have to worry about that. Pussy too good for me to stray or use my hand," he told her honestly, causing her to blush.

"I miss you."

"I miss you too. Shit's crazy, but I won't be gone long. I need to straighten this out with my brother, and once that's squared away, I'll head home. It could take a day or two."

"Okay," she pouted. "Make sure you tell him to get his shit together with Mikayla, too, or he's going to lose his best friend. He hurt her feelings."

"She not about to stop being nobody's friend. But tell her I got her. I'll talk to him."

"Okay. Well, call me later, and I love you."

"That shit sounds good as hell coming from your mouth. I love you too." Jermaine ended the call and embraced the warmth that Riley brought over him. It had been a while since he'd been in love, and although the single life had its benefits, there was nothing like having a consistent and real woman by his side. It also felt good to know that they were dating with a purpose, and he was certainly seeing a future with her wearing a ring gifted from him. He smiled at the thought of her. His dick got hard at the thought of kissing her. He didn't see any of that getting old, and that made him even more excited for the future.

He allowed himself to feel mushy for a few more moments before shaking the feeling off and getting serious. He was now only minutes away from his mother's and needed to get in the right headspace to deal with Jeremiah. The moment he pulled in front of his mother's house, he felt more than ready to set some things straight. He hated that he and his brother were having communication issues again, especially since things between them were getting better and had ended on a high note when he dropped him off.

He exited the car and thought about using his key to let himself in as a way to shock Jeremiah, but he decided to knock instead. Though he was there to have a conversation with his brother, he wouldn't pin his back against the wall to do so.

"One minute," he heard his mother yell from the other side of the door. Although this trip was about his brother, catching up with his mother was on his list, too. He wanted to make sure that Jeremiah's attitude hadn't spilled over to her.

"Who is it?"

"It's me, Ma," he said right before the door swung open.

"Why didn't you use your key?" she asked with her hands on her hips.

"And why didn't you look on the expensive-ass security system I pay for to see it was me?"

"First of all, watch your mouth, and you know I do not like all that techy stuff. Your brother tried to show me, and I still don't get it."

"Speaking of my brother, where is he anyway?"

"Went to the store for me. He should be back soon."

"That's why I didn't see your car. I thought it was in the garage."

"No, I let him take it."

"Mom, he doesn't have his license yet. If he gets pulled over by the police—"

"Boy, stop it. He has his permit, and he's scheduled to take the driver's test Monday. A trip up the block isn't going to hurt him," she said, dismissing his worries no matter how valid they were.

"All right," he conceded, slightly irritated as he took a seat on the sofa. His mother did the same, sitting across from him. "How have things been between you two?" he asked, although now he had a feeling, given she let Jeremiah take her car and had him scheduled for his license test.

"Good. I thought he was a little homesick at first, but he's been moving around like he never left. I know the little girl he's dealing with now is happy he's home. She was heartbroken when he left."

"Who he been—"

Before he could finish his question, the front door opened, and in walked Jeremiah with a handful of grocery bags. Jermaine was going to ask his mother who besides the young lady Jeremiah was kicking it with, but since his brother had walked in, he decided to save the question for their conversation.

"You get everything?" their mother asked as Jeremiah got closer to them.

"Yes, they had everything on your list." His eyes traveled to Jermaine. They remained on him for about ten seconds before he turned and walked off into the kitchen. There was no "hi, hey, what's up," or even a nod. He looked right at his brother and kept it moving.

"I'm going to go put the groceries away." His mother stood and gave him an uncomfortable look before she kissed him on top of his head and headed to the kitchen. It was obvious what she was trying to do when Jeremiah stomped out of the kitchen, but instead of sitting to speak with him like he was pretty sure their mother told him to do, he headed up the stairs to his bedroom.

"This dude," Jermaine grumbled as he got up from the sofa and went to his brother's bedroom. Luckily, the door wasn't locked, and he let himself in. "You not speaking to me?"

Jeremiah turned around and looked at him without saying a word.

Chuckling, Jermaine swiped his hand down his face and took a deep breath to relax his nerves. He felt himself about to get irritated, and he didn't want that, nor would it help what he was trying to do.

"Tell me what your problem is. I can't fix it if I don't know what you need."

"Now why would I give you something else to fix when you haven't done anything about the reason I'm out here?" He made eye contact with his brother and felt a weight off his shoulders when he finally said what he had been thinking over the last couple of weeks.

He had gone over in his mind on numerous occasions how he would get his feelings toward his brother off his chest. And though what he said wasn't what he had rehearsed, it still penetrated the way he wanted to. He was sure of it by the look on his brother's face. He wasn't done, though. He wanted Jermaine to feel so bad that he moved quicker to get him back home.

"I am trying. I had to let stuff die down first."

"No, it seems like you've been more concerned with being in your relationship with Riley than trying to get me back out there."

"Is that what you think for real?"

"That's what I know. How many dates have you been on, and how many times have you put your ear to the streets to figure out what needs to be done to get them off my ass, especially since they talking shit about me on social media now?"

The information hit Jermaine like a ton of bricks. He had stepped back to allow things to die down, yes, and he and Riley were getting closer in the process, but he had never forgotten his true mission, which was to fix things for his brother. Now hearing that he was possibly being bullied on social media had him upset, because if he'd never gotten caught on his way out by Riley, there would be one, maybe even two, fewer 619 boys to bother his brother.

"Why didn't you tell me?"

"I'm telling you now, and what difference would it have made whether I told you now or later? Either way, you not making any moves for me." Jeremiah grabbed his jacket and exited the room, leaving his brother sitting there looking dumb.

Jermaine decided to let him run off and blow off whatever steam he was feeling because his brother had made too many valid points for him to try to push any further understanding upon him. Instead, he was about to go and do what he promised with more fire under his ass than before. He got up and closed his brother's door behind him.

"Ma, I'll be back," he yelled out to her.

"Okay, baby, because I made enough food for all of us, and I want us to sit at this table and eat as a family," she yelled back to him.

Jermaine made sure to lock the door behind him, opting not to reply to his mother because he'd already said he would be back. He was on his way to speak to one of his homies he hadn't spoken to in a while and hoped that it would be accepted, although his visit wasn't going to be an expected one. It has been years since he'd been in the streets, and beef with some youngsters was never something he even thought would be a problem of his, and because it was, he now needed some insight on what he should do.

Jermaine turned left on Martin Luther King Drive and was surprised to see not much had changed. The neighborhood was clean, and though the homes were old, they had been kept up pretty good. He pulled directly in front of the home they called the Row House and felt a sense of calm wash over him. As grimy as the neighborhood used to be, he had always felt safe there. Even the few enemies he had back in the day knew better than to step to him there.

Jermaine exited his car and walked up to the door, knocking with the code he hadn't used in years. He was almost surprised at how easily it came back to him: two slow taps, three fast, and one hard. He heard some movement on the other side of the door and then nothing. He waited a few moments, and right as he lifted his hand to knock again, the door swung open.

"Look what the damn wind blew my way," Big Ace said with a large smile on his face as he opened his arms for a hug that Jermaine immediately sank into.

"What's up, Ace?" Jermaine said as he pulled back from their embrace.

"You tell me. I thought I told you not to come back here."

"I know, man, and I would have listened if I didn't need to talk to you about something."

"Your phone don't work?"

"Not for this conversation."

"Come on."

Jermaine followed him through the house and noticed how he had upgraded the inside. The paint was fresh, the furniture was modern, and even the floors were done.

"Have a seat." They sat at the coffee table, and Jermaine sat across from him. "Tell me what's going on."

Though Jermaine would have preferred to engage in some small talk first, he got to the point and told him all about the beef Jeremiah had with the 619 boys. By the time he put it all out there, he felt relieved and optimistic. The sad thing was, after speaking about it all, he realized how dumb the entire situation was and hated that his brother hadn't avoided the whole situation by not befriending or joining the gang.

"I got a solution for you."

"You do? 'Cause each time I think of one, it comes down to me bodying some little niggas, and I know that ain't the right choice."

"The old me probably would have told you that was the route to go, but who I am now and the position I'm in allows for me to tell you to take a different route."

"And what's that?"

"I know exactly who the gang is even though they are way out there where you're living now. I'm their supplier. So I'm going to let them know to leave your brother, who is also my brother, alone, or I'm cutting them off. I've needed an excuse to stop dealing with their dumb asses anyway because of shit like this. Beef and staying on the cops' radar does not make money, and it brings unnecessary drama."

"Damn, you supply they ass. I didn't even know they were into selling and shit. That's something my brother kept from me."

"I don't think they all sell. I supply the leader of their crew. Either way, I'm helping all they ass eat, and if they want to keep eating, they gonna catch what I throw. Tell your brother to give me some time to iron some things out and you'll be able to take him home."

"Thank you so much, Big Ace, but this conversation will stay between us if it's coo' with you. Little bro don't need to know anything."

"I'm fine with that too."

"Thank you, man. You've always had me, and I can't thank you enough."

"You have. Staying out of bullshit and making a life for yourself is enough thanks for me," Big Ace told him.

Every time Jermaine needed something, Big Ace had been there, and this time was no different. He would forever feel indebted to him and appreciate him as well. They sat and talked until Jermaine was sure his mother had finished dinner and would be pissed with him for being late.

Chapter 20

"Where are we going?" Mikayla asked Riley as she noticed they had driven for much longer than she anticipated. She had dozed off during the ride and awakened to find they were still moving.

"You'll see when we get there. Our destination isn't much farther, so just enjoy the rest of the ride."

"Maybe I could if you weren't playing music that put me to sleep," she told her.

"Ain't nothing sleepy about some nineties R&B music. If you listen closely, it'll teach you a few things. The music was pure, authentic, evolving, but most importantly, teaching. Like, music then made sure men give women the utmost respect. The stuff y'all listen to nowadays is exactly why the boys of your generation have no pizzazz about them."

"If you say so." Mikayla shrugged because an argument about music with Riley was one she knew she could not win. Multiple arguments proved it. Besides, she did like the music Riley played when they were home, cleaning the house, or just chilling. It wasn't fit for a five-hour car ride, though, especially when she had already been going through it because things were still a bit off with Jeremiah.

He had gotten better with returning her calls and texts, but she seemed to always be the one reaching out first. And then it broke her heart when he said that she may as well find another best friend because he doubted that he would be coming back home. She was sad for two days behind that. It wasn't until Riley and Jermaine assured her that things would turn around really soon that she came out of her funk. She kept the information to herself because if things didn't work out, she didn't want Jeremiah's feelings hurt once again.

"I do say so. Now can you enjoy the rest of this ride? I can't wait until you get your license so you can drive me around."

"I have my permit. One more month and I can take my driving test. Plus, since you're being all secretive, there's no way I could have driven us to wherever it is we're going." Mikayla sat up in her seat and looked out her window and Riley's as much as she could in hopes to see a familiar landmark that would tell her where they were, but it was primarily rural, so she honestly had no idea where they were or where they were headed.

Riley silently chuckled at Mikayla's curiosity, all while hoping she would be receptive to what she decided to do. This trip had been a long time coming, but it was also one she knew Mikayla had to be in a better space to take. She knew she was a bit wrong to determine that for her cousin, but she truly felt that now was the best time. If she turned out to be wrong, she would do whatever she needed to do to make it up to her. The closer they got to the location, the more nervous she became.

"Your boo is calling," Mikayla teased as Jermaine's contact name popped up on the car's screen. My Boo was exactly what she had him saved under, and she smiled at how he had called at the right time.

"Hold on, babe, let me connect you to my AirPods," she told him as soon as the call connected. He knew where they were headed, and she didn't want him to accidentally give it away.

"Please, because I do not want to hear Jermaine crying like Jodeci because you've been gone for a few hours," Mikayla teased.

"Man, g'on somewhere with that," he said, and Riley and Mikayla laughed.

"Yeah, I see you been taking notes while hating on my music," Riley told her as she placed her second AirPod in her ear. "Hey, babe."

"Y'all made it?"

"Almost," she said, not purposely being short with him but not wanting to say too much because she didn't want Mikayla to know he knew their destination before her.

"You feeling okay?"

"About the same as I told you before." She had told him her reservations about taking this trip without providing Mikayla a choice. But he assured her she was doing the right thing, and when she went over the pros and cons, she too found it to be the right thing to do.

"It's going to be fine, trust me. We've discussed this, and after everything you've told me, this trip is going to be one Mikayla didn't know she needed but will be grateful to have had in the end. Get out of your head about it."

"How did you know that's where I was?"

"'Cause I know you. Still learning you, but I know you."

"I can't deny that. I'm glad you called. It was right on time."

"You know I got you. Couldn't let you keep second-guessing a good decision."

"How's everything on your end?"

"It's cool. Preparing to get this knucklehead-ass boy back. Just talked to the principal at the school, and since he's been turning in all his work and his grades are fine, the transition from homeschool back to regular sessions shouldn't be an issue."

"That's amazing. You always do what you say you're going to do, Mr. Stately." She smiled. Even though he couldn't see her, he could hear it in her voice.

"I try to. A man ain't nothing if he can't keep his word."

"Riley, what is this building?" Mikayla asked, sounding almost like she was panicking.

"Babe, we're pulling up. I'll call you later."

She ended the call so fast that she barely heard him say, "Okay."

"Riley," Mikayla called out to her again as they entered a parking lot and got in the line of a bunch of cars.

"I'll tell you everything once I park," she told her, keeping her eyes on the road. From the corner of her eye, she could see Mikayla sit back and fold her arms across her chest.

"Visitor?" the guard asked when they pulled up to the guard shack.

"Yes," Riley told him and took the orange ticket he gave her to put in her car window. The car was silent as she followed a group of cars into the parking lot, where she circled for almost five minutes looking for a spot.

"Don't be mad at me," Riley said as she unbuckled her seat belt and turned to face Mikayla.

"Why are we here?"

"I thought this would be good for you. But if you want to leave, we can."

Mikayla looked up at the big gray brick building and felt herself becoming emotional. This was a trip she didn't know if she would ever take, and although she wanted to be upset with Riley for making the choice for her, she knew Riley wouldn't put her in a situation she didn't think she was ready for.

"What am I supposed to say when we get in there?" she asked her, and Riley could see the nervousness written all over her face.

"You don't have to say anything. You can sit there and listen if that's all you want to do. Whatever happens, though, I'll be right there beside you."

"Why now? And without asking me?" she wanted to know. She couldn't say for sure, but it was a big possibility that Riley's answer would determine whether she stayed.

"He asked to see you. And with everything that's been going on with Jeremiah, and with you becoming a young woman who's still learning so much about herself, I felt like you were still missing a piece that can help you along your journey. I don't know if it's selfish that I want you to have something I didn't, even if it's from somewhere like this because I feel like it'll add something of value for you. And me wanting this for you made me move in a way that disregarded how you might feel, and I apologize for that."

"It's okay. I've thought about visiting my dad. I never knew if I would, so I guess now is as good a time as any." She shrugged like this was no big deal, but it was a huge deal. She hadn't seen her father in years. They seldom communicated, whether in letters or sometimes phone calls. He communicated with Riley more than her, and even with their small communication, she still felt they didn't know each other.

"So we're doing this?"

"Yes. I just hope for your sake it goes well, because if not, you have a lot of making up to do."

"I'd spend the rest of my days making it up to you if it happens to go any way other than how I believe it will." Riley extended her hand with her pinky up and waited for Mikayla to raise and connect her pinky to hers. A pinky promise could not be broken, and Mikayla knew she meant every word.

"Okay, let's do this."

They both took deep breaths before exiting the car. Hand and hand, they walked through the parking lot toward the entrance, balls of nerves. Check-in went smoothly. Mikayla was taken aback to learn that she and Riley had been on the visitor list since her father got to the prison. Although he never made it a secret that he would love to see her, there was never any pressure either. So for him to have her listed as a visitor and never knowing if she'd take advantage meant something to her.

"Wait over there. You'll be called from that door," the guard told them as he handed Riley back her things.

Mikayla took the time to observe the room. This was very different from the jail they visited Jeremiah in. Most of the people in the waiting room were women and children. Some had one kid, and others had multiple kids. There were teens who she assumed were with their mothers, and none of their faces displayed that they were happy to be there. There were a few males who lingered around, mostly older men. One thing she noticed on the faces of the majority of those in the room with her and Riley was they all looked tired. She wondered if it was from taking the visit too often or missing their loved ones. It could have also been from lack of sleep, but she saw enough movies to know that most people coming to see someone they knew took a toll on them as well.

"Visiting room B." The door the guard told them to look out for opened, and multiple people stood and got in line.

"That's us," Riley said, and they followed the small crowd.

As she had done when they visited Jeremiah, Riley held Mikayla's hand and went through all of the checks first. This check, however, was very different. It was more thorough, and she assumed it was because adults tended to take advantage of the system more by sneaking things in for their loved ones. She hoped that the pat down wouldn't discourage Mikayla from visiting again if this visit went well. She knew that making visitors feel uncomfortable, even if it was only a little bit for a short amount of time, was a way to make them want to make this trip less and less. She was proud of those who could endure such a thing to keep their loved ones on the inside feeling important and loved.

"Do you see him?" Mikayla asked as she looked around the room. Some inmates were already seated, and she wasn't sure if her father was among the crowd.

"Not yet. Let's choose a seat. Maybe he isn't out here yet." Riley led them toward the back of the room, closest to the door where the inmates entered and exited the room. As they walked, they looked at the men sitting alone just to be sure they hadn't missed Mikayla's dad.

"Do you remember what he looks like?" Mikayla asked. She hated that she was really drawing a blank when trying to picture her father. She did have photos of him that he'd sent over the years, but they were in a photo album she rarely pulled out.

"It's been so long, but I guess I'll know him when I see him."

The clanking of the doors and visitors standing let them know they wouldn't have to wait much longer to lay eyes on Mikayla's dad. One by one, inmates entered the room in their tan attire.

"Well, I'll be damned," Riley said as her mouth dropped in shock. She was the first to lay eyes on him. He had stepped out the door, and his eyes roamed every direction of the room except where they were. And as if her energy screamed at him, he quickly turned and advanced their way.

"What?" Mikayla wanted to know what had her cousin so stuck, and then her eyes turned from Riley to the direction Riley was looking in. And she too would be damned. It was like looking at the grown male version of herself. She didn't need to see any photos from an album to know the man coming their way was her dad. He had this stern yet calm look on his face until their eyes met, and it changed. His lips spread into an enormous smile that made her feel warm inside. It was then that she knew this was a good idea on Riley's behalf, and she needed it.

"Girl, your mother ain't do nothing but carry you," Riley spoke through clenched teeth.

"Look at my beautiful girls," he greeted them once he was inches away. His arms were open to give and receive hugs, and as much as he wanted the first one to be from Mikayla, he noticed her step back and Riley step up, embracing him.

"Uncle Mikey, you in here staying young, I see. You don't look a day over twenty-nine," Riley teased as she backed away from their embrace.

"Oh, but my body reminds me that I am every bit of forty-five." He smiled as he swiped his hand over his goatee. "Hey, baby girl." He turned his attention to Mikayla with the same open arms while his heart thumped from nerves, hoping she didn't reject him.

Slowly Mikayla walked into her father's open arms and took in the feel of his arms around her as she hugged him back. So many years, at least five, had gone by since she felt an embrace like this, and she'd forgotten how necessary it was. How much she needed it. Mikayla felt herself revert to the little girl who loved getting hugs from her father. She remembered the last being two days before he was locked up. They'd just come from shopping for clothes and toys, and she remembered it being one of the best times she had with her father. They always had fun, but there was something about that day that made her feel extra special. What she wouldn't give to go back to that day. She would have begged him to not leave her, and given the effect she had on him back then, he may have stuck around. She cherished that last hug until she became angry and resentful that jail took him away. As he held her now, she realized how the memory was way more filling than the anger. The levee broke. A flood of tears spilled from her eyes as her emotions got the best of her.

Seeing how emotional her baby cousin was caused Riley to shed a few tears also. It felt like hours had passed when they pulled away from each other. Had it not been a stupid rule of the prison that contact could only last for so long, she probably would have spent the entire visit hugging her father and crying into his chest.

He sat down right next to her, with Riley across from them both.

"You're so beautiful, baby girl," he said with tears running down his face as he wiped away hers with his thumbs.

"Thank you," she sobbed. Using the sleeve of her shirt, she wiped her face, not caring that she'd ruined the small amount of makeup she had on.

"All right, we have to stop this crying. I'm in prison. Niggas will try me if I'm out here looking soft."

"Really?"

The sad yet shocked expression on Mikayla's face told him just how green his daughter was, and he knew it was one of the reasons she had let young knuckleheads get away with too much. He hadn't been privy to everything his daughter engaged in, but hearing family members call her fast and say they were surprised she hadn't gotten knocked up yet made him highly disappointed in himself for not being there. His daughter was practically made out to be a little jezebel, yet all he saw was his baby girl. And as he looked at the young woman before him, he could see those rumors—that was exactly what they were since he saw none of it with his own eyes—had not defined her nor given him any indication they were true. He was an OG and had been around many whores and fast-living women to know one when he saw her. Sure, he was biased because Mikayla was his daughter. He just figured that if things were as bad as he was told, he would see it.

"No one will do anything to me, baby girl. My name means something around here." He smiled at her. "How's school?" he asked, wanting to start the conversation off light.

"It's going good. I'm one of the best students in the entire school, and I'm not just saying that. There is a list of all the students who do well throughout the year, and I'm in the top two, and I ain't number two." She beamed, and it filled Mikey with so much pride to see his daughter proud of her accomplishment.

"And what about you, niece? How are things?" he turned and asked Riley.

"Ooh, Riley's got a boyfriend, and she's in love," Mikayla teased while her cousin blushed.

"Is that so? You know, if my brother and I were out, neither of y'all would date until we were too old to fight. Nah, I take that back 'cause I'd shoot me one about my girls."

"Blame your daughter. If she hadn't become best friends with his brother, I wouldn't have even met him."

"Seems more like a good thing than bad the way your behind is over here turning redder than a cranberry."

"You won't get an argument out of me on that one. He's truly a good guy, and our future wants align, so it's not like we're dating without a purpose."

"Then that's good, niece. Do not let a man date you without a purpose, and honestly, if all y'all doing is dating, then remember you kinda single until you're married."

"I mean, that does make sense and all, but I won't put out there something I wouldn't be happy with if done to me. 'Cause if he goes on a date with another person, then he can surely forget about me."

"I know that's right," Mikayla chimed in.

"You, young lady, shouldn't even worry about dating until you're at least thirty-five," he said to Mikayla.

"Thirty-five?" she gasped before they all fell into a fit of laughter.

"Nah, I'm joking, but seriously, I need you to know how precious you are. Every part of you means something and is to be respected and cherished. It doesn't take a man multiple chances to figure that out. Yes, we may fuck up at times, but never let that make you feel any kind of way about your worth. You are priceless, baby girl. And I know there are many things my absence did not allow me to show you, but understand that, even behind these walls, I am and will always be here for you."

Emotional again, all Mikayla could do was nod her understanding while wiping away tears. She felt the sincerity in her father's words, and it felt amazing to know from his mouth that he had her and was in her corner.

"Now, although I don't want you talking to boys, you're a teenager, so I know it's inevitable. So though I may not like any of them, you can talk to me about whoever you're dating. I'm going to always keep you on your toes when it comes to men, all right?"

"All right." She smiled.

The rest of the visit went smoothly, and Mikayla couldn't believe how easily she fell into conversation with her dad. When it was time to leave, she was everything but excited. However, knowing she had built this amazing bond with her father in one sitting, she looked forward to his phone calls, letters, and their next visit until he was a free man.

Riley drove them home feeling an abundance of emotions, many of them good, but they weren't strong enough to overshadow the hurt she was also feeling. She was glad the visit went well, but it reminded her how Mikayla needed her father and how she needed her father as well. She vowed that they would make the trips more often. Letters and phone calls were cool, but the only way they would feel what they felt today would be in their presence.

Chapter 21

"Hey, Mrs. Jennifer, is Jeremiah home? His phone is going straight to voicemail."

"Yes, baby girl, he's here. Let me take him the phone. How have you been? I can't wait to get to see your pretty little self in person. FaceTime doesn't allow me to hug you for being such a great friend to my son."

"Aw, thank you. I can't wait to see you too."

"All right, let me give him the phone."

Mikayla chuckled hearing Jeremiah's mother yell his name while telling him to charge his phone. There was some shuffling on the other end, and then a groggy Jeremiah said, "What's up, Mikayla?"

"How'd you know it was me?" she teased.

"Because no one else has the house number and Mama wasn't gon' do all that yelling for anyone else. Not even Jermaine."

"Why are you sleeping in the middle of the day?"

"I went to a party last night after we got off the phone, came back, and have been out ever since. I can't party like a young'un no more," he said like he was sad.

"Boy, please, ain't nothing wrong with you. If the party bored you to death, just say that," she laughed. Jeremiah followed suit.

"What are you doing this weekend, more parties?" As soon as the question left her mouth, she felt a pillow hit her in the head. "Jeremiah, hold on." She didn't wait for him to oblige as she turned around and looked at Riley like she had lost her mind. "Why'd you do that?"

"Because you bet' not say anything about this weekend," Riley fussed.

"I'm not."

"Sounds like you're giving out hints." Riley rolled her neck before placing her hands on her hips.

"Not doing that either. Bye, Riley." Mikayla rolled her eyes and placed the phone back to her ear.

"What's up with Riley?" Jeremiah asked, and his question made Mikayla's heart drop. She hoped he had not heard their conversation.

"Nothing. Getting on my nerves about some dishes," she easily lied.

"Sounds like Riley," he chuckled.

"Hey, I called because I wanted to know if I could wear your letterman jacket. Jermaine wouldn't let me take it without asking, even though we both know you're going to say yes."

"Who told you that lie? Nah, girl, you can't wear my jacket. For what and to where?"

"Really?" she fussed.

"You still didn't say to where and for what."

"A party and because it matches the new Jordans Riley bought me."

"Ay, you really can't wear it. I copped the new Jordans too, and you're right, that jacket go perfect with them bitches," he laughed as Mikayla grumbled into the phone. "I'm joking, crybaby-ass girl. Don't get my jacket dirty, either. I'll text bro. It's good when my phone charges."

"He's here. I'll tell him you said it," Mikayla said loud enough for Jermaine to hear. She knew he and Riley were ear hustling to make sure she didn't slip up and tell him about their upcoming visit. As much as she told Jeremiah, she would not tell him this because she too wanted to surprise him.

"All right, well. I'm about to rest up a little longer, and I'll hit you as soon as I get up. I'm putting my phone on the charger now."

"Okay. Thanks again, bestie," she said excitedly, ending their call.

"Your brother is lucky I still love him because the way he's been treating me since he's been gone is not okay," Mikayla said to Jermaine from the back seat of his car. The weekend had finally arrived, and she would be lying if she said she wasn't excited that they were on the road to him.

"I thought he got better and y'all were communicating more," Riley said as she turned as much as she could in her seat to face her.

"Yes, he has. We spoke this morning, but that doesn't mean I'm not holding the past against him." She laughed.

As close as they were, she did not like when Jeremiah put distance between them. When she told him about it, he said she was overthinking. She let him have it because she did not want to be a nag. And thankfully, her telling him was enough for him to attempt some change.

"You didn't tell him we were coming out there, did you?" Jermaine asked, wanting to make sure she didn't ruin the surprise.

"I'm not dumb. Besides, I heard you and Riley the fifty times y'all told me not to tell him."

"Just checking," Jermaine said. The time had finally come for his brother to come back home, and he hadn't told him. They were talking a bit more, but he knew his brother was still upset with him. The complaints Mikayla were making about her and Jeremiah communicating he'd love to have. He had to have his mother give Jeremiah the phone on multiple occasions because his brother would blatantly ignore him. It hurt because during their ride there they had reconnected. He guessed the distance did not make the heart grow fonder. He often wanted to remind Jeremiah that it was his dumb mistakes that landed him back at their mother's just as they had landed him at his home five years ago, but he refrained. There was no reason to throw salt on an open wound.

"How much longer until we get there?" Mikayla wanted to know. Though she was comfortable in the back seat, she was tired of being in the car.

"We're a few minutes away."

When Jermaine said they were a few minutes away, he wasn't lying. Both Riley and Mikayla found themselves a bit nervous when he pulled in front of the nicely painted two-story home. It was a larger version of Riley's townhouse with a well-manicured lawn and a beautiful flower garden out front.

"This is your childhood home?" Riley asked. She was kind of shocked. From what she'd learned about Jermaine and some of the trouble he got into growing up, she couldn't believe that he did all of that while living in a home as gorgeous as this one.

"It is. I've had some work done on it. It didn't always look like that. It also wasn't raggedy or anything. It needed minor work, and I got it done for my mother."

"Well, this is a nice house. I could see myself living in something like this with my future husband. Oh, but there has to be a white picket fence added," Mikayla said from the back seat.

"Do you not remember what Uncle Mikey said to you about men?"

"Girl, nobody is talking about getting married anytime soon. I can still know what I want my future home to look like." She rolled her eyes.

Opting to not entertain Mikayla any further, Riley turned to Jermaine. "Babe, we'll wait here. Just leave the keys in the car."

She knew they were picking Jeremiah up and would be going to a hotel. She hadn't even considered going inside the home. She was nervous about the trip for reasons unknown because they had never even discussed meeting each other's parents. After all, her father was incarcerated, and his mother lived so far away.

"Man, y'all not about to wait in this car. Get the hell out. What you scared of?" he asked with a smirk on his face.

"Nothing." She frowned as the pace of her heart sped up.

"Well, then get out."

"Yes, let's go inside. Mrs. Jennifer is super nice."

Riley hated to admit that she was a little jealous that her cousin had a good relationship with Mrs. Jennifer. She had been dating Jermaine for months and she hadn't even gotten a chance to say hi to his mother over the phone, and she had called a few times when they were together. She was trying not to allow negative thoughts invade her mind right before entering his mother's house, but she couldn't help it. If she meant as much to Jermaine as he said she did, why didn't he introduce them? When she stepped inside his childhood home, who would he tell his mother she was? Mikayla already had a title. Who would Riley be? If he called her a friend, she would be heartbroken and would probably end things with him and catch the first train she could back home. Staying in the car felt much safer to her. But as he and Mikayla stepped out of the car and Jermaine made his way to the passenger side to open her door, she knew she had no choice but to get out.

With her nerves getting the best of her, Riley walked on wobbly legs hand and hand with Jermaine up the steps of his childhood home. She wondered if he could tell that she would have fallen if she hadn't been holding on to him, or if he could make out the sound of her heart rate because it was beating loudly and rapidly. She hadn't felt like this in a while, like a teenage girl going to meet a boy's mother for the first time. As the grown woman she prided herself on being, this should have been an easy task. Whether his mother liked her shouldn't matter. Not only did she bring a lot of great qualities to the table—her beauty, being goal driven, and having her own money were enough to fill the table alone—but those qualities weren't even the icing on the cake of how dope of a person she was. Knowing these things about herself should have been enough to not care about validation. But she did. She wanted to make a good impression on a woman she didn't know, and she didn't like feeling like that.

"Calm down," Jermaine whispered in her ear before placing a kiss to her cheek.

With wide eyes she looked at him, shocked he could tell she was nervous.

"And breathe. My mom is cool." He chuckled while shaking his head. He wasn't worried about his mother liking Riley. There was no doubt in his mind that she would.

"What the hell?" Jermaine mumbled, surprised at the front door being sprung open and Jeremiah rushing out, heading straight for Mikayla, whom he lifted off her feet and spun around.

"The fuck made you come flying out the house?" Jermaine asked once Jeremiah put Mikayla back on her feet and came toward them, hugging Riley next.

"I saw y'all approaching on the security system that Mom never uses. What y'all doing here?" His excitement was barely containable.

"Shit, we just came to visit and take a quick trip," he told him with a nonchalant shrug.

"Y'all staying here?"

"Nah, we gon' chill with Mom for a bit, then head out. So you might wanna pack some clothes."

"Cool. Come on, Mikayla, let me show you my room."

"Dang, shouldn't I say hi to your mom first?"

"Man, as much as y'all talk, she can wait." He pulled her inside the house and toward the stairs, ignoring her protest.

The last thing Riley and Jermaine heard her say was, "I'm telling her you kept me from speaking first," before they completely disappeared up the stairs.

"Mom," Jermaine called through the house as he shut and locked the front door behind them.

"I'm in the back, and who is making all that noise?"

She sounded irritated, and that only added to the horrible case of nervousness Riley was feeling. She wanted them to run out the front door, but the grip he had on her hand prevented it. And just like Jeremiah had done to Mikayla, he pulled her toward the back of the home, minus the protesting.

"Oh, hey, baby." Her face lit up when she laid eyes on her son. Riley wasn't even sure she noticed her standing right next to him because all eyes were on her oldest. Riley noticed her, though, and could not deny her beauty. She saw some of Jermaine in her but knew Jermaine and Jeremiah were actually spitting images of their father per photos she saw.

Jermaine released her hand to greet his mother with a hug that seemed to last forever yet was only moments long.

"And who is this beautiful young lady you have here?" she asked once their embrace ended.

Beaming with pride, Jermaine turned toward Riley then back to his mother before speaking. Riley unknowingly held her breath as she waited for his answer.

"This is my girl . . . woman, Riley." He subtly inched her toward his mother.

"Riley. You are gorgeous, and I've heard so much about you from my son and your cousin Mikayla." She smiled and pulled Riley into a hug. And Riley felt something she hadn't felt in a while—a mother's touch. Even though it wasn't her mother, she still felt comfort and welcomed it.

"Thank you. It's nice to meet you, Mrs. Stately."

"Oh, girl, we are going to have to get you more comfortable. Mikayla calls me by my first name. That's my girl. She's the sweetest. Where is she, matter of fact?"

"With Jeremiah. He pulled her off to go grab his things."

"Yes, the time has come. He's going to be so excited. You haven't told him, right?"

"Told me what?"

"Damn, you was ear hustling?" Jermaine asked.

"No, I just walked in. Now tell me what?"

"That we're going to Great Wolf Lodge, nosy ass."

"Ooh, I've always wanted to go there. It's going to be fun," Mikayla said as she popped her head from behind Jeremiah.

"There's my girl."

"Mrs. Jennifer." Mikayla sang her name as she walked toward her with open arms. The two hugged like long-lost sisters, and once again, Riley felt a tinge of jealousy.

"Y'all aren't leaving right now, are you?" Mrs. Jennifer asked as she released Mikayla.

"Nah, we can sit for a bit, but we have a check-in time, so not too long," Jermaine told her.

"That's all I need to get acquainted with my girls. Y'all come on." She took them by the hand and pulled them toward her lady's den.

"You better hope she doesn't show your baby pictures," Jeremiah said.

"Yours are in that book, too."

"Yeah, but it ain't my girlfriend she showing. And I was a better-looking baby than you."

"You looked just like me."

"Eh, that's debatable. Besides, you picked out most of my clothes back then, so I stayed fresh. Now, what Mama chose for you . . ." He put his fist to his mouth to stifle his laugh.

Jermaine hated that his brother had made one too many good points, so instead of acknowledging them, he rushed off toward the den, hoping he could stop his mother before Riley and Mikayla heard too many jokes about him as a kid.

"Babe, you had the cutest high-top fade," Riley gushed from the passenger seat as she reached across the armrest and rubbed the side of his face with the back of her hand.

"So you're just going to skip the part where his red sweater was too tight and he looked like a little butterball?" Mikayla chimed in. She and Jeremiah snickered.

"My baby was the cutest looking butterball I've ever seen in my life."

"We not that far from Great Wolf. It would not be wrong if I made all y'all ass walk from here." He was still salty that his mother had set him straight and allowed Riley and Mikayla to see his baby photos. Not all of them were bad, but the few that were had been enough to keep them talking.

"Okay, we're done. Mikayla, not another word."

"Okay," she whined.

The rest of the car ride was silent. They seemed to have nothing to talk about since they weren't making fun of him, and he welcomed the silence. It wasn't until he pulled into the parking lot of Great Wolf that the noise resumed, and he thought Jeremiah and Mikayla were a couple of preadolescents instead of the damn near graduated teens they were. He had barely put the car in park before the teens exited the back seat and anxiously stood at the trunk, waiting for it to open so they could grab their luggage.

"I should make their asses stand there for ten minutes," he said, looking in the rearview mirror.

"As funny as it seems, that wouldn't be a good idea. As soon as you get us checked in, we can send them out, and I can make it up to you for making fun of your baby pictures." She rubbed his thigh suggestively.

"You know you really hurt my feelings, so you got a lot of making up to do."

"I got you."

"In that case, let's go." He unlocked the door and shut off the car.

Riley chuckled as she sat in her seat, waiting for him to open the door for her. If she opened it herself, he'd have a fit.

After she got out, he grabbed their luggage and made Jeremiah take Mikayla's bags. Their check-in went smoothly, and not long after, Mikayla and Jeremiah changed into their swim clothes. Riley made it her business to fix the feelings he claimed she'd broken. She spent over an hour making up to him, and by the time they were done, both were hungry.

"They are going to meet us at the restaurant," she told Jermaine.

"In wet clothes?"

"No, they have coverups."

He shrugged and finished getting dressed, and within minutes they were headed to meet the teens.

"I'm definitely taking advantage of all this place has to offer tomorrow," Riley promised, looking around.

"How long are we staying?" Jeremiah asked.

"Until Monday."

"Then y'all going back home?" he asked in a sad tone.

"Yeah, we are."

"Oh." The solemn look on Jeremiah's face caused Riley to kick Jermaine under the table. She didn't want to see Jeremiah look like a wounded puppy anymore.

"You're coming home with us," he told him.

"What?"

"Yeah, man, shit is straight. You can come home."

The look on his face could've lit the darkest room in one of the darkest buildings.

"Damn, bro, thank you." He stood and embraced his brother, not worried about who was watching. Finally, he could get back to his life. Living with his mother was cool and all, but home was with Jermaine.

Epilogue

"Can you believe that we're here?" Riley asked, looking over at Jermaine, who was looking good as ever dressed in all black. This time it wasn't to go commit a crime. It was for a celebration. His black button-down and black slacks complemented his muscular build perfectly, and she found herself standing in front of him more than usual because the print in his pants was on display—not purposefully, but it was something he'd been blessed with that was hard to conceal in the pants. She was excited to be standing where they were but would be happy when it was over so she could show her man just how much she appreciated how handsome he looked.

"I mean, for Mikayla definitely, but my brother . . . There were times I wasn't so sure if we'd make it to this day. Not because he isn't intelligent, but because he was caught up in some dumb shit," he said honestly. If there was anyone in the world he could be that honest with when it came to his brother, it was her.

"Listen, Mikayla's grades were never a worry. It was her ability to be easily influenced that kept me on edge about this day. You remember how you acted and what you thought when you first met her." They, too, had plenty of obstacles to overcome, and she was happy they were able to do so. All of them. For priceless moments like this one.

"And I was wrong as hell. But at the end of the day, everything played out just like it was supposed to." He leaned in and kissed her on her forehead.

"Aw, babe," she gushed, loving when he showed public affection, which he did often. Still, each time felt like it was new.

"Oh, I did that because ol' girl keeps staring and winking at me. I was trying to show her we're together." He smiled, watching Riley's eyes get big before she snapped her head around to see who was flirting with her man behind her back, literally.

"Who?" she asked with aggression, and he tried to keep a straight face, but he failed tragically.

"What'd I miss?" Mrs. Jennifer asked as she rushed toward them.

"Nothing with the kids, but your son is about to get himself and whoever is playing behind my back messed up."

"Mama, I was joking with her, and she ready to go crazy. I've never seen this side of her, and it's cute," he chuckled, pulling Riley into him.

"Leave her alone. We are here for my babies. Don't go getting her in a bad mood."

"The class of 2022 will be entering any moment. Thank you for your patience," the announcer spoke over the loudspeaker.

"Finally. I've been waiting for this day," Mrs. Jennifer said, getting excited. The day had finally come for Jeremiah and Mikayla to graduate, and they were all excited and ready to watch them walk across the stage.

"I'm so glad there's reserved seating. At your graduation, your dad almost went to jail for seats close to the stage. Your brother did great with these seats."

"He sure did. Mikayla was not trying to strong-arm anybody like I told her to," Riley said as they made their way down the aisle to where their seats were.

Jermaine sat between his mother and Riley, and not long after he was seated, the lights of the auditorium dimmed. Loud music started, and Jermaine and Riley smiled once they caught on to the beat. "Swag Surfin'" was being played by the marching band, and behind them entered the class of 2022 swaying to the beat. The entire room was standing and cheering them on as they grooved onto the stage. With blurred vision from tears in her eyes, Riley snapped as many photos as she could get of Mikayla and Jermaine. She wished her uncle Mikey could be there, especially since his and Mikayla's relationship had grown tremendously.

"They look so grown up. I am not ready for them to grow up," Riley said as she patted her watery eyes.

"Girl, imagine how I feel. I carried his bighead behind for ten months. He's my last baby. Now he's leaving for college." Mrs. Jennifer wiped the lone tear away, and they all sat and watched the ceremony.

"That was so beautiful."

Mrs. Jennifer and Riley gushed as they moved through the throng of people who were also waiting to greet their graduates.

"He said they are in the front to the left," Jermaine announced, looking at his phone. He took Riley by the hand, and Riley grabbed Mrs. Jennifer's, and they made their way through the people faster since they now had a specific destination.

"There they are." Jermaine was the first to spot them, having a height advantage. He practically released Riley's hand as he made his way to his brother. Any other time that may have upset her, but she had done the same to Mrs. Jennifer, making her way to Mikayla.

They rushed into each other's arms, and the floodgates opened.

"I'm so proud of you," Riley cried, hugging her little cousin tightly.

"Thank you. This feels so weird, but I am so happy. I wouldn't have been able to do this without you."

Her words touched Riley deeply, and even though she had played a major role in Mikayla pulling her life together, she wanted her to know that it was she who had done the work. Slowly she separated from their embrace and cupped Mikayla's face with her hands.

"I am so proud of you. I appreciate what you said, but make sure you give yourself credit, Mikayla. You've overcome so much, have grown so much, and none of that would be possible if you didn't do the work."

"I wouldn't have had the courage to do the work without you. If it hadn't been for you, I'd probably be a teen mom dropout with a baby daddy in jail with a statutory rape case," she said honestly but made sure Riley was the only one able to hear her.

"You still did the work." Riley pulled her back into a hug. Mikayla hadn't lied, and it hurt that, at one point, that could have been her cousin's reality, and she was so grateful that it wasn't.

"Okay, our makeup is more than likely severely ruined by now," Mikayla joked, pulling away from her cousin. "Aw, look at them." She turned and looked at Jeramiah and Jermaine, who were both misty-eyed while embracing. It was such a beautiful moment.

"I'm so proud of you, man," Jermaine said loud enough for everyone to hear. He was prouder than he'd ever been and had no problem letting anyone in earshot know it.

"Thank you, bro. You really went hard for me, and I appreciate you so much. I told you I was going to make shit up to you."

"And you have. Not including how proud I'm going to be at your next graduation."

"Yep. Howard U, here I come."

"Here *we* come," Mikayla corrected him.

"Okay, I've enjoyed watching you all have a moment, but I am here too," a teary-eyed Mrs. Jennifer said, reminding them all of her presence.

"My bad, Mom." Jeremiah walked up to her with open arms and hugged her tightly as she cried on his shoulder.

"Mikayla, I'm proud of you too," Jermaine said, pulling her into a hug.

"Proud enough to get me a car too?" she joked.

"For what? You gon' be wherever Jeremiah is, and he'll let you use the car when you need it."

"I know that. Just wanted to see if you were proud enough to say yes. Obviously not."

"Man, I can only afford one car with this baby on the way." He rubbed Riley's growing stomach. Because of her stature and the snacks she couldn't stay away from, she was showing a lot sooner than expected, but it was the cutest bump they all had ever seen.

"That's a lie. However, you can definitely get away with that excuse because I am so excited about my little cousin. We will be on the first flight home before he or she is born."

"Yes, my nephew about to be so fly."

"Um, no one said it's a boy," Riley corrected him.

"If you did a gender reveal like I suggested, we'd all know."

"That's the new stuff y'all are doing. I want to be surprised. Now can we head to the restaurant? I am starving."

"Me too. Mikayla, you riding with me?" Jeremiah asked.

"Duh. You should let me drive."

"You playing. You went over three curbs the last time we took Riley's car. You not doing that in my shit."

"You did what?" Riley asked.

"Whew, thanks for dry snitching, Jeremiah. Nothing happened." She took him by the arm and pulled him toward the student parking lot, where his car was.

"Did you know about her jumping my car over curbs?"

"Not at all, babe. Let's go eat."

"He didn't even ask if I wanted to ride." Mrs. Jennifer faked hurt.

"Mom, you rode with us."

"So? I would have declined. It would have been nice to be asked."

"It's okay, Mrs. Jennifer. Soon you'll have another baby to spoil, and they are going to be jealous when your grandbaby gets here."

"Sure are, because I'm going to be like, 'Son who?'" She laughed, extending a high five to Riley.

The ride to the restaurant was quiet as they all were lost in their own thoughts. Riley felt happy and sad at the same time. She would be sending her cousin off to college and welcoming a new baby. Everything happened so fast, and no one could have paid her to believe this would be her life. Love, growth, and happiness were all abundant in her life, and she was so thankful for it all.

A Note from the Author

Hello, everyone. If you took the time to read my debut novel, I'd like to thank you. This story is a journey I hope you all enjoyed. Besides those of you who decided to take a chance on a new author like myself, I want to thank my super-agent, Diane Rambert, for believing in me and always having my back. I'd also like to thank Urban Books for welcoming me with open arms. I hope you all are ready because Raevyn Renee is just getting started.